Big Lake Wedding

By Nick Russell

Copyright 2019 © By Nick Russell
All rights reserved. No part of this book may be reproduced in any form or by any means, electronic or mechanical, including photocopying, recording, or by any information storage or retrieval system, without permission in writing by the publisher.

Nick Russell
E-mail Editor@gypsyjournal.net

Also By Nick Russell

Fiction
Big Lake Mystery Series
Big Lake
Big Lake Lynching
Crazy Days In Big Lake
Big Lake Blizzard
Big Lake Scandal
Big Lake Burning
Big Lake Honeymoon
Big Lake Reckoning
Big Lake Brewpub
Big Lake Abduction
Big Lake Celebration
Big Lake Tragedy
Big Lake Snowdaze
Big Lake Fugitive
Big Lake Wedding

Dog's Run Series
Dog's Run
Return To Dog's Run

John Lee Quarrels Series
Stillborn Armadillos
The Gecko In The Corner
Badge Bunny
Mullets And Man Buns
Strawberry Slugbug

Standalone Mystery Novels
Black Friday

Nonfiction
Highway History and Back Road Mystery
Highway History and Back Road Mystery II
Meandering Down The Highway; A Year On The Road With Fulltime RVers
The Frugal RVer

Work Your Way Across The USA; You Can Travel And Earn A Living Too!
Overlooked Florida
Overlooked Arizona
The Gun Shop Manual

Keep up with Nick Russell's latest books at www.NickRussellBooks.com

Author's Note

While there is a body of water named Big Lake in the White Mountains of Arizona, the community of Big Lake and all persons in this book live only in the author's imagination. Any resemblance in this story to actual persons, living or dead, is purely coincidental.

Prologue

While it was one of the most anticipated weddings in the town of Big Lake's history, there was no question that it was also one of the most unusual. The bride wore a traditional modified white A-line dress with lace on the shoulders, a modest scoop at the neck and an open back. The groom wore a simple light gray suit with a dark blue tie over a sky-blue shirt. The bridesmaid was dressed in a dark green dress with a mid-length hem, while the best man also wore a gray suit of a darker shade than the groom's.

As the bride walked slowly down the aisle on her father's arm, the people gathered for the event couldn't help noticing the hastily applied safety pins that were holding the bodice of her dress together, or that her left eye was black and swollen shut. There were bandages on two of the fingers on her left hand, but fortunately, the ring finger was bare.

Standing at the front of the room, the groom's two black eyes made him resemble a raccoon. One of his trouser legs was torn halfway to the knee, a white gauze bandage covered part of his forehead, and dried blood caked his split bottom lip.

When they reached the front of the room, the bride's father kissed her on the cheek, shook hands with the groom, and sat in a chair in the front row. He was by himself because the bride's mother refused to take part in the spectacle, choosing instead to sit outside in their car.

Judge Harold Ryman, who was officiating, looked at the man and woman in front of him affectionately and smiled, then shook his head.

"I've heard of brides or grooms that needed to be dragged to the altar before, but I have to say that this is the first time it looked like both of them put up a fight."

There was laughter from the audience and from the wedding party. When the groom laughed, he revealed a missing front tooth.

"It looks like these two are off to a rough start," the judge said. "Let's hope that things get better for them because I've got to tell you, it doesn't look like it could get much worse."

His comment was greeted with more laughter, the groom putting a hand to his side and pressing against what he was sure was a cracked rib as he did so.

"I've asked both the bride and groom if they wanted to proceed with things today, or if they would prefer to put it off for another time. Both of them have told me this *is* the right time. Actually, I think the bride said, and I'm quoting her here, 'Can we just get this the hell over with?'"

Now the entire room was laughing loudly at the absurdity of the scene before them. Yes indeed, it was like no other wedding the little mountain community had ever seen, and people would be talking about it for a long time afterward.

"Well, all right then. Let us proceed," the judge said. "But before I do, the bride asked me if I was going to go through that whole love, honor, and obey thing. I told her I normally do, it's just part of the tradition, and she let me know that she was okay with the first two, and that she would obey her new husband from 9 to 5, but the rest of the time, that idea was out the window."

In spite of herself, the bride started to laugh so hard that she snorted. By now any sense of decorum had long since left the room and people were wiping tears from their eyes and slapping their legs at the judge's last statement.

When she managed to get control of herself, the bride said, "Like I asked you before, can we just get this the hell over with?"

"Yes, ma'am," the judge told her. "I make it a point never to argue with brides. Especially brides that carry guns."

He went through the usual thing about two people joined together in the eyes of God, talked about the bond they were making to each other for evermore, and then asked if there was anybody who felt the couple should not be joined in holy matrimony. Everyone in the audience held their breath for a moment, wondering if someone would actually raise an objection, and both the bride and the groom watched the door, expecting her mother to storm inside and try to put a stop to the proceedings. But when there was only silence, the judge said, "Very well then, James Alan Weber, do you take this woman, Robyn Abigail Fuchette ....

Chapter 1

Two Weeks Earlier

"I swear to God I must have been adopted! There's no way that woman and me are related!"

"That bad, huh? What's she done now?"

"What hasn't she done, Jimmy? Yesterday she chewed out the florist because he didn't have a sample made up of the bridal bouquet. Then she went over to the church and pitched a fit because she thinks the carpeting is going to clash with Marsha's dress. Since they can't change the carpet, she went to Marsha's store and told her she needed to find a new bridesmaid's dress. Like she can just drop everything and go to Phoenix and find something on short notice like that this close to the wedding! And then today, because she hasn't created enough chaos, she jumped all over the fellow from Show Low that has the limousine because he wouldn't drive it here so she could inspect it. I didn't know anything about it until he called me and told me to find somebody else because he was canceling. I just want to forget the whole damn thing!"

Seeing the look on her fiancé's face, Robyn Fuchette quickly tried to put him at ease. "I don't mean the wedding, Jimmy. I just mean I want to be done with all the stress and problems. I don't *need* a big wedding, I don't *need* a limousine, I don't *need* a bouquet. That's all my mom's doing. She thinks because she had a big fancy church wedding, I have to have one, too. I just want us to be married and done with it. Do you understand where I'm coming from?"

"I do," Sheriff Jim Weber said, getting up from his chair to put his arms around her. "It's going to be okay, I promise you."

Robyn wiped a rare tear from her eye and turned her face into his chest. A moment later she seemed to compose herself and stepped back.

"Sorry, I know we don't do public displays of affection when we're on the job. I'm just so frustrated right now."

"It's okay, it's not like anybody's gonna come barging in here. Look, I know your mother is difficult, to say the least, but…"

As if to make a liar out of him, there was a knock on his office door and it opened, his administrative assistant, Mary Caitlin poking her head in.

"I'm sorry to interrupt you guys, but Christine Ridgeway just called from SafeHaven and said there's a guy there pounding on the door, trying to get in and making all kinds of threats. I've got Buz and Jordan on the way out there, but Christine called back and said he's kicking in the door now and threatening to kill somebody if his wife doesn't come out and talk to him. Judy's still got her on the line and told her not to hang up."

"Tell her we're on our way," Weber said, heading for the door with Robyn close on his heels.

They jumped in the Sheriff's Ford Explorer and he paused for just a moment before pulling onto Main Street to make sure no other traffic was coming, then sped through town with his roof lights flashing and siren wailing.

"It's got to be Donald MacGregor," Robyn said. "I know that Cindy left him after he started in on her again, and she's at SafeHaven."

"When did that happen?"

"Last week, Monday or Tuesday, I can't remember which," Robyn said. "Coop and I took the call and he was ready to take us both on. Coop drew his Taser and told him he was not going to play his silly ass games and that if he didn't shut up and stay where he was he was going to zap him. I guess Donald could tell he was serious because he toned it down a little bit. I tried to get Cindy to file a charge on him but she wouldn't do it. She claimed all he was doing was being verbally abusive. I'm sure he hit her, but there were no physical marks so we had to take her word for it. Donald told me he was going to get me for interfering in his life, and I think if Coop hadn't had that Taser in his hand he might have tried something."

"That guy needs a good ass kicking," the sheriff said, "and I'm just about fed up enough to give him one."

"I'm glad she finally left him. I can't tell you how many times we've had to go out to their place because the neighbors called to report that he was drunk and beating on her. And each time she swore up and down that she fell and bumped her head or tripped and landed on her face. Maybe now that she's out of that situation she won't try to cover up for him anymore."

Weber pulled into the oncoming lane to pass a slow-moving pickup truck pulling a camper trailer, and once he was past it he moved back into the right lane and floored the accelerator.

"This time it doesn't matter if she files a complaint or not," he said. "I know Christine will. Maybe if he spends some time in jail he might get it through his head that he can't keep this crap up."

Donald MacGregor was well known to the Big Lake Sheriff's Department, whose personnel had dealt with him since he was a small boy. Donald was only six or seven years old the first time he got into trouble when he was caught shoplifting candy bars at the grocery store. A few months later he was in trouble again for the same thing. As he grew older, his crimes became worse. At ten years old he was beating up smaller children in the neighborhood and stealing their toys. Two years later he was making schoolmates give him their lunch money to avoid a beating by him. The first time he was caught window peeping he was fourteen, and from there he graduated to vandalizing cars, driving without a license, and truancy. But of all his many misdeeds, it was the bullying that stood out more than anything else. Donald was big as a boy, standing head and shoulders above most of his classmates, and he grew to become an intimidating man with broad shoulders, thick biceps, and iron-hard fists that he didn't hesitate to use on anyone who crossed his path when he was in a bad mood. Which seemed to be all the time. And if nobody was nearby to punch his frustrations out on, he would find someone.

Some people had hoped that when he married Cindy Schofield, he might mellow out somewhat. Cindy was a nice girl from a good family who unfortunately had been taken in by Donald's bad boy reputation. But as often happens in situations like this, instead of changing him like she hoped she could, Cindy had become his favorite punching bag. Weber hoped that now that she had finally found the courage to leave her abusive husband and seek refuge at the women's shelter, she might finally escape his control. And it was obvious that Donald was going to do everything he could to put a stop to that.

They were still a mile away from SafeHaven when Deputy Buz Carelton's voice came over the radio. "We need backup here now, it's getting physical!"

Robyn picked up the microphone from the hook on the Explorer's dashboard and said, "We're almost there."

Less than a minute later Weber slowed down long enough to turn into the long gravel driveway that led to SafeHaven, then punched the accelerator again. When they roared onto the scene he slammed on the brakes and skidded to a stop next to two Sheriff's Department vehicles and an old Ford pickup that might have been white at one time, but was so dirty, dinged, and dented that it was hard to tell for sure.

The sight before them was enough to get anybody's blood pumping. Deputy Jordan Northcutt had his arms locked around Donald's waist and was trying to pull him away from the door while the bigger man rained punishing blows down on his head and shoulders. Buz, his shirt torn open and blood dripping from his nose and mouth, was methodically punching the enraged man anywhere he saw an opening. Neither of them seemed to be having any effect at all.

Weber and Robyn joined the melee, Weber delivering a hard sideways kick to the back of Donald's left leg while Robyn flicked open her 26 inch expandable ASP baton and went for the enraged man's head and neck. The struggle continued for a moment or two longer, but between the four of them they were finally able to subdue their opponent and force him to the ground, where Weber put a knee on the back of his neck, and Dolan and Jordan managed to handcuff his hands behind him. Even then Donald continued to struggle, kicking out one leg to catch Robyn on the upper leg, knocking her backward. Pressing harder with his knee on Donald's neck, the sheriff grabbed his head and pushed it into the wooden floor of the porch as hard as he could.

"Stop resisting!"

"My wife's in there!"

"I said stop resisting. You're only making it harder on yourself."

"I'll kill you, you son-of-a-bitch," Donald roared. "I'll kill all of you, and then I'll kill those bitches inside, too."

"You're not killing anybody today," Weber told him. "But if you keep this nonsense up, you're going to be the one that's dead."

Robyn went back to Weber's Explorer and returned with heavy nylon leg hobbles. With Weber holding down his neck, Buz kneeling on the prisoner's back, and Jordan sitting on his legs, Robyn was able to get the hobbles on his ankles, then they secured the hobbles to his handcuffs. Trussed up like a pig ready to go to market, Donald still tried to struggle, but it was impossible. So he began hurling verbal abuse at Weber and his deputies, his wife, and the staff at SafeHaven.

"How about you just calm down? This isn't getting you anywhere," Weber said.

Donald's response was to curse him and then spit at the sheriff.

"Okay, we can do it that way if you want. Robyn, would you get a spit hood, too?"

Donald tried to lunge at her and bite Robyn's arm when she put the mesh cover over his face, but his restraints wouldn't allow him to do so.

"That's enough of that bullshit," the sheriff said, gripping the man's arm and pressing his fingers hard into the nerve in his armpit. Donald shrieked in pain and Weber said, "That's enough, damn it!"

Weber, Buz, and Jordan carried the prisoner to Jordan's car, shoving him across the back seat. He was still cursing when they closed the doors on him.

Weber looked at his deputies, who were both disheveled and had marks on their faces where Donald had hit them. "You guys okay?"

"I'm getting too old for this crap," Buz said, wiping at the blood that dripped from his nose.

"Did he break your beak?" Weber asked, referring to his long-time deputy's hawk-like nose that, along with his skinny neck, had earned him the nickname Buzzard when he was still a schoolboy. "Do you need an ambulance?"

"No, I'm fine. But if you two hadn't got here when you did, I might've had to shoot that dumb ass."

"You okay, kid?"

Jordan, Big Lake's newest deputy, nodded. "Yeah, but I'm sure glad backup got here. Buz and I were giving it everything we had and the guy didn't seem to even notice we were there. I didn't know what we were going to do."

"You did a fine job," Buz said to the other deputy, "Any time I get in a jam, I want you covering my back. He's a keeper, Jimmy."

Jordan hung his head for a moment to try to hide it, but the young man's face was beaming at the praise from the more experienced deputy.

"Why don't you guys get this idiot out of here and put him in a cell, then get yourselves cleaned up. Robyn and I will handle things here, and you can write your reports later. Buz, are you sure you don't need to get checked out?"

"I'm good, Jimmy. I'll talk to you later."

The heavy front door of SafeHaven had been bowed inward by Donald's attack, but it had held. It opened as Weber and Robyn returned to the porch and Christine Ridgeway, the director of the women's shelter, poked her head out. "Is it safe yet?" She was holding a four-inch barreled Smith & Wesson Model 10 .38 revolver.

"Yeah, he's gone," Weber said. "Put that thing away before you shoot one of us by mistake."

"That's one crazy man, Jimmy. I thought sure he was going to come in here and kill us. I was standing here inside the door ready for him."

"As out-of-control as he was, you might have had to use it," Weber said, watching the trail of dust from the two police cars driving away.

"I hope we've seen the last of him!"

"Me, too," the sheriff said. "And if I can do anything to make sure of it, I will."

Unfortunately, things were not going to work out that way.

Nick Russell

Chapter 2

"How does your leg feel?"

"It's okay, just a little bit tender."

"You could have been killed out there today."

"I could get killed driving to work, Mother. It's no big deal."

"It is a big deal! And you," Renée Fuchette said, pointing an accusing finger at Weber, "I can't believe you let Robyn get involved in something like that!"

"Mother, don't start."

"No, Robyn, I'm going to have my say. How dare you put my daughter in a situation where she can be assaulted like that? My God, what kind of man are you, Jim Weber?"

"Stop it, Mother. It's part of the job. I've told you that a thousand times."

"And I've asked you a thousand times why you can't do something else with your life? Rolling around in the dirt fighting with somebody? That's not the way you were raised, Robyn."

"It's what I do, Mother. It's what I'm good at. Now just drop it."

"It's what you're good at? You've already gotten shot working for this man, and now this? That's what you call being good at your job? Well, I'd hate to see what would happen if you were bad at it! You could be a schoolteacher or a nurse, or a business executive. Instead, you choose to spend your life dealing with the dregs of society. Why is that, Robyn? Are you doing it just to impress this man who isn't worthy of you under the best of circumstances? Because I can tell you right now, he's not worth it."

"Enough, Renée," Bill Fuchette said, slapping the table with the palm of his hand so hard that the silverware laid out next to their dinner plates rattled. "We've been through this before, and it doesn't accomplish anything except to get everybody all riled up. Robyn is doing a job she loves, and I agree with her, she's good at it."

"Good at it? She got shot, Bill! Have you forgotten about that? Some maniac shot our daughter. What is good about that?"

"It wasn't a maniac, Mother. It was a scared old man."

"Yes, a scared old man with a gun. And he was scared because a maniac was on the loose and this man here let you go out and look for him! That's a terrible way to treat a woman you say you love, if you ask me."

"Nobody asked you, Mother."

The woman opened her mouth to say something again and her husband glared at her. "I said enough, Renée. Not another word out of you. I mean it."

Robyn's mother glared at her husband, then stood up and threw her napkin on top of her plate. "Fine, if you want to encourage this, it's on you, Bill. Whatever happens is all your fault."

She stormed out of the room, and a moment later they heard the bedroom door slam. The three of them sat at the table in uncomfortable silence, then Bill said, "I'm sorry, honey. I've talked to your mother until I'm blue in the face. She just won't listen. I know you're doing good work up here, and I know you're a good cop. And as for you, Jim, ignore all that BS. You two are a good fit together and I could see that right from the start. And as for you trying to protect Robyn or keep her from doing her job, I know my daughter. If you tried something like that, there'd be hell to pay. So both of you just ignore Renée and keep on doing what you're doing."

"Thank you, Daddy," Robyn said. "I wish Mom would come around, but I don't think it's ever going to happen."

"I wish she would, too, Kitten, but I don't think either one of us should be holding our breath waiting for it to happen."

After her mother's outburst, none of them had much of an appetite left but they picked at their food and tried to make small talk. Afterwards, Bill shooed them out of the kitchen while he did the dishes. Sitting on the front porch swing, Robyn was quiet and brooding. Weber had known her long enough to know that nothing he could say would change things right now or lighten her mood. So, he just sat quietly, his arm wrapped around her shoulder, holding her close. Finally, Robyn broke the silence, asking him, "Are you sure you want to marry into this mess? She's never going to get any better."

"That's okay, I'm up for it," he assured her, kissing her forehead. "Just promise me you won't turn into her someday."

"If I do, you have my permission to shoot me. How about that?"

Weber chuckled and said, "Let's hope it never gets that bad, okay?"

"Seriously, Jimmy, sometimes I worry I'll end up being just like her. And I hate even thinking about it."

"Don't worry, Baby. If nothing else, I'll keep a Taser handy, just in case."

"I don't know how you put up with it and don't say anything when she attacks you like that, Jimmy. It's not fair."

"Hey, I've got broad shoulders. She can pile on as much as she wants to. At least when she's doing that she's giving the rest of the world a break."

"Maybe you should Taze her. That might do the trick."

"I think I'll pass on that one."

"I've seen you walk into bars alone and break up fights. You shot a bear with your pistol. Compared to that, you should be able to take her down."

"Are you kidding me? That woman scares the hell out of me," Weber said with a grin. "I'd rather fight a bear in my underwear than tangle with her!"

~~~***~~~

When he left Robyn's house Weber stopped by the Sheriff's Office. Kate Copley was holding down the dispatcher's desk and looked up when he came through the door.

"How are you doing, Jimmy?"

"I'm fine, Kate. Anything happening?"

"Archer is out at the Town Pump on a call for a beer run. Couple guys came in and grabbed a twelve-pack each and made a run for it without paying. Chad and Coop just cleared from breaking up an argument between a couple of flatlanders at the Redeye Saloon that looked like it was going to get physical. And every so often that guy back in the cell starts ranting and raving so loud I can hear him out here, but that's about it."

As if on cue, the sound of Donald MacGregor cursing came to them.

"See what I mean? He does that every half hour or so and goes on for a while, then he runs out of breath and shuts up for a while before he starts again."

"I guess it would be a waste of time trying to talk some sense into him, wouldn't it?"

"Be my guest," Kate said. "That or have Steve Harper come by with the fire truck and hose him down like you did that guy from Mohave County that time. That shut him up pretty quick."

"I wish I could," Weber said. "But the Town Council might take a dim view of that. I guess that's considered cruel and unusual punishment. Go figure."

He walked down the hall and unlocked the heavy steel door that led into the cellblock. MacGregor was standing at the bars of his cell shouting and threatening to kill somebody if they didn't let him out of there. Unimpressed by his tirade, Weber stood with his arms crossed watching him, not saying anything. The sheriff's presence didn't slow the prisoner down at all. It just gave him someone to yell at besides the empty walls around him.

"You let me out of here right now, Sheriff. I know my rights and I'm warning you, if you don't, you're gonna be sorry!"

When Weber didn't reply, MacGregor said, "You think you're so tough, but you're nothing. It took four of you assholes to get me down!"

The sheriff shrugged his shoulders and said, "It was worth the effort just to see a girl put pink handcuffs on you, Donald. Are you ever going to grow up?"

"You go to hell, Weber. You and that bitch deputy of yours that you've been screwing so long. Next time I see her I'm going to…"

"You need to watch your mouth if you know what's good for you, Donald."

"Or what? What are you going to do about it? How about you open the door of this cell and say that again?"

"I'd love to. I really would. I'd love to come in there and kick your ass so hard and for so long that all there'd be left is a big pile of puke and pus. But I'm not allowed to do that. No, I have to treat you nice because you're a prisoner and you have all those rights that you're talking about. But that's okay. And I'll tell you why. Because tonight I'm going to go home and I'm going to take a nice long hot shower and then I'm going to sleep in my own comfortable bed. And tomorrow I'm going to brush my teeth and get dressed and have a nice breakfast and go about my day. But you? You're going to sleep on that bunk with its thin mattress, and you're going to take a dump in that stainless steel toilet attached to the wall there, and tomorrow you're going to eat whatever we decide to bring you, whenever we decide to bring it. Then we're going to take you to see the judge, and he's going to give you a nice long sentence and you get to enjoy our accommodations even longer. That is, unless he sends you down to Florence for a while. And I promise you, you're not gonna like it there. Nope, not one bit. Because down there they've got some real bad ass cons, and the first time you mouth off to one of them or try shoving somebody around, one of them is going to take a shiv and gut you. Of course, they may put you face down on a bunk and use you for their bitch for a while first. And that's okay with me. I've got no problem with that. So, you have yourself a nice night, Donald. Scream and holler and rant and rave and cuss and piss and moan all you want. The dispatcher can just turn that little stereo she's got up front up a little louder and drown you out. Sleep tight, don't let the bedbugs bite."

And with that the sheriff turned and walked out of the cellblock, locking the door behind him as Donald began shouting again.

Chapter 3

"It's time to see the judge," Weber told the prisoner the next morning as he finished eating the bacon and scrambled eggs in a Styrofoam container from the Frontier Café. "You have two choices. We can handcuff you and put cuffs on your legs and you can walk in there like a man, or you can start the same crap you did yesterday and we'll truss you up again and carry you in. Which is it going to be?"

As was often the case with Donald MacGregor, once he finally screamed out the last of his rage somewhere in the middle of the night, he seemed to have calmed down somewhat. He was still surly and Weber knew just how dangerous he could be, but he didn't seem to have any fight left in him at the moment.

"Just cuff me and let's go get it over with."

"Okay. I want you to turn around and put your hands behind your back. I'm going to open the cell door and Deputy Wright and Deputy Northcutt are going to hook you up. And if you so much as take a deep breath or act like you're going to resist in any way, I'm going to put you down with this Taser. Do we understand each other, Donald?"

"Yeah, whatever. Just do it."

Weber nodded at his two young deputies and unlocked the cell door. Knowing the man's propensity for violence, they approached cautiously, but he remained docile while they cuffed his hands and feet and ran a chain between them to restrict his movements.

"Okay. Good man," Weber said, though he felt there was nothing good about MacGregor, and never would be. They led him out of the cell and out the back door of the cellblock, where a police car was waiting. After they loaded the prisoner in the back, Weber said, "I'll meet you there in a couple minutes."

As the deputies drove away he went back inside, locked the door behind him and went out into the main office, immediately wishing he had stayed back in the cellblock.

"Sheriff Weber, I need a moment with you."

"Sorry, Chet, I'm on my way to court."

"But this won't take but just a minute."

The sheriff sighed. He had hoped that when Chet Wingate resigned as mayor of Big Lake the man wouldn't be such an irritant all the time. He had been wrong. Though the mayor had relinquished his position, citing health reasons though everybody knew it was just a move to avoid being humiliated by public recall election, he still managed to be underfoot all too often.

"Make it quick."

"I was wondering about the upcoming nuptials."

"Nuptials?"

"Yes, when you and Robyn get married."

"What about it, Chet?" Weber thought the prissy little man was angling for an invitation to the wedding but he was wrong. Chet Wingate wanted more than that. Much more.

"Who is officiating at the ceremony?"

"Reverend Collier. Why?"

"Well, as my wedding gift to you and your lovely bride-to-be, I wanted to offer my services on this special day."

"Services? It's not going to be a big deal with ushers and things like that, Chet. And Larry Parks is my best man. So I'm not sure what services you're talking about."

"Well," the former mayor said, with a self-satisfied smile as he drew himself up to his full height, which wasn't much more than his width, "I would be willing to perform the marriage ceremony."

Big Lake Wedding

"You? Don't you have to be a minister or a judge or something like that to perform a wedding, Chet?"

"I believe I can as mayor."

"I'm not sure about that, but it doesn't matter since you're not the mayor anymore, Chet."

"Technically, I am. My term in office doesn't expire for three more months."

"But you resigned. That means your term is over with, as I understand it."

"I resigned for health reasons. I'm feeling much better now and I'm going to resume my position as mayor."

"Have you talked to the Town Council about this yet?"

"Myself and Councilwoman Smith-Abbott have discussed it at length. We think it's best for the town."

Weber was pretty sure the former mayor couldn't just walk back into a Town Council meeting and take over again just because he wanted to, but he didn't feel like continuing the discussion and he needed to get to court. "I don't know how all of that works. You might want to talk to Bob Bennett and Kirby Templeton before you start making too many plans. And as for the wedding, thanks but no thanks. Robyn and her mother have got that all worked out already."

"Well, I'm sorry to hear that you're not having a say in what's happening with your own wedding, Sheriff. I know we have had our difficulties in the past, but just think about how this will help the town to heal. You and Robyn getting married and me up there with the two of you in front of the congregation, putting past conflicts aside and embracing the future. A wonderful, happy future not just for the two of you, but for all of us."

If Weber had any reply to that it was cut off by the door closing behind him as he went out.

~~***~~

"We've got a problem," a grim-faced Buz Carelton said when Weber got out of his Explorer at the courthouse.

"Tell me that idiot didn't start fighting with you guys again."

"No, he's not the problem. Judge Ryman isn't here."

"What do you mean he's not here? Where is he?"

"Over at the hospital in Show Low. The court clerk said he's got a kidney stone lodged someplace and it was hurting so bad they took him to the hospital last night."

"So everything today is postponed?"

"No, and that's the problem," Buz told him. "Judge Burton from Springville is filling in for him."

"Oh, shit."

"I know."

Weber shook his head with resignation and said, "Well, all we can do is all we can do."

The sheriff didn't know of anyone sitting on the bench who he thought was less suited for the job than Judge Walter Burton. He always thought of the man as a leftover flower child from the 60s who had held onto his unrealistic view of how life should be in spite of the harsh realities that sometimes existed. He truly believed that everybody was kindhearted and wholesome inside, even if their actions sometimes belied that truth. Furthermore, he had never abandoned his antiestablishment mindset from those days so long ago, in spite of his position. Judge Burton believed that the best way to change the system was to become part of it and force change from within. To say he was soft on criminals and hard on the law enforcement community would be an understatement. Weber had listened to more than one Springerville cop rail on about how they had a perpetrator dead to rights and the judge had dismissed the case over some triviality, or else given them a light slap on the hand and sent them home when they promised never to break the law again. The man saw the world through rose colored glasses and that was never going to change.

After Bob Bennett, the Town's Attorney, read the charges of disorderly conduct, resisting arrest with violence, four counts of assault on a police officer, and making terroristic threats, the judge sat patiently while Weber described what had taken place at the women's shelter.

By the time he was done, there was a frown on the judge's face. He folded his arms across his chest and shook his head. "Sheriff Weber, can you tell me why in the world you thought it was appropriate for yourself and three of your deputies to pile on this man at once?"

"Because it took four of us to subdue him."

"And you didn't think there might be some way to de-escalate the situation by talking him down instead of immediately resorting to violence?"

"When they first arrived on the scene, Deputies Carelton and Northcutt found the defendant kicking in the door of SafeHaven, trying to get to his wife, who had sought shelter there from his abuse. They ordered him to stop but he continued, and things went downhill from there."

"They went downhill because they immediately started fighting with him. And then, according to the report, you and another deputy arrived on the scene and jumped right into the scuffle without even trying to ascertain what was going on first. Isn't that right, Sheriff Weber?"

"With all due respect, Your Honor, you weren't there. We had a large man who was out of control, threatening to kill people and attempting to break into a building where his wife was hiding. When myself and Deputy Fuchette arrived, my other two deputies were already engaged in a physical confrontation with the defendant and they weren't having much success getting him under control. There wasn't time to "ascertain what was going on" as you put it. We took action to stop him before things got even worse."

"I know you're talking, Sheriff Weber, but all I can hear in my mind is four to one. I just don't see how that is fair."

"Your Honor, in a situation like that, if it took twenty officers to get control of the perp and end the threat, so be it. Mr. MacGregor could have stopped what he was doing at any time and there would not have been a physical confrontation. That's the route he chose, sir, not us."

The judge scowled at Weber and said, "No matter how you try to justify it, Sheriff, in my opinion four officers on one person is uncalled for. No matter what the situation is. Mr. MacGregor, do you have an attorney present?"

"Yes, sir, Your Honor," said a tall Hispanic man as he stood up. "I am Renaldo Ortiz and Mr. MacGregor's mother has hired me to represent him."

"Have you had a chance to talk to your client, Counselor?"

"Only briefly, Your Honor."

"This is a an arraignment. Do you need more time to confer with your client before he enters a plea?"

"No, sir. Mr. MacGregor pleads not guilty."

"I see. Mr. Bennett, what are your thoughts on bail for the defendant?"

"Your Honor, this man is a danger to the public. He has repeatedly assaulted members of this community, his wife, and now these police officers. I would ask that no bond be permitted at this time."

"Has Mr. MacGregor ever been convicted of a crime of violence, Mr. Bennett?"

"No, sir, but that's only because people are too intimidated to…"

"That's speculation, sir. I deal in facts. Has his wife ever filed a complaint against him for assault?"

"No, sir. But that's only because…"

"Stop it," the judge said, raising his hands to cut off any further comment from the Town's Attorney. "If all you have to go on is hearsay, Mr. Bennett, save your breath. I see no reason to hold someone in jail based on what you're telling me about this defendant."

"But, Your Honor…"

Ignoring him, the judge turned to the defendant and his attorney.

"Mr. Ortiz, what say you?"

"Your Honor, there's no question my defendant was out of control yesterday. He's not denying that and he deeply regrets it. But that was not normal behavior for him. He was so distraught over coming home to find his wife had left him out of the blue, for no reason at all, that he lost it. Was it right for him to go to

Big Lake Wedding

the women's shelter and act like he did? No, it wasn't. Was it right for him to resist arrest? No sir, it wasn't. He freely acknowledges that. But at the same time, the actions of the officers involved only served to further escalate the situation. As you, yourself, have acknowledged, sir, four on one is not exactly fair odds."

Weber shook his head in disgust as the defense attorney began to list his client's many positive qualities.

"Your Honor, Mr. MacGregor is a son, a brother, and a loving husband with deep roots to the community. If anything, he is as much a victim here as anyone. Four officers beating on a distraught man who only wanted to see his wife and save his marriage. I would ask that he be released on his own recognizance."

Bob Bennett started to object but the judge gave him a warning look and shook his head.

"Mr. MacGregor, if I release you pending trial, do I have your word that you will stay out of trouble?"

"Yes, sir, I promise."

"I'm going to release you on $500 bond, sir. I'm going to add a condition to your release, and that is that you have no contact with your wife or anybody on the staff at SafeHaven. I would also tell you I think you need to consider anger management counseling. Do you agree to those terms?"

"Yes, sir. Thank you, sir."

The judge looked back at Weber and shook his head. "Four on one? Really?" He rapped his gavel and said, "Court is adjourned. See the clerk to pay your bail, Mr. MacGregor."

Nick Russell

Chapter 4

"Seeing that jerk strut out of court like he didn't have a care in the world just pisses me off," Weber said bitterly an hour later.

"You can't win them all, bubba," his best friend, FBI Agent Larry Parks said. "Knowing what I know of that guy, you'll get another shot at him. Some people can't keep out of trouble no matter what they do."

"I can't believe how much of an idiot that judge is. Condemning us because it took four of us to get him under control. He could have stopped resisting at any time. He was the one that wanted to fight."

"Well now, maybe that judge was onto something. Did you ever think about that? Maybe you're doing things all wrong. How about the next time you get a situation going on, you forget the pepper spray and the Tasers and all that and just whisper sweet nothings in the perp's ear? Who knows, maybe it'll work?"

"The only thing I want to whisper in this particular perp's ear is "you're dead," just before I pull the trigger," the sheriff replied.

"See, there you go again, acting like a Neanderthal. I think there's way too much red meat in your diet. I really do."

"And I think you're as full of shit as a Christmas turkey," Weber told him.

Parks laughed and said, "Be that as it may, it's a brave new world my friend. Embrace it."

Before Weber could reply, his cell phone buzzed and he pulled it out of his pocket. Pushing the button to answer, he asked, "What's up, Mary?"

"I think you should come back to the office," Mary Caitlin said. "Something's come up you need to know about."

~~***~~

The air seemed subdued when Weber walked in the office and he noticed that everybody had uncomfortable looks on their faces and no one would meet his eye.

"Geez, you guys are acting like somebody died. What's going on?"

"Let's go in your office," Mary said.

"Okay."

Weber followed her into his office and Mary closed the door.

"Sit down, Jimmy, there's something I have to show you."

"What is it that's so bad that I have to sit down?"

"It's just easier to show you this way," Mary said, moving the mouse to his computer until the screen saver cleared. "Check your email."

Weber logged into his email account and Mary pointed to an unopened email titled From Robyn To You. "Open that one."

Weber did and was startled to see a photograph of a braless Robyn holding her shirt open and flashing her breasts.

"What the hell?"

"Everybody in the Department got the same email. See, it's addressed to you but then it's cc'd to everybody else."

"Why would Robyn send me something like that?"

"I don't know. That's between you and her. But I don't know how she goofed up and sent it to everybody else, too."

"No, Mary, something's wrong here. Robyn wouldn't send a picture like that in the first place."

"I couldn't believe it when I saw it either, Jimmy. Not that I'm judging or anything, but…"

"No. She wouldn't send a picture like that. She wouldn't even take a picture like that. Or let anybody else take one of her."

"Well, that's her, isn't it?"

"Yeah, that's her, but I just don't understand this."

"Maybe she got a little silly and decided to send you something special as a goof," Mary said. "It wouldn't be hard to make a mistake and click Send All or something so that everybody in the department got it."

"I know Robyn, and I know she wouldn't do that."

"I didn't think so either, but it's her email address in the return line, Jimmy. RFuchette@biglakeSO.AZ.gov."

"Then somebody must have hacked it or something. Have you talked to Robyn about this yet?"

"No," Mary said. "It popped up on Tommy's email and he got white as a ghost when he saw it. At the same time, I got it, and so did Chad. That's when I saw that it was mailed to everybody in the Department. I wanted you to know first because I wasn't sure how to handle it."

Weber pulled his phone from his pocket and pushed the speed dial number for Robyn. When she answered, he asked, "Where are you?"

"I'm just leaving the house to run some errands. Actually, I'm just trying to get away from my mother. What's up?"

"I need you here at the office, ASAP," Weber told her.

"I'm on my way. What's going on?"

"I'll tell you when you get here. Don't be long."

~~***~~

"That's not me! I don't know who that is, Jimmy, but it's not me."

"That's what I told Mary. But it looks like you."

"I don't care who it looks like, that's not me! I don't understand what's going on. You said everybody in the department got this?"

"I'm afraid so," Mary said.

"How could this happen?"

"I have no idea," Weber said.

"Robyn, please don't take any offense, because I'm not judging you at all," Mary said tentatively. "Is it possible that you were goofing off or something and took a picture like this and forgot all about it?"

"No, Mary. No way. And besides, if it was a selfie I'd be holding the camera with one hand, wouldn't I? In this picture I'm holding my shirt open with both hands. I mean, *I'm* not holding my shirt open, but the woman in the picture is. So somebody else had to have taken it. And even if it was me, which it's not, would I then forget that I sent it to the whole damn department?"

There was a sound at Weber's office door and Chet Wingate opened it.

"Sorry to interrupt, Jimmy, but I wondered if we could continue our conversation from this morning."

"Not now, Chet," Weber snapped. "And don't be opening my damn door without an invitation!"

But it was too late, the unwelcome visitor had already seen the image on the computer screen. "What's the meaning of this? This is disgusting! How dare you look at photos like this on a department computer?"

Mary got up and quickly ushered the unwelcome visitor into the outer office.

"Jimmy, that's not me in that picture," Robyn repeated, shaking her head.

"I believe you. I'm just trying to figure out some explanation for it."

"I don't know what the explanation is. I just know that's not me."

Weber looked at the image on the screen. If Robyn wasn't the woman in the picture, whoever it was was a dead ringer for her. She was wearing jeans and a light blue or white shirt, standing in the forest somewhere, a smile on her face as she exposed herself to the camera.

"Robyn, is there any chance that someone else could've taken a picture of you like…"

Big Lake Wedding

"No, Jimmy. No chance at all. My God, we're supposed to be getting married in two weeks and you don't know me any better than that?"

"I'm not saying it's you, Robyn. I'm just saying..."

"What? What are you saying, Jimmy?" Robyn was staring at him with her arms crossed and an angry look on her face.

"All I mean is... hell, Robyn, I don't know what I mean. I just wondered if some old boyfriend or somebody from the past..."

"I've never asked you how many notches you've got on your bedpost from before we got together, Jimmy. But I can assure you, it's a hell of a lot more than I have. And I never let anybody take a picture of me when I was naked or partially naked or anything like that. And I damn sure didn't pose for one!"

By then she was shouting. Mary knocked on the door and came back in.

"I'm sorry about that, I had no idea Chet was here," she said.

"I'm sure by now he's already broadcasting this to the whole town," Robyn said.

"Robyn, I don't know how to tell you this, but he doesn't have to."

"What do you mean, Mary?"

She looked at the younger woman with apprehension in her eyes when she said, "I just got a phone call from Kirby Templeton and he received the same email. Apparently so did every member of the Town Council."

~~***~~

"Okay, it looks like Robyn sent the emails, but she didn't," Larry Parks said. "The return address says it's from Robyn, but see here when I hover the mouse over the sender's email address? It actually says it came from WXHK@soonta22459.net."

"Who the hell is that?" Robyn demanded.

"I have no idea," Parks replied. He did a quick Google search and said, "Nothing comes up. My guess is that it's a spoof email address leading back through a bunch of blind IP addresses, and we are almost certainly going to hit a dead end trying to find where it originated from."

"Well, you'd better find it," Robyn said. "And stop looking at my boobs! Or whoever's boobs those are in the picture."

"Hey, it's all innocent. I'm just doing research."

"Whatever you're researching, it's just creepy. Could you please close that screen before somebody else walks in here and sees it? It's bad enough Chet Wingate did!"

"Well, we know one thing at least," Parks said.

"What's that?"

"We know all that nonsense about him having a bad heart isn't true. Seeing this picture about knocked me out of my shoes. If I had a bad heart it would kill me. But what the hell, I'd die with a smile on my face."

"Not funny, Parks. Not funny at all."

"Robyn, I know you're really pissed off, and I can understand that. But trust me, a year from now this really is going to seem funny."

"I swear, Parks, you look at that picture one more time and you won't be alive a year from now."

He closed the screen and said, "Okay, we confirmed what we already knew. Robyn didn't send the picture. Now we just need to figure out who did, and why?"

"And how do we do that?"

"I'll call down to the field office in Phoenix and talk to some people who know more about computer forensics than I do," Parks told her. "Meanwhile, Robyn, can you think of anybody who would have sent a picture like that? Could someone have taken a picture of you when you…"

Weber winced at the explosion that he knew was coming, but Robyn surprised him when she said evenly, "Let's get this straight once and for all. That's not me in that picture. No boyfriend or anybody else ever took a picture of me like that, or any other pictures even close to it. So, if you're going to start looking up old boyfriends and checking their photo files, you're wasting your time. And no, I didn't go out in the middle of the forest and strip down and some passerby took a picture. It's not me!"

"I believe you," Parks told her. "I believe you, and Jimmy believes you, and Mary believes you. We all believe you. So now that we've established that it's not you, we've got to figure out who this woman is and why whoever's behind this sent those emails."

"Let's get this done as fast as we can," Mary said. "We've already had phone calls from every Town Council member and a couple dozen people who heard about it through the grapevine."

"The grapevine being Chet Wingate," Robyn said bitterly. There were tears in her eyes and Weber wrapped his arms around her and said, "We are going to get to the bottom of this. I promise you."

"And meanwhile, everybody in town thinks I'm some kind of crazy flasher or something. How can I ever look anybody in the face around here again?"

"You do it the way you do everything else," Mary Caitlin told her. "You hold your head high and you take care of business, Robyn. You know what they say, those who really know you don't need an explanation, and those who don't know you probably won't believe an explanation anyway. Just keep being you. This too shall pass."

"God, Mary, you sound like you're repeating passages from some twelve-step program or something."

"Believe me. After being married to Pete Caitlin as long as I have, I know a lot of passages to help me get through the day."

Nick Russell

Chapter 5

Robyn stayed in the office and did not go out on patrol that day, busying herself with paperwork.

When Weber returned later that afternoon, one look at his face told her there was more bad news.

"What is it, Jimmy? Tell me."

"I'm sorry, Robyn. It wasn't just people here in our Department and the Town Council that got that email. Paul got one at the newspaper, Juliette Murdoch got one at the Chamber of Commerce, Judge Ryman's Court Clerk got one, and I'm sure there's one in the judge's email inbox, too."

"How could this be happening, Jimmy? Why is it happening?"

He shook his head. "I don't know. I really don't. Now, don't go off on me, hear me out, okay? I believe that you never let anybody take a picture of you like that. It's got to be some kind of photomanipulation or something. What do they call it... Photoshopping something? Where they take a picture of a person and put them someplace else or with somebody else. Parks thinks that's what's happening, and so does Dan Wright, and they both know a lot more about computers than I do. Hell, you probably know as much as they do. So, setting the fact that it's a fake photo aside, we need to look at who did this. Is there an old boyfriend with a grudge about something that might have been able to create a picture like that and send it?"

"No, nobody would do that, that I can think of. Why would they?"

"I have been at this job long enough to know that people do things for a lot of reasons," Mary said. "Sometimes it's jealousy, sometimes they're mad about some insult or whatever. Was there ever a guy that you broke it off with that you thought was okay with things, Robyn? Somebody that you'd didn't think had a problem, but maybe they secretly did?"

She thought for a minute and shook her head. "I haven't exactly been in a lot of relationships, okay? And no, I don't know of anybody I was ever involved with who would do anything like this, or would feel they had a reason to."

"Honey, I don't know how to say this, so please don't take it the wrong way," Weber said. "I'm in a bad position here because I don't want to intrude on your privacy, and you're right, the past is the past. Unless the past shows up in the present to cause problems. But, we need to know who you were dating just so we can check them out. If it were somebody else that this was happening to, you know that would be one of the first steps we would have to take."

"Jimmy… never mind. I'll make a list. But don't get your hopes up, it's a pretty short list."

"Can I say something?" Dan Wright asked.

"Unless it's a comment on my boobs, go ahead," Robyn replied.

"We also need to look at people that you've interacted with on the job. You may not have an old boyfriend who's carrying a grudge, but I don't know a cop in the world who hasn't got at least a few people who would love to find some way to get even with them for whatever they got busted for."

"He's got a point," Weber said. "I guess we need two lists. And we both know that second one is going to be a lot longer."

~~***~~

"Do we really have to do this? Because all I want to do is run away," Robyn said when they returned to her house that evening.

"It's okay, honey. You can't hide out at the office forever. You're going to have to face the world, and your mother, sooner or later."

"How about later? Like a lot later? I don't know if I can deal with her right now."

"Do you suppose she's heard about it already?"

"I doubt it. If she did, we would have heard her shrieking all the way from the office."

Weber laughed and said, "Might as well get it over with. Remember, you're not alone. I'm here."

"So, what am I supposed to do? Just go in and say, 'Hi Daddy, hi Mother. How was your day? Oh, by the way, everybody in town has looked at pictures of my boobs that aren't really my boobs, just somebody who looks like me showing their boobs.' How do you think they're going to take that, Jimmy?"

"I think your mother's probably going to put on a display of histrionics that would wake up the dead, and I think your father is going to be concerned about you and how you are handling things."

"You know, Jimmy, there was a time when I would just turn around and run. It was how I dealt with things."

"I know."

He did know that. He knew it firsthand, because early in their relationship Robyn had done a disappearing act when she couldn't cope with the stress. Weber had always wondered why she would never hesitate to wade into the middle of a bar fight or domestic disturbance to break things up, but got a deer in the headlights look and bolted when things became uncomfortable on a personal level away from the job.

"Don't worry, I'm not going to do it now."

"I hope you never do it again, Robyn."

She closed her eyes for a moment, then opened them and looked at him and said, "I wish I could promise you that. In my heart, I don't think I will. But right now, that's my first instinct."

Before he could reply, the front door of her house opened and her mother came out on the porch, demanding to know, "Are you two ever going to come inside, or do you just plan to sit out there all night?"

~~***~~

If anything, Weber had been generous in his response to the question about how Renée Fuchette would react to the news that someone was sending a fake photograph of her half nude daughter to many of the movers and shakers in Big Lake. The woman stood with her mouth agape and Weber wondered if they might be so lucky that she had been stunned into permanent silence. A moment later she proved him wrong.

"That's it! No more! You pack some clothes right now, Robyn, because we're going back home and you're never coming back to this disgusting town!"

"Mother, this *is* my home and I'm not going anywhere."

"Are you out of your mind, Robyn? It doesn't bother you that people are seeing a picture of you like that?"

"Yes, of course it bothers me, Mother. But it's not a picture of *me*. Like Jimmy said, it's Photoshopped, or whatever they call it."

"I don't care what they call it or how they made it look like you. It's disgusting! And as for you, Jim Weber, this is one more example of the terrible lifestyle you have exposed my daughter to. Well, I can tell you something, mister. It stops right now!"

"Mother, please, would you just stop?"

"No, Robyn, I won't stop. I don't know what's wrong inside your head that you are willing to put up with things like this, but I will not stand by and see you ruin your life."

"If you want to leave and go back to Phoenix, have at it, Mother. But stop treating me like a child. I'm an adult. I'm a police officer. And I'm engaged to be married. I don't need you making my decisions for me."

"Well, obviously you do, because the decisions you have been making lately are insane. I don't know what kind of spell this man has cast on you, but you need to open your eyes, Robyn. He's no good for you."

Big Lake Wedding

"That's enough," Robyn's father said. "Just drop it, Renée."

"Don't you try to silence me, Bill Fuchette! This girl has tried to ruin her life ever since she was sixteen, and all you've done is stand by and smile at her and tell her 'it's okay, Daddy's here.' Somebody has to try to talk some sense into her."

"Stop bringing up the past, Mother."

"What? You're afraid your boyfriend is going to find out your dirty little secret? Well maybe it's time he knew. Have you told him, or do I have to do it?"

"Shut up, Renée," her husband warned, but there was no quieting down the enraged woman.

"Jim, do you know that when Robyn was…"

"Yes, Mother, he knows I got pregnant when I was a teenager. And he knows I went to Mexico and got an abortion that screwed me up inside so badly I can never have children. We don't have any secrets from each other."

"No secrets? Really? Well, isn't that precious?" She turned to Weber and asked, "And you have no problem with that? How many secrets are you holding onto that Robyn won't know about until it's too late? Well, guess what? I know about all the womanizing you did. I know about that little drinking problem of yours, too. And that the Town Council has tried to fire you repeatedly. Not to mention your sister the murderer. Oh yes, I know all about you, mister!"

"Everybody has a past," Weber said, "and Robyn knows all about it. I never pretended to be an angel. And to answer your first question, no, I don't have a problem with anything about Robyn. She wasn't the first young girl to make a mistake, and she won't be the last. In fact, one of my deputies' daughter was in that exact position a while back. Except there was one exception. Do you know what that exception was?"

"No, I don't know, and I don't really care."

"It doesn't matter, I'm going to tell you anyway. The difference was, that girl had a mother and father who stood by her. Who instead of criticizing and demeaning her, put their arms around her and loved her and gave her support when she needed it most. Now, Bill here, I'm pretty sure that's what he did, because that's the kind of man he is. He's a father in every sense of the word. On the other hand, you're a bitch, lady. Maybe if you would have been a mother for your daughter when she needed you, she wouldn't have felt like she had no other choice than to go to Mexico and risk her life to do what she did."

Renée seemed speechless for the second time that evening, but it didn't take long for her to react. She slapped Weber's face hard enough to rattle his teeth, and said, "How dare you speak to me that way!" Then she stormed down the hall, slamming the bedroom door. A repeat of the previous evening's events.

The three of them stood quietly in the kitchen after her departure, then Weber said, "Bill, I'm sorry. That was out of line, but…"

Robyn's father shook his head and waved the comment away. "No apology necessary. You said what everybody who knows that woman has thought for years."

There was a platter of uncooked hamburger patties sitting next to the stove, preparations for the dinner her mother had been making when they arrived. Bill started laying them out in a pan and said, "If she keeps getting mad and skipping dinner like she's been doing, maybe she'll starve to death and all of our problems will be over."

Weber smiled and Robyn laughed, appreciating the man's attempt to lighten the mood. Little did any of them know that their problems were just beginning.

Chapter 6

The minute he walked in the door the next morning Weber could tell by the look on Mary Caitlin's face that there was more bad news waiting for him. Without a word she nodded her head toward his office. He followed her inside, waiting to hear what she had to say. Instead of telling him, she opened his email program and clicked on a new message.

This picture was more explicit than the first. The woman was standing facing the camera totally nude, her hands cupping her breasts.

"Son of a bitch. Please tell me everybody didn't…"

"I'm afraid so. We've all gotten it. And the Town Council, and the newspaper, and the Chamber of Commerce, and Steve Harper at the fire department. Along with Joyce Taylor at the bank and at least three business owners I've heard from already this morning."

"Oh, Mary. This is going to kill Robyn."

"I know, Jimmy. I can't imagine what she must be feeling right now."

There was a knock on his door and when Mary went to see who it was, Larry Parks said, "I got another picture."

"So did everybody else," Mary told him. "Come on in."

The FBI agent looked at his friend and shook his head. "Sorry, Jimmy."

"Tell me that you guys can figure out who is sending this crap."

"The problem is, this isn't a federal crime. So officially, the Bureau can't do anything about it. But I think it falls under the category of revenge porn, which is a felony under Arizona law. In fact, it's a Class 4 felony if the person is recognizable and if the photos are sent without that person's permission, with the intent to harm, harass, or intimidate them. If the people were in a relationship or living together, it also falls under the domestic violence category."

"Even if the pictures aren't actually Robyn?"

"They aren't Robyn, but she is obviously the target. The pictures are meant to make people believe it's Robyn, so that's obviously harming and harassing her, in my opinion. But keep in mind, I'm not an attorney."

"If I catch the asshole doing this, he's going to need more than an attorney," Weber said.

"But how do we figure out who it is?"

"Like I said, Mary, officially the Bureau can't do anything. But I've got a couple of friends who are willing to do some snooping around unofficially, as a favor to me. So far, they've run into brick walls, which is to be expected. Remember when I told you yesterday that the real email address of whoever sent the pictures is going to lead back through a bunch of blind IP addresses? That's what's happening."

"So what does that mean? Can they find this guy or not?"

"I think they can find him," Parks replied. "But it's going to take some work, and like I said, these folks are doing it on the side for me, and keeping it unofficial."

"In the meantime, the person doing it keeps destroying Robyn's reputation."

"I know it's frustrating as hell, Jimmy. No matter how many paths the email address gets routed through, I think it's a pretty safe bet that they are originating from right here in Big Lake, don't you? Unless there's someone from someplace else that would have a reason to hurt Robyn. Can she think of anybody like that?"

Weber shook his head. "No, she's been over it a thousand times in her head and she can't think of anybody, anywhere, who would do this."

"What about old lovers, things like that? I don't mean to be indelicate, but..."

"No, you're right, and that's something we're looking into right now. She gave Mary a list. I haven't looked at it, trying to respect her privacy. Did you guys find out anything, Mary?"

"She told us yesterday it was a short list, and it is," Mary replied. "I put Coop and Chad on it. So far, nothing."

"There was also a list of people she may have crossed paths with on the job that are holding something of a grudge. Anything there?"

"Yeah, that's the longer list by far, Jimmy. Three names from that list come to mind right now, but there may be more."

"Who are they?"

"Levi Bischoff, Shane Wilder, and Donald MacGregor."

"MacGregor? Our last run-in with him was just a couple of days ago. He was just in court yesterday, and that's when the first picture came. Could he have done something that fast?"

"I don't know, Jimmy. But yesterday wasn't the only time he and Robyn have crossed paths. She's been out to their house two or three times when he was beating on his wife."

"Come to think of it, when we were on our way out to SafeHaven the other day she told me that her and Coop were at the house last week on a call, and that he told her then that he was going to get even with her."

"So maybe he had been planning this all along," Parks said. "Because whoever did this, they put some time and effort into it. Look at that picture on the screen, we all know it's not Robyn, but it sure looks like her."

"It looks like her, but it's not her," Weber said.

"Like I said, we all know that."

"No, I know it better than anybody else. I mean, I've seen her naked. There are differences."

"I don't really think you have to elaborate, Jimmy," Mary told him.

"No, I don't need to go into detail. But I can tell you right now, that's not Robyn."

"Okay, putting that aside, look at this." Parks did something with the mouse to zoom the picture in. "We're going to assume this is somebody else's body, which is obvious, but if that's not Robyn's face she has one of those, what do they call them? Doppelgängers? An exact double. Usually when somebody manipulates a photograph to put a different head on a body you can tell it here, around the neck. Maybe a slight twisting or something, depending on the angle, or a slight difference in skin tones or some pixilation. Whoever did these was very good, because you're not seeing that here."

Weber studied the picture again. In the first picture, the woman seemed to be in the forest somewhere. In this one she was standing in a bedroom. There were no photographs on the wall or anything else that might identify where it was located. Just an unmade bed, a bare nightstand in the background, and a dresser on the wall behind her.

"Does Donald MacGregor know enough about computers to do this?"

"I don't know, Jimmy. It's not that hard to Photoshop a picture like this, but to do it with this kind of quality, that's someone who has had some practice."

"All right, we've got MacGregor on the list. Who are those other two that stood out to you, Mary?"

"Levi Bischoff and Shane Wilder. Robyn and Levi tangled back in December when he got drunk and rowdy at the Brewpub and she took the call to remove him. He was drunk enough to shove her, and Robyn took him down to the floor and arrested him. He spent a night in jail and his buddies ragged on him for a couple of weeks about how that little woman made him do a faceplant, then put her pink handcuffs on him and dragged his ass out the door."

"I'd say if he made the mistake of shoving her, he got what he had coming," Weber said.

"Nobody's disagreeing with that," Mary replied. "I think Levi definitely learned his lesson. I know Robyn took another call a while back when he was drunk and being obnoxious at the Town Pump. But the way I hear it, as soon as Robyn showed up, he settled right down and apologized to the store manager and that was it."

"I know Levi pretty well," Weber said. "When he's not drinking he's a pretty decent guy. I think he'd give anybody the shirt off his back if they needed it. But like with a lot of people, when he gets boozed up he becomes a completely different person, and he'll argue with you about anything and everything."

"Is it possible he's still fuming inside about being embarrassed by a girl arresting him?"

"I don't see it, Parks. But what the hell do I know? I think somebody needs to talk to him for sure."

"What about this last guy, Mary? Shane Wilder."

"Shane's a real piece of work, Parks. He comes from a long line of losers and he's doing everything he can to carry on the family tradition."

"Didn't his dad do time?"

Mary nodded her head. "Back when Pete was sheriff, George Wilder was a young man. About same age Shane is now. He was always in some kind of trouble. Joy riding, stealing gas, nothing major until he was 19. That's when he got caught breaking into the IGA. He got six months for that, and he wasn't back home more than a month or so when he got caught stealing batteries from cars parked right in the owner's driveways. Judge Abernathy was on the bench back then, and he didn't waste any time violating George's probation and sending him back behind bars. He got out and settled down after that, but Pete always thought he was just as bad, he had just learned how to hide it better. Both of his boys, Shane and Destry, have been in and out of trouble for as far back as I can remember."

As far back as Mary Caitlin could remember was a long time. The wife of the former sheriff seemed to have an encyclopedic knowledge about every family in and around Big Lake. Someone once joked that not only did Mary know where all the bodies were buried, she knew who supplied the shovels. That wasn't far from the truth.

"What's Shane's beef with Robyn?"

Mary looked at her notes and said, "Three months ago Robyn pulled him over on a routine traffic stop for no brake lights. Turned out the license plate on the car he was driving was from another vehicle that was registered to somebody else, he didn't have any proof of insurance, and his driver's license was suspended. Robyn also said in her report that she could smell alcohol on him and asked if he had been drinking. Of course, according to him he only had one or two drinks"

"I don't think I've ever stopped a drunk driver who didn't tell me he had only had one or two." Weber said.

"Maybe they forget how to count after that first drink," Mary said. "After he failed the field sobriety test, the breathalyzer showed he was way past the legal limit. She arrested him, then searched his car and found pot in the console. He claimed she planted it, but her body cam showed otherwise. He started giving her grief and was making all kinds of threats until she let him know who was boss. I don't know if he's smart enough to even know how to turn on a computer, let alone do something like this. But you never know."

"All right, I think we need to have a talk with all three of these clowns. In the meantime, Mary, keep digging to see if you can find anybody else who might be responsible for this."

While he was speaking the telephone on his desk rang and Mary picked it up. She listened for a moment and said, "I'll tell him" before hanging up.

"Tell me what?"

"That was Kirby Templeton. He's on his way over here, said he needs to talk to you."

~~***~~

Kirby Templeton, senior Town Council member and Big Lake's interim mayor, had a troubled look on his face when he arrived at the office a short time later. Mary showed him into Weber's office and left them alone.

"I guess I know what this is about, don't I?"

"This is bad news, Jimmy. It seems like almost everybody in town has seen those pictures of Robyn, and if they haven't seen them, they've darned sure heard about them."

"Kirby, I know it looks like her, but that's not Robyn in those pictures."

"That's what Mary said, too, and I'm not calling either one of you a liar. But the fact is, even though it may not be Robyn, it looks like her and everybody thinks it's her. I've had at least a dozen people come in the pharmacy and say something to me about it already."

"We're trying to get to the bottom of it, Kirby, believe me."

"Oh, I believe you. I just hope you can do it fast. Do you have any idea who might be sending these pictures yet?"

"We're looking at a bunch of different angles. So far, nothing positive."

"How is Robyn handling all this, Jimmy?"

"About like you'd expect. She's humiliated, she wonders what everybody's thinking about her, and she's really mad at whoever's doing this. Like the stress of the wedding wasn't already enough."

"I can understand that. Look, Jimmy, I hate to be the bearer of bad news, but the Town Council's called an emergency meeting for 3 o'clock this afternoon. We need you and Robyn to be there."

"Kirby, please don't rake her over the coals. Robyn's a very private person and this whole thing is taking a toll on her."

"I understand that, Jimmy. I really do. But this isn't my doing. And to be honest, the Council can't just ignore a situation like this. We have to be able to tell the people of this town something when they ask us why photographs of a naked deputy are showing up in their email inboxes."

"It's not Robyn," Weber replied evenly, though both men could hear the tension in his voice.

"It doesn't matter who it is, Jimmy. Everybody who sees those pictures *thinks* it's Robyn. And until you can prove it isn't her, we need to take some action."

"Take action? What kind of action, Kirby?"

"I don't know. That's something that the whole Council has to decide."

Weber wanted to say that if they would really believe it was Robyn in those pictures, the whole Town Council could go to hell as far as he was concerned. But he knew that wouldn't accomplish anything. Kirby Templeton had been a good friend for many years, and the sheriff knew he was an honorable man who was only doing his duty.

"3 o'clock. We'll be there."

Chapter 7

"What do you want with Shane? He ain't done nothing wrong."

Judy Wilder was wearing a thin, faded green terrycloth robe and her lank hair looked like it had not known shampoo or felt the touch of a comb or brush in days, if not weeks. She was a thin, stoop shouldered woman who had been beaten down by life ever since she was a little girl. Growing up in a dysfunctional home where her alcoholic father couldn't keep a job and her mother drank just as much to fuel her constant need to criticize and belittle her children. She had been more than happy to marry George Wilder when he asked her to. If he hadn't proposed, she had no idea what she would have done, being fifteen and three months pregnant with his child and all. She knew being married to George was not going to be a picnic, but at least it was a way to escape her situation at home.

George had proven to be just as bad at providing for his family as her own father had been, and though he didn't drink as much, he was certainly no stranger to alcohol. At least he didn't hit her or go into fits of rage like both of her parents had done. Things like that would take too much effort. George preferred to park his ass on the couch as soon as he got out of bed in the morning, and stayed there most days. Well, except for those days when he did leave whatever shabby house they were living in at the moment to go and try to scrounge up a few bucks. More often than not, he did that by stealing something and selling it to whoever would buy it. At least George had gotten better at his petty thievery and wasn't getting arrested all the time like he did when he was younger.

Their union had produced four children; Lila, Destry, Shane, and Susie. Like her, Lila had married the first guy who asked her, and was back home again in less than two years holding a little one on her hip and with another in her belly. Destry and Shane had both inherited their father's aversion to honest work and sometimes accompanied him when he was on the hunt for car batteries, tires, or anything else that wasn't nailed down that they could pilfer. They also both inherited their parents' penchant for strong drink.

And then there was Susie. Judy had heard stories before about babies being switched at birth, and in Susie's case she truly believed that might have happened. While she and George were both slender, as were their other three children, Susie was… well, as much as Judy hated to put it in those terms, the girl was a blimp. She had been a pudgy baby who became a pudgy toddler, and then a pudgy child, and by the time she hit her teens, she was fat. There was no other way to say it. Not just fat, but really fat! Her blouses always gaped open at the buttonholes and showed a roll of blubber, so by the time she was fourteen she had taken to wearing shapeless dresses that looked like someone had thrown a large blanket over her head. Not that many people ever saw her anyhow. Susie stayed in her room reading books about horses and fairies and dragons and nonsense. Except when she had to go to school, which wasn't all that often. It was always a battle to get her out the door. Neither Judy or George put much stock in all of that classroom nonsense, so as often as not when Susie ignored the third knock on her bedroom door telling her to get ready for school, Judy stopped trying to get her in gear.

The only other place Susie ever went was to the town's little library. Every week she brought home an armload of books the librarians had ordered for her from other libraries in the region that they were connected with. Books, horses, and Oreo cookies seemed to be the only things Susie cared about in life. And her mother was pretty sure that if the Oreo supply ever ran dry, the girl might actually eat a horse! Or at least one of her books.

Now, standing in the doorway blocking the sheriff's entrance, Judy tried to think about what her husband and sons might have done lately to bring the law to their door.

"I didn't say Shane did anything wrong," Weber told her. "I just need to ask him a few questions."

"Right. That's what you guys say every time you come around here, and then you haul somebody off to jail. I'm telling you right now, whatever you think Shane did, he didn't do it."

"Really, Mrs. Wilder? You don't know why I'm here, but you know Shane's innocent of anything. That's interesting. How do you know that?"

"I know that every time you people show up, you're here to cause us trouble. That's how I know it."

"Look, Mrs. Wilder, I'm not here to give you any problems. I just need to ask Shane a couple of questions."

"Who is it, Ma?"

Weber couldn't tell which one of the Wilder sons was yelling from inside the house trailer, but instead of waiting for the woman to reply, he called back, "It's Sheriff Weber. If that's you, Shane, I need to talk to you for a minute."

He almost expected to hear the sound of the back door slamming and was glad a deputy was back there in case the man they were looking for decided to make a run for it. But instead, a shirtless young man with unruly black hair and a scraggly beard appeared behind his mother. "Whatever it is that you think I did, it wasn't me."

"Hi there, Shane. That's the same thing your mother told me."

Shane scratched at the thick mat of hair on his chest and Weber couldn't help but wonder what might be living in there and tried not to shudder.

"Would you mind stepping out here on the porch for a minute?"

"Whatever."

His mother moved aside and Shane sauntered out onto the porch. His arms and belly were covered in poorly done tattoos, and he had three or four piercings in his lower lip and face.

"What's up?"

"Shane, do you have a computer?"

"Do I look like a computer geek to you?"

"No, sir, you don't. But sometimes looks are deceiving. Hell, for all I know, you might be the next Supreme Court Justice."

"Whoever said I stole a computer is lying. I never touched one. Don't have any use for the damn things."

"Really? That surprises me. They're small and easy to transport, I'd think you'd be stealing them right and left every chance you got."

"Me? You got me all wrong, Sheriff. That must be somebody else you're thinking about."

"You think? Well then, let me ask you this, Shane. Do you have a problem with Deputy Fuchette?"

"That's your squeeze, right?"

"Answer the question, Shane. Do you have a problem with her?"

The man stretched nonchalantly and then smirked when he said, "Only problem I have is that she never sent me any of those nudie pictures like she did everybody else in town. Shit man, maybe I need to get myself a computer after all. I'm missing all the action."

Weber knew Shane was trying to provoke him and as much as he would like to slap the smirk off the punk's face, he maintained control.

"I heard there was an incident a while back where Deputy Fuchette arrested you and you didn't take too kindly to that."

"Hey, that bitch set me up!"

"Watch your mouth, Shane."

"Okay, whatever. But I didn't have any pot on me. She planted it. And I wasn't drunk, either."

"That's not what the field sobriety tests and the breathalyzer showed."

"I don't give a rat's ass what your tests showed. I wasn't drunk and I didn't have any pot. She just needed to arrest somebody to make her quota or something. I know how you guys do things."

Weber didn't see any point in standing there arguing over the validity of the arrest, so instead he asked, "Are you sure you don't have a computer, Shane? If I come in and look around, I wouldn't find one?"

"Unless you got a warrant, you ain't coming in this house," Judy Wilder said.

"Naa, there's no need for that," Shane told her. "You want to come in and look around? Be my guest, Sheriff. I got nothing to hide."

He stepped back and waved his hand toward the door.

"Shane, I don't want that man in my house!"

"Get out of the way, Ma. The sooner he looks around, the sooner he'll be gone."

The woman grudgingly backed away from the door so her son and the sheriff could enter. The first thing that hit Weber was the smell. A combination of dirty diapers, body odor, and filth that had been evident from the doorway assaulted his nose when he was two steps inside. George Wilder, wearing only a pair of faded boxer shorts, was asleep on the couch and never roused. A naked toddler was holding onto a small dog of indeterminate breed that had been barking since Weber knocked on the door. When he saw the sheriff the child began crying. Weber wasn't sure if it was because he was a stranger, or because he had inherited his family's natural dislike of law enforcement. The end tables, furniture, and floors were littered with clothing, empty beer and soda cans, dirty paper plates, and other trash.

"Lila, would you come in here and get this screaming kid and this damn mutt? I can't hear myself think for the noise," Judy shouted down the hallway. When there was no response she banged on a closed bedroom door and called, "Lila, get your ass out here!"

The door opened and a young woman with almost as many tattoos as her brother came out wearing a dirty T-shirt and short shorts that showed that both of her legs were also heavily inked. Without a word she walked into the living room and picked up the child in one arm and the dog with the other and returned to her bedroom, closing the door behind her. If she had seen the sheriff standing in her family's living room, she gave no indication of it.

"See, no computer," Shane said.

"How about I look in your bedroom?"

"Have at it."

They moved down the hall and Shane opened the door to a small room that contained two beds, a battered nightstand and dresser, and walls covered with pinups of big pickup trucks and women with even bigger breasts. Like the rest of the house, the place was a mess. And there was no computer.

Shane indicated an open door at the end of the hall and said, "That's my parents' bedroom, take a look. Weber poked his head inside to see that while the room was not as dirty as those he had already viewed, there was no computer on the nightstands, the dresser, or the unmade bed.

"What about these two rooms?"

"Those are my sisters' rooms." Shane opened the door to the one Lila had gone into and they caught his sister wearing only a purple thong as she changed clothes. Even more ink covered the rest of her body.

"Shane, what the hell? Don't you know how to knock?"

While Lila may not have appreciated her brother and the sheriff barging in on her privacy like they did, she didn't take any actions to cover herself, either.

"Sorry," Weber said, backing away from the door.

Wanting to avoid any further embarrassment, he put his hand on Shane's wrist to stop him from opening the door across the hall and knocked,

When he received no response, Shane said, "Susie, open the door. I said open the damn door!"

When there was still no response he opened the door and Weber saw an overweight teenager laying on her stomach on her bed reading a paperback book. She looked up at them but didn't say anything.

"See, no computer? Do you want to take a look in the crapper, too, just to be sure?"

"No, I've seen enough."

Weber realized he had been taking shallow breaths ever since he walked into the mobile home and he wasted no time going back out onto the porch, with Shane following him.

"What's this all about, anyway? I told you I didn't steal any computers."

"I'm not here about any stolen computers," Weber told him. "I want to know who is sending those pictures of Deputy Fuchette out." He didn't figure it was worth the effort to explain that they were doctored images in the first place.

"What? You don't like people looking at your woman's body?"

Seeing the look Weber gave him, Shane said, "Hey, trust me, Sheriff, no disrespect meant. But if I had a woman who looked like her naked, I'd be too busy doing other stuff to worry about taking pictures."

Weber wondered how he could possibly take offense to a statement like that.

"See you around, Shane. Stay out of trouble."

Nick Russell

Chapter 8

"Sure, I know Deputy Fuchette. She's a nice lady."

Levi Bischoff was stacking 50 pound bags of Purina horse feed in the warehouse at Taylor's Farm and Ranch Supply. He was wearing a white T-shirt that was streaked with dirt and was sweating heavily from his efforts. He paused to wipe his arm across his forehead and asked, "Is this about those pictures everybody is getting?"

"That somebody wouldn't be you, would it, Levi?"

The young man was just bending down to pick up another bag from the forklift and he paused and looked at the sheriff quizzically. "Me? Why in the world would I do something like that?"

"I heard you two had a problem at the Brewpub a while back," Weber said.

Levi smiled ruefully and said, "Yeah, I had a few too many and was being a horse's ass. Mike told me I had to leave and I mouthed off to him, so they called the cops. She came in and I shoved her, but I swear to God, Sheriff I wasn't trying to hurt her. I just wanted to get the hell out of there and she was blocking the way. I know that's no excuse, and I'm lucky she didn't charge me with assault or something. Just disorderly conduct, and I damn sure deserved it, too. I can be a jerk when I get to drinking. The next day I apologized to Deputy Fuchette for the way I acted, and I went to the Brewpub and apologized to Mike and Sherry, too."

"The way I heard it, your buddies gave you some grief about a girl taking you down and putting pink handcuffs on you."

Levi laughed and said, "Yeah, they did. I still hear about it now and then."

"And that didn't piss you off, Levi? Strong guy like you that can carry those heavy bags of feed around all day long like it's nothing, and a woman as small as Deputy Fuchette did that to you? Some guys would hold a grudge about that."

Levi picked up the last bag of feed from the forklift and added it to the stack, then wiped his hands and shook his head. "Not me. I had it coming for being such an asshole. And I really did feel bad about shoving her. Sometimes when I drink I do stupid stuff."

"So maybe you wanted to get even with her for embarrassing you like that in front of everybody?"

"What can I say? She got the best of me. Like I said, I had it coming. I damn sure don't have any bad feelings towards her about it. I apologized to her the next day. And I have to admit, if it would've been any of my buddies she took down the same way, I'd be laughing my ass off."

"I heard you and her had another run-in not long ago at the Town Pump."

"That? There was no problem there. I was drunk again and being a jerk and she came in and told me I had to leave. She even gave me a ride home so I wouldn't be driving my truck and getting popped for DUI. She's good people."

"It sounds like you get into a lot of trouble when you drink, Levi."

He nodded his head sheepishly. "Yeah, it's a problem and I know it."

"Maybe you ought to think about getting some help."

"I can handle it on my own, I don't need to sit around in a room full of drunks talking about how much they feel sorry for themselves and expecting everybody else to feel sorry for them, too."

Weber wanted to tell him that it didn't work that way, but at that point he was pretty sure he would be wasting his time and his breath. Besides, he had other things to worry about.

"Let me ask you this, Levi. Do you have a computer?"

"A computer? Yeah, I've got a computer. Why?"

As soon as he said it realization of where their conversation seemed to be heading kicked in and he opened his eyes wide and shook his head. "Hold on there, Sheriff. If you think I'm the one that sent those pictures out, you're wrong. There's no way I would do anything like that."

"So you wouldn't have any objection to me checking out your computer?"

"Hell no, help yourself! We can go to my place and get it right now if you want. There's no way I would post pictures like that of Deputy Fuchette or any other woman. I swear to you, Sheriff, I didn't send those pictures out. I'll take a lie detector test or whatever you want. Like I said before, Deputy Fuchette is a nice lady, and she gave me a couple of breaks even when I didn't deserve them. I don't know who is sending those pictures of her around town, but it's not me. And if I knew who *was* doing it, I would tell you."

Weber had been a cop long enough to know when somebody was lying to him. And based on that experience and his knowledge of the young man, he was pretty sure Levi was being truthful.

"I appreciate your time, Levi. I'll get out of your way so you can get back to work."

"I mean it, Sheriff. We can go get my computer right now. I've got nothing to hide."

"I believe you," Weber said. "But do me a favor, Levi. The next time you have a drink or two, stop before you get yourself in trouble again. It's all about moderation, my friend."

He left the young man there in the hot, dusty warehouse, mentally checking him off their list of suspects.

~~***~~

The driveway was empty and nobody was home at Donald MacGregor's house when Weber and Dolan arrived there. After knocking on the doors and checking around the back of the house, stepping carefully over piles left by at least one large dog, they were returning to their units when a tall, rawboned woman with a mass of curly dark hair that hung down past her shoulders yelled at them from across the street.

"What do you want?"

"We're looking for Donald. Have you seen him around?"

"Why are you bothering him again? Haven't you people done enough to him?"

"We just need to talk to him for a minute," Weber said. "Do you know where he is?"

"No, but if I did, I wouldn't tell you. You guys are always coming around here hassling him and he ain't done nothing wrong!"

"We're not here to hassle him, Mrs. MacGregor," Dolan told her. "Like the sheriff said, we just need to ask him some questions."

"You just leave him alone," Sally MacGregor demanded, marching across the street and pointing her finger at them. "Ever since he was a little boy you cops have been picking on him. There ain't no excuse for it!"

"There's no need to get hostile, ma'am," Weber said. "All we want to do is talk to him."

"If you want to talk to my son, you do it through his lawyer! We know our rights and I'm not going to stand for any more of this bullshit." As if to emphasize her point, she poked Weber in the chest with her finger.

"Ma'am, I'm only going to tell you this once. Keep your hands to yourself and don't touch me again."

"What are you going to do about it? I pay your salary."

"And I appreciate that," Weber told her. "But that doesn't give you the right to assault me."

"Assault? What assault? You're out of your damn mind if you think I assaulted you. If I ever assaulted you, you'd know it!"

"You touched me. That's assault. Don't do it again. Now, if you can't answer our questions and tell us where your son is, how about you go back across the road where you belong?"

"Where I belong? I own this house and mine over there, too. So I belong here. You're the ones that don't belong! Now get off my property."

She raised her hand again, finger pointed toward the sheriff, but saw the look on his face and seemed to think better of it, dropping her hand back to her side.

"We're going," Weber said. "But when you see Donald, tell him I want to talk to him."

"I ain't his damn secretary. Now get out of here."

Weber wasn't in a mood to deal with the irate woman, but as much as he was tempted to let her know who was boss, he didn't. He had learned as a young lawman that you need to choose your battles, and this one wasn't worth it.

"You have yourself a nice day, Mrs. MacGregor."

They got in their units and drove away. Big Lake was a small town, and Weber and Dolan both knew it wouldn't take long for a ne'er-do-well like Donald to show up somewhere, usually looking for trouble.

Nick Russell

Chapter 9

It was past noon and Weber's stomach was growling, so he called Parks to ask if he wanted to meet for lunch at the ButterCup Café. The restaurant was busy with locals and out-of-town visitors, but they managed to snag a table in the back corner near the double doors to the kitchen.

"Tell me your people found something," Weber said as he sat down.

"Sorry, Jimmy. I just talked to somebody down there. Nothing yet."

"Dammit. We've got to put a stop to this, Parks. It's ruining Robyn's life."

"I know," his friend said sympathetically. "I hear the Town Council is holding some kind of special meeting this afternoon about all of this."

"Yeah, at 3 o'clock. Kirby Templeton told me about it this morning."

"How did Robyn take that news?"

"About like you'd expect. She wasn't happy at all."

"This sucks, man. Have you had any luck on your end?"

"Not yet. We talked to Shane Wilder and Levi Bischoff, and I don't think either one of them had anything to do with it."

"What about that Donald MacGregor?"

"I haven't managed to get with him yet. I figured I'd try again after lunch. Do you want to ride along?"

"Wish I could, but I've got month-end reports that have to be filed this afternoon."

"You know, if you didn't put that stuff off until the last minute it would make your life a lot easier."

"Look who's talking," Parks said. "How many times have I heard Mary nagging on you to do your paperwork?"

He had a point there. Weber hated any kind of paperwork and only tackled it when his administrative assistant cornered him and gave him no other alternative.

"Maybe you need a Mary Caitlin of your own."

"No, thank you. It's bad enough with Marsha ordering me around all the time."

The waitress came and took their orders. As she left Weber noticed four women at a table across from them looking at him as they whispered among themselves and shook their heads with disapproval. He knew all of them, old biddys with nothing more to do with their time than gossip and find fault with others. And he was pretty sure what their conversation was about. His mood had not improved since the encounter with Sally MacGregor and he knew he was probably spoiling for an argument when he got up and walked over to their table.

"Afternoon, ladies, how are you doing?"

"Ummm, we're fine, Sheriff," said Edith Delong, surprised that he would approach them.

"That's mighty fine, Ms. Delong. I'm glad to hear that. How about you, Mrs. Miller? You doing okay?"

"Yes, Sheriff, just fine."

"How's Harvey?"

"He's fine, too."

"Well that's good to know. How about you two ladies, Mrs. Ettinger and Ms. Coleman? You doing okay?"

"Just fine," Rachel Ettinger said, not meeting his eyes. Jackie Coleman simply nodded and didn't reply.

"Great. Sounds like the whole world is fine. That's good to know. You all seem to be involved in a conversation, I didn't mean to interrupt. I just wanted to say hi and make sure you're all okay."

"Doing good," Edith Delong said. "Real good, Sheriff, thank you."

"No problem," Weber replied. "I'll let you ladies get back to whatever it was you were talking about. It seemed pretty important to you."

"We were just passing the time of day, Suzanne Miller said.

Weber smiled and nodded his head at them and returned to his table.

"What was that all about?"

"Just hobnobbing with the citizenry," Weber said. "Letting them know the sheriff is out here doing his job and keeping an eye on everybody."

Before Parks could reply the waitress returned with their orders.

"Sheriff, I don't mean to be nosey, but how is Robyn doing? She's such a nice person and I think whoever is doing this stuff to her with those pictures needs to be caught and needs a real butt whipping."

"Thank you, Sarah," Weber said. "She's having a hard time right now, but we'll get to the bottom of it."

"Well, you tell Robyn that the people who care about her know better than whatever those gossip hounds are whispering about," Sarah said casting her eyes towards the table where the foursome of women were seated. "You tell her that she doesn't have anything to be ashamed of."

"Thank you, Sarah. I'll let her know. I'm sure it will mean a lot to her."

When the waitress left their table, Parks asked, "Aside from all of that, how are things going with Robyn's parents being in town?"

"About as badly as you'd expect," Weber told him.

"That mother of hers is a real piece of work, isn't she? She came into Marsha's shop demanding that she go down to the Valley and buy a new dress for the wedding because it clashed with the flowers or the carpet in the church or something. Marsha pretty much blew her off."

"That woman is a real piece of work," Weber acknowledged.

"You better watch out, bubba. My daddy always used to tell me that if you get interested in a woman, check out her mother, because that's your future. Robyn could turn into her someday."

"God, if I thought that was true I'd beg you to shoot me right here and now."

"If you insist. Anything for my pal."

"Why do you seem just a little bit too eager?"

Parks laughed and said, "Seriously, I don't know how Robyn can be such a sweet thing after growing up with a mother like that."

"I think she gets that from her father. Those two are about as different as any couple I've ever known. Bill is pretty mellow about everything, and Renée is like the Wicked Witch of the West."

"How does Robyn put up with that?"

"Better than I do, unfortunately," Weber admitted. "She was going off on one of her tirades last night and I called her a bitch."

"Whoa! That's never a good move."

"No, but sometimes it needs to be said."

"What happened then?"

"She slapped my face and went in the bedroom and slammed the door."

"How did Robyn and her dad take that?"

"I guess they agreed with me," Weber said. "At least neither of them slapped me."

The foursome at the table across from him had finished their meal and were getting up to leave, casting glances Weber's way as they did so.

"You ladies have a great day," he called out to them. Only one, Edith Delong, acknowledged him with a guilty smile and a nod of her head.

The women had barely got out the door before a portly man approached their table and asked, "You guys mind if I join you?"

"Make yourself comfortable, Paul. What's up?"

Paul Lewis, the editor and publisher of the weekly *Big Lake Herald*, was a good natured man who never took himself or life seriously. A friend of Weber's since their boyhood, Paul was always quick to support the sheriff and his deputies when someone complained about being arrested or taken to task for their misdeeds. Even when the person complaining was a member of the Town Council.

"You all set for the meeting this afternoon, Jimmy?"

"As ready as I'm going to be."

"How's Robyn?"

"She says she never wants to leave her house again. Can't say as I blame her, right now. And this Town Council meeting is bullshit. Anybody with half a brain knows Robyn didn't pose for pictures like that."

"That's all Adam Hirsch's doing," Paul said. "He was in my office an hour ago telling me how disgraceful those pictures are and how Robyn is ruining the reputation of the whole town."

"Adam Hirsch can kiss my ass," Weber said.

"What's the story with this guy anyway? It seems like he's as bad as Chet Wingate was when it comes to you, Jimmy. What did you do, make him eat an earthworm when you were kids or something?"

"I never did anything to him, Parks. The guy's just a dickhead."

"Now that's not exactly true, Jimmy," Paul said. "Here's the thing, Parks. Adam was a nerdy little guy in high school who grew up to be a nerdy little man. Back when we were all teenagers, Adam had the hots for some girl in high school and she wouldn't give him the time of day. But Jimmy here? That girl had her eyes on him and she wasn't about to take them off the prize. I guess Adam asked her to a school dance or something and she laughed in his face in front of everybody in the school cafeteria."

"Teenage girls can be pretty cruel sometimes," Parks said. "Lord knows, I got turned down more than once back in the day."

"Yeah, but then she showed up at the dance with Jimmy. I guess she kind of threw it in his face. As far as Adam is concerned, he broke them up even though there was never anything between them. He's been carrying a grudge ever since. I honestly believe the only reason he got on the Town Council was because he thought it would give him an opportunity to stick it to Jimmy now and then."

"Wait a minute. You're telling me this all dates back to high school? Didn't the guy ever grow up and get a life?"

"Life can be rough when you're a teenage nerd," Weber said. "But apparently he never developed past that stage in his life."

"Only if you make it rough," the newspaperman replied. "I wasn't a great catch back then either, believe it or not."

"That's not hard to believe," Weber said. "And are you implying you're a great catch now?"

Paul smiled at the waitress when she set his iced tea in front of him but waved away a menu. "No, I've got a mirror in my bathroom. I accept me for who I am. The difference between Adam and me is that instead of resenting Jimmy for being the hunk he is, and was even back then, instead I buddied up to him. You'd be surprised how many girls I managed to date among the hangers around."

"So what you're telling me after all these years is that you weren't really my friend, I was just a tool to help you score?"

"Yeah, pretty much," Paul said, with a grin plastered across his face.

"Is that why you still hang out with him? I mean, there has to be a reason."

"Don't cast stones, Parks. You hang out with him, too."

"Yeah, but I do it because I lost a bet."

"Maybe we should start a support group or something. Call it The Friends of Jim Weber."

"Screw both you guys," Weber said.

"I'll pass, Jimmy. Nothing personal, but as an adult I took a vow of celibacy so I could devote myself to my work, chronicling the lives and times of our little mountain community."

Weber smiled at his friend and shook his head. "If bullshit was gold you'd be so damned rich you'd have supermodels crawling all over you, Paul."

The fat man shrugged his shoulders and said, "Maybe so, but it is what it is. By the way, Robyn doesn't have a sister, does she?"

Chapter 10

The driveway was still empty when Weber drove past the MacGregor house after lunch. Not sure what else to do, he drove out to SafeHaven. Maybe Cindy MacGregor could tell him if her husband had a computer and the skills necessary to send the doctored pictures out over the Internet.

Christine Ridgeway opened the door when he knocked and Weber said, "I see that you got the door fixed."

"Yeah, Frankie Stepanov came out and made it all better. He's a nice guy."

Weber knew Frankie, a retired gentleman who was an excellent handyman and often helped out his neighbors and friends by doing simple repairs around their homes and property. Frank would never take a penny for his work, but he never turned down a free meal or a plate of cookies given to him in thanks.

"So what brings you out here, Jimmy? Tell me you came to rescue me from all this and take me away to someplace where we can sit on the beach and drink mimosas all day."

"Only if you promise to wear a thong bathing suit," he told her.

The large woman laughed and said, "Oh Lord, that's a sight nobody wants to see! Big girls don't wear thongs, Jimmy. Especially not sitting on a beach. I'd get enough sand in my coochie to fill a tiger's litter box."

"That's probably more about your coochie than I need to know. Actually, the reason I'm here is I'd like to talk to Cindy MacGregor if I could."

"Sure. She's vacuuming upstairs. Let me get her."

Only then did Weber become aware of the sound of the vacuum cleaner on the second floor of the old farmhouse. The women who came to SafeHaven were never charged a penny for staying at the refuge as long as they needed, but they were expected to help with the housework when they could.

Christine went upstairs, and a moment later the sound of the vacuum died away and Cindy came back downstairs with Christine.

"Hi, Sheriff. You wanted to talk to me?"

"Yes, ma'am, if you could spare me a few minutes."

"Why don't you two go sit in the living room there," Christine said. "You want coffee, Jimmy?"

"No, thanks, I just had lunch."

"I've never known you not to have room left for coffee. I'll get some."

Weber watched as she walked out of the room and shook his head. That was Christine, large and in charge. They had been friends since they were kids. It was Weber who had given her the nickname Hillbilly because she grew up on her family's ranch in the foothills outside of town. Living in a small town and serving as its sheriff, he knew just about everybody on at least a nodding basis and got along with most of them quite well. But there were only a handful of people he considered true friends, people that he could bet his life on, and Christine was one of them. It was he who had lured her away from her social worker's job in Southern California to come back home and set up and run SafeHaven. He didn't know of anybody better suited for the role, and Christine had proven him right more than once.

"What did you want to talk to me about?"

"Cindy, I need to know if your husband has a computer."

"A computer? Yeah, we've got a couple of them. A laptop and a desktop. Why?"

"Does Donald use the computer very much?"

Big Lake Wedding

She shrugged her shoulders. "I don't know, I guess. Why?"

"What all does he do on the computer?"

"I'm not sure what you mean, Sheriff."

"Well, for example, does he do email?"

"Yeah."

"So he knows his way around the Internet and things like that? Would you say he's very skilled in doing things on the computer?"

"I guess. But I don't know what you're getting at."

"Have you heard about those pictures of Deputy Fuchette that have been showing up around town?"

"Yeah, Christine told me about them." She suddenly seemed to understand where he was going with his line of questioning and said, "Wait a minute. Do you think Donald's the one sending those pictures to people?"

"I don't know, to be honest with you," Weber admitted. "It's obviously somebody who's got it in for her, and I know that he didn't appreciate Deputy Fuchette showing up at your house a couple of times. He said she was interfering in your marriage."

Cindy shook her head and said, "The only person interfering with our marriage was Donald. Well, him and that crazy mother of his. She thinks her little boy walks on water and can do no wrong. One time she happened to walk in when he was wailing on me and saw I had a bloody nose and a split lip, but do you think she made him stop or yelled at him for beating on me? No, instead she wanted to know what I did to set him off. Like it was my fault!"

"Cindy, do you think Donald could be the one sending those pictures?"

"Honestly, I don't know, Sheriff. He looks at a lot of… a lot of porn online. He was always wanting me to do the things those women in the videos were doing. And I tried." She hung her head and said, "I did things I never thought I would do, just to keep him happy. But no matter what I did, it was never enough. Either he'd start pounding on me because I didn't do things right, or because somebody pissed him off at work, or just because he felt like it."

Weber looked at the woman and realized that physically she was built very much like Robyn. He wasn't sure how to ask his next question and he tried to put it delicately. "Cindy, did Donald ever take any nude pictures of you?"

Even though her head was still downcast, he could see her face reddening.

"I'm not here to judge you, Cindy. What happens between a man and woman behind closed doors is their own business. I just need to know if it could be Donald that's sending these pictures to everybody."

She nodded her head but still didn't look up at him.

"Yeah, he took pictures. Lots of them." She looked up and there were tears in her eyes. "I'm not like that, Sheriff. I'm not, I swear. But I thought if that would make him happy and keep him from going into one of his rages, it was worth it. But instead, all he did was throw it in my face. He'd show me pictures online of women that were better built, had bigger boobs or whatever, and tell me what a loser I was because I didn't look like them or wouldn't do the things they did. But I tried. I tried so hard to make it work."

Weber put his hand on her shoulder to comfort her and said, "Like I said, I'm not here to judge you. Can I ask you to do something for me, Cindy?"

She shrugged her shoulders and said, "If I can."

"Would you look at these pictures that were sent out and tell me if it's you in them?"

"Me? I thought they were pictures of Deputy Fuchette."

"We think that whoever is doing this took her head and put it on pictures of another woman. I just noticed you and her are about the same build and I wondered if that's something that Donald could have done."

"I don't know how hard it is to do something like that."

"I don't either," Weber admitted. "But somebody's obviously doing it."

"And you think it's Donald?"

"It's a possibility."

"Let me see."

He pulled out his phone and opened the file where the pictures were saved, handing it to her. Cindy looked at the pictures carefully, then shook her head."

"No, that's not me."

"Are you sure? Like I said, whoever's doing it put Deputy Fuchette's head on somebody else's body. Could these be pictures of you that Donald took and then manipulated somewhere like that? Do you recognize the backgrounds, maybe?"

She shook her head and said, "All the pictures he took of me were inside, not out in the woods. And wherever that bedroom is, it's not at our house or anyplace I've ever been. And besides..." her face colored again and she said, "besides, I know that's not me because there's no tattoo."

"A tattoo? You have a tattoo?"

"Yeah. Donald wanted me to get a tattoo on my boob. It's a heart with his name and my name across it. I didn't want to do it, but he said that was the only way I could prove to him that I was really his. I hated it from the minute I got it. It wasn't about love, it was about him marking his property. He might as well have branded me," she said bitterly.

Christine came back with their coffee and said, "Don't you worry about it, dear. You're out of that mess now and you don't ever have to go back to it."

"Oh, I'm not going back, don't worry about that. Just in the time I've been away it's been enough to clear my head and know that nothing is ever going to change with Donald. It's over between us. I want to go see that attorney you talked about, the one that helps with women in my situation. I want a divorce."

"If that's what you want, I know that Miss Jensen will handle it for you," Christine assured her.

"I'm just afraid of what he's going to do when he gets served."

"Don't you worry about that, Cindy. He's not going to bother you, is he, Jimmy?"

"He might try. But if he does, we'll make sure he gets the message to stay away."

The old grandfather clock in the hallway chimed twice and Weber said, "I need to get back to town. We've got a meeting with the Town Council in an hour."

"In the middle of the day? That's odd," Christine said.

"They want to discuss those pictures," Weber told her.

"Oh no. Tell me they're not going to try to make Robyn's life even more miserable than it already is."

"I think that's the game plan," Weber said. "At least among some of the members."

"Robyn doesn't deserve this, Jimmy. No woman deserves it."

He drained the last of his coffee from the cup and set it down, then stood up and said, "You're right. And the sooner I can figure out who's been sending those pictures out and put a stop to it the better. Cindy, thank you for your time and for opening up to me. I appreciate it. And don't you worry about Donald. If he comes around bothering you, he's going to answer to me."

Chapter 11

"This is an executive session of the Town Council," Kirby Templeton said, opening the meeting. "Since we will be discussing a sensitive personnel issue, it is not open to the public. I'm sorry, Mr. Lewis and other members of the audience, but I'm going to have to ask you to leave now."

"We've got a right to be here and know what's being said," Reba Hayes said from her chair in the front row. "I don't want my tax dollars being used to pay someone who conducts herself like a common streetwalker."

"That's enough," Kirby said. "I don't want to hear that kind of talk from you or anybody else, Miss Hayes. Now, everybody, get out of here."

There were probably 15 or 20 people in the room, and they left, some grumbling. When they were gone Kirby looked at Chet Wingate, who was sitting in the front row. "Chet, didn't you hear me say this was an executive session? What are you still doing here?"

"I'm the mayor. I'm supposed to be here."

"Chet, you're not the mayor anymore. You resigned, remember?"

"I didn't resign, I took a leave of absence due to my health issues. Now I'm better and I'm back to resume my duties as the duly elected Mayor of Big Lake."

"It doesn't work that way, Chet."

"Says who?"

"Says me. Says the rules of protocol. The mayor's office doesn't have a revolving door. You resigned, end of story. Now you have to leave like everybody else."

"I have a right to be here," the former mayor said defiantly.

"No, sir, you don't. I'm asking you once again to leave."

"I suggest the Council take a vote on that," Chet said. "That will settle the matter once and for all."

"We're not taking a vote, Chet," Kirby said irritably. "We all know the reason you left the Council was because of the recall election people were talking about, not for some drummed up health crisis. And you're not coming back now. If you want to retake your seat on the Council, you're more than welcome to put your hat in the ring when election time comes around. Meanwhile, get out."

"You can't make me leave. I have a right to…"

"Sheriff Weber, please remove this man from the Council chambers."

"Gladly," Weber said, putting his hand on Chet's shoulder. "You heard the man, let's go."

"No," Chet said folding his arms across his chest like a petulant child.

"Come on, Chet. Don't make this harder than it has to be."

"You wanted me gone for a long time, Jim Weber. Well guess what? I'm not leaving!"

Weber looked at Kirby who rolled his eyes, then back at the former mayor and said, "You have two choices, Chet. You can get up on your chubby little legs and walk out of here, or I can pepper spray you and drag your butt out. Which is it going to be?"

There was a gasp from the dais and Councilwoman Gretchen Smith-Abbott said, "You can't talk to him that way, he's the mayor!"

"No, Gretchen, he's not the mayor," Kirby said. "Enough nonsense. Sheriff, get him out of here."

Grasping Chet under one flabby arm, Weber hauled him to his feet and used his other hand to grab his shirt collar at the back

Big Lake Wedding

of his neck and ushered him out of the room, with the former mayor protesting all the way. Closing the door, Weber locked it and turned back to the Town Council and said, "Let's get this over with."

After the formal rollcall, which showed all Town Council members present, Kirby said, "We've called this meeting to discuss the photographs that have been circulating around town that appear to be of Deputy Fuchette. Is there anybody here who has not seen the pictures I'm talking about?"

"Yes, we've all seen them and they're disgusting," Councilwoman Gretchen Smith-Abbott said. "Deputy Fuchette, you should be ashamed of yourself. You've ruined the reputation of this community forever."

Kirby rapped his gavel and said, "That's enough of that kind of talk. We're not here to chastise Deputy Fuchette. We're here to find out what we can about where these photographs are coming from."

"I don't know where they're coming from, but I got two more today, just before this meeting," Councilman Adam Hirsch said. "And they're even more disgusting than the first two."

"You did? I didn't get one. Did anybody else?"

Everybody pulled out their cell phones, and when Weber saw he had a new email with Robyn's return address he felt his heart sink. He clicked on the icon to open the attached pictures. There were indeed two of them this time. In one, the woman who looked like Robyn was on her hands and knees, her rear end pointed toward the camera. In the second picture she was on her back, nude, with her legs spread and knees bent, a lascivious smile on her face. Both pictures looked like they had been taken in the same bedroom as in the earlier photograph that had circulated around town.

He looked over toward Robyn, seated next to him in her uniform. Her face paled when she saw the images on his phone and she closed her eyes. From the looks on the faces of the assembled Councilmembers, Weber was sure they were all looking at the same thing.

"That's not Robyn," Weber said.

73

"Of course it's her," Councilwoman Smith-Abbott said. "Who else could it be?"

"I don't know, but it's not her."

"And you're saying that because of your intimate knowledge of her body?"

"As a matter fact, Adam, yes, I am."

Weber knew Robyn was blushing beside him, but he didn't know how else to handle the matter except to take it head-on.

"All right, enough," Kirby said. "Deputy Fuchette, please understand that we're not here to harm you or your reputation in any way. You and Sheriff Weber have both said that's not you in these pictures. We need to figure out who it is and why this is happening."

"We know who it is," Councilman Hirsch said.

"Enough, Adam. You're out of order."

The little man scowled but didn't say anything else.

"Okay, Deputy Fuchette, do you mind if I call you Robyn?"

She stood up and said, "That's what you do any other day of the week."

"Thank you. Robyn, we know this is a delicate matter and I'm sure you can understand that we can't just ignore what's been happening. Is there anything you can tell us about these pictures or who might be sending them? Anything at all?"

"I don't know who is sending them and I don't know why they're sending them. But they're not me."

"It *is* you," Councilwoman Gretchen Smith-Abbott said. "All you have to do is look at the pictures and look at you. It's the same person."

"It's not me!"

"If it's not you, then who is it?"

"I don't know, but it's not me. I can prove it."

"How?"

"Open that picture the woman with her butt poked out," Robyn said. "Go ahead, all of you, open it. Now, look at this."

Unbuckling her gun belt, she took it off and set it on the chair behind her, then loosened the belt on her trousers and pushed the waistband down on one side a few inches.

"What are you doing? Stop that! You can't take your clothes off in this meeting," Councilwoman Smith-Abbott said. "It's bad enough you're showing your body to the whole town in pictures!"

Robyn ignored her and pointed her finger at the scar along her right hip, the reminder of when she was shot by a frightened old man with a .22 rifle who thought she was a killer on the loose.

"You see that scar? The woman in that picture doesn't have a scar, does she?"

"Pull your pants back up. This is disgusting."

"It's not like she's doing a striptease, Gretchen," said Councilman Mel Walker, who owned the Arby's franchise. "You wanted her to prove it's not her in those pictures. I think she just proved it."

"That doesn't prove anything," Adam Hirsch said. "These pictures could have been taken before she got shot for all we know."

"It's not me!"

"I'm sorry, Deputy, I have no reason to believe anything you say."

As Robyn pulled her waistband back in place, Kirby rapped his gavel again and said, "Stop with the accusations! Deputy Fuchette has been a loyal and dedicated employee of this town for a long time. No matter what you think you're seeing in those pictures, she deserves the benefit of the doubt as far as I'm concerned."

"That may be the way you feel about it, but I think she needs to be fired," Councilwoman Smith-Abbott said. "How can she do her job when everybody knows she's nothing more than a... a strumpet?"

"I won't tolerate any more talk like that," Kirby said. "I mean it, Gretchen. There will be no name calling in this meeting."

"I agree with Councilwoman Smith-Abbott," Adam Hirsch said. "For the good of the Town, and to protect the integrity of the Sheriff's Department, I move that Deputy Fuchette be fired right this minute."

"I second that motion."

"Nobody's getting fired," Kirby said.

"There's a motion and a second before the Council. We need to take a vote on it."

"We're not voting on anything until we hear all the facts. You two stop that nonsense right now or I'll adjourn this meeting."

The pair sent him hateful looks but didn't say anything else.

"Okay, let's get back on track. Robyn, you say that's not you in those pictures and that you don't know who's doing this, and I believe you. I really do. But we need to figure out who's behind this, and why. Sheriff, have your people been able to find out anything so far?"

"We've interviewed several persons of interest and we have a couple of leads that we're following up on."

"But you don't know who has been doing this yet?"

"No, sir, not at this time. I'm not a technical person, but according to Special Agent Parks from the FBI, whoever's doing this has more than a basic knowledge of photomanipulation. We know that the email address they are coming from is a spoof. Parks is having a couple of people from his Phoenix office looking into it unofficially, seeing if they can trace the emails back to their source. So far they haven't had any success, but I'm confident that it's only a matter of time."

"Meanwhile, while all this investigating is going on, people are whispering across back fences all over town about how disgraceful this whole thing is. This Council owes it to the citizens of Big Lake who put their trust in us by voting us into office to take action, and to take action now."

"And what action are you suggesting, Gretchen?"

"Councilman Hirsch has already put forth a motion to dismiss Deputy Fuchette. I have seconded that motion. I think it's the only choice we have."

"May I speak?"

"Of course, Mr. Bennett. What do you have to say?"

Big Lake Wedding

"Thank you, Kirby," the Town's Attorney said as he stood up. "Legally, we have no grounds to fire Deputy Fuchette at this point. Personally, I agree that these pictures are not her in the first place. In my opinion, she is a victim. But setting that aside, legally you can't just fire somebody based upon an assumption. There is no proof that the person in those pictures is this young woman. And ethically, don't we owe it to her, as a loyal servant of this community, to circle our wagons and protect her from these attacks instead of turning our backs on her in her time of need?"

"I've been against this whole thing between the sheriff and Deputy Fuchette right from the start," Adam Hirsch said. "How can a supervisor legally have a personal relationship, a romantic relationship I might add, with his subordinate? That right there is enough reason to send both of them packing, in my opinion."

Councilman Frank Gauger looked at the other man and shook his head. "This has come up before. There is nothing in the Town Charter that prohibits it."

"The Town Charter," Councilwoman Smith-Abbott said sarcastically. "The Town Charter was drawn up by Mike Washburn over 100 years ago. Just because he was a Neanderthal who did things his way doesn't mean we have to live with any of that in this day and age."

"Actually, we do," Bob Bennett corrected her. "When Mr. Washburn founded Big Lake and donated the land it sits on, he specified that things be done a certain way. When he drew up the Town Charter he laid out how he wanted things done. Among them was that he appointed Isiah Tillman as the first sheriff, and his son George as his deputy. That set a precedent right there."

"So what? That's ancient history."

"No, Gretchen, it still applies today. One caveat that Mr. Washburn included was that if at any time in the future the Town tried to change anything in the Charter, the very land Town Hall sits on, the courtroom, the schools, the parks, and any other public property would revert back to his family, including all structures and improvements to the land. That is just as enforceable today as it was back in the 1880s."

"His family? The last of his family died when Lucy was killed."

"The family trust that Miss Lucy set up long ago is still in place. Miss Lucy reiterated her father's wishes again in her will. If you start changing things, it's going to cost this town a fortune trying to contest the original Charter, and we're still going to lose."

"That's nonsense," Adam Hirsch snapped.

"No, it's the law."

"Okay, let's get back on track," Kirby said. "Do you have anything else to say relating to today's issue, Mr. Bennett?"

"No, not officially as the Town's Attorney. But I will say again that as far as I am concerned, Deputy Fuchette is a victim. Instead of trying to persecute her, we should be doing exactly what Sheriff Weber is doing. Trying to find out who is behind these pictures and how to put a stop to them."

"Thank you," Kirby said. "I've given this a lot of thought, and I've talked to Councilman Gauger and Walker at length. I don't feel that we can just sit idly by while the investigation goes on. While I'm in agreement that these pictures are fakes and are not of Deputy Fuchette, we still have a bunch of very upset citizens who are demanding action. And while I appreciate Special Agent Parks' unofficial help, I think we need to call in somebody from an outside agency to conduct an independent investigation."

"Somebody like who?"

"My thought was the Department of Public Safety. How would you feel about that, Robyn?"

"I don't care who you have investigate, I just want this over and done with. The sooner, the better."

"All right. Sheriff Weber, can you make a call to the DPS?"

"I'll do it as soon as I get back to the office," Weber said.

"I demand we take a vote on my proposal to dismiss this woman and get it over with."

"Adam, just stop, okay?"

"No, I won't stop. Just because you and Sheriff Weber are friends doesn't mean she gets a pass on behavior like this. I demand a vote!"

"Fine," Kirby said, the exasperation showing in his voice. "All those in favor of firing Deputy Fuchette without an investigation and completely disregarding her rights, say aye."

"Wait a minute. You're trying to skew the voting results. That's not fair!"

"None of this is fair," Frank Gauger said. "You want to vote? My vote is nay. As Bob Bennett pointed out, Deputy Fuchette has been a loyal employee of this town for a long time, first as a dispatcher for the Sheriff's Department, and now as a deputy. My God, people, she took a bullet for us! She deserves our support and she has mine. What about the rest of you? Are you going to show the same loyalty to her that she has shown to us or are you going to throw her to the wolves because that's the easy thing to do? And maybe because it helps somebody settle old childish scores." With that he gave Adam Hirsch a stern look.

"I vote aye," Hirsch said, avoiding Gauger's eyes.

"My vote is aye also," Gretchen Smith-Abbott said, her hands folded primly atop the dais.

"Nay," said Mel Walker.

"Nay for me as well," said Kirby Templeton. Then he looked at the two of newest members of the Town Council. "Ms. McGill, Ms. Clarkson, what say ye?"

"Aye," responded Valerie Clarkson. "I'm sorry, I don't know when these pictures were taken or who is sending them, but there's no denying it's Deputy Fuchette. I don't believe this crazy story about someone putting her face on another body for a minute."

"Ms. McGill?"

"I've certainly gotten an education on how small towns work in the short time I've been on this Council," said Janet McGill. "When I moved here from San Francisco I expected a quiet life where the biggest concern might be a barking dog or somebody playing their car radio too loud. That's certainly not the case. And while I fully support an independent investigation, I feel it would be a travesty to dismiss an employee who has such a fine record as Deputy Fuchette's until we know all the facts. My vote is nay."

"There you have it," Kirby said, wrapping his gavel. "Motion is denied."

"Then I think we should at least suspend her without pay until the investigation is completed," Adam Hirsch said. "You said yourself that a lot of people in this town are very upset. We can't just ignore their concerns."

"Nonsense," Frank Gauger said. "Why don't you grow up, Adam?"

"I don't have to take that from you!"

Kirby rapped his gavel hard and said, "Enough already! As much as I hate to admit it, Adam has a point. We have to answer to the citizens of this town. So, here's a compromise. How about if we place Deputy Fuchette on paid administrative leave until the independent investigation is completed and we have the results?"

"You want to pay her to sit on her ass," seeing the look he got from Kirby, Hirsch amended his comment. "You want to pay her to set on her butt all day long while this investigation drags on and on?"

"Yes, Adam, that's what I want. It only seems fair. You may have never heard of a concept that's been popular throughout our history where someone is innocent until they are proven guilty. But that's the way things work. I want a vote on my proposal for putting Deputy Fuchette on paid administrative leave. Aye or nay, and we don't need any comments. Just cast your vote."

Again the voting was the same, three Councilmembers opposed to Kirby's proposal and four in favor. "The motion is passed and this meeting is adjourned. Sheriff Weber, keep us posted on what the outside investigator has to say, please."

With that he rapped his gavel a final time, ending the meeting.

Chapter 12

Robyn walked out of the Town Council meeting with tears in her eyes. Several people had been lingering on the sidewalk, waiting to hear what had taken place. She ignored them and held her head high, but Weber could tell that her heart was breaking. She didn't say a word until they were back at the Sheriff's Office.

"I guess you need my weapon and badge, right?"

"No, the weapon belongs to you. You paid for it. As far as I'm concerned, the badge is still yours, too. You're on leave, Robyn. You're still a deputy here."

"For now."

"For now, and forever," he told her.

"Not if Hirsch and Gretchen have their way."

"But they didn't get their way. That's what you have to keep in mind. Bob Bennett and the other members of the Council made it very plain that they support you."

"But they still suspended me, didn't they?"

"No, you're not suspended, Robyn. You're on paid leave pending an investigation. Just like I was after I shot Steve Rafferty. It's procedure, that's all."

"Yeah? Well, procedure sucks."

"Yes, it does. I'm sorry. If there was any way I could change things, I would."

The door opened and Kirby Templeton entered the office, accompanied by Frank Gauger and Mel Walker.

"Robyn, I know this hurts and I know you feel put upon right now," Kirby said. "We want you to know that we are behind you 100%. It may not feel that way, but we are. You're not going to lose your job, and we are going to get to the bottom of this and find out who has been sending those pictures. And when we do, we're going to see to it that that person is punished."

She took a deep breath and nodded her head, her eyes closed.

"I appreciate that. I really do. And I know that putting me on leave was the right thing to do. But right now, I just want to scream. I'm sorry if I'm coming across like an emotional woman instead of a professional, but that's how I feel."

Mary Caitlin put her arm around the younger woman and hugged her. "You have every right to feel the way you do, honey. But don't forget that a lot of us love you, and we have your back. All the way."

Robyn nodded her head, unable to speak.

"Anyway, we just wanted you to know that if there was any other way of handling things, we would have," Mel Walker said. "I'd like to say that someday we'll look back on this and laugh, but it's no laughing matter. I guess the good news is that at least now you'll have more time for you and your mother to take care of all of the last-minute details for your wedding. That's a good thing, right?"

Robyn laughed in spite of herself, though there was no humor in it. "Obviously you've never met my mother, have you?"

~~***~~

"This is so unfair," Marsha Perry said an hour later as they waited for the waitress at the Ming House Chinese restaurant.

"I know, and Jimmy keeps reminding me that life isn't fair."

"What can I do to help you, Robyn?"

"I don't suppose you'd go stuff a gag in my mother's mouth, would you? That would help."

"Sorry, girlfriend, it's one thing to gag Parks here now and then to spice things up in the bedroom, but your mother scares me."

"That's what I said just the other day," Weber told her.

"Yeah, and I heard you called her the B word and got slapped, too."

"It had to be said."

The waitress, a pretty young Asian woman named Mei, whose raven black hair hung to her waist, brought glasses of water and two bowls of crisp fried noodles to their table and took their orders. When she left them, Marsha said, "No offense, Robyn, but I don't know how you can put up with that mother of yours. She's a real piece of work."

"Why do you think I live up here and not down in the Valley?"

"I thought she was going to tear my head off because I wouldn't close my shop the minute she said so and drive back to Phoenix to pick up a new dress for the wedding."

"Ignore her," Robyn said. "Your dress is just fine."

"Was she always like this?"

"I don't know about always, but she has been as long as I can remember. Once when I was a little girl I was visiting a friend of mine, and her mother had different things that she had drawn hung up on the refrigerator. When I got home, I asked my mother why she never hung up any of my pictures and she said it was because they were childish and showed no talent."

"Gee, childish? How old were you?"

"I don't know, six, maybe seven."

"How dare you be a child at that age, you slacker!"

"For some silly reason, I thought she might at least try to be on her best behavior while she was here helping me with the wedding. That lasted for maybe five minutes after they pulled into my driveway. I don't know why I even considered that to be a possibility."

"Hey, don't blame her," Parks said. "It's really not her fault. Crazy is like diarrhea. You can only hold it in for so long."

"Oh, I blame her. I blame her for a lot of things. Before I left the house to go to that Town Council meeting she was complaining about the wedding invitations."

"The invitations? What's wrong with them?" Marsha dug in her purse and pulled out an envelope with their wedding invitation in it and said, "They look great to me."

"Apparently the printer didn't use quite the right shade of blue here," Robyn said pointing to the cover of the invitation. Then she opened it and said, "And she didn't like the type style, either."

"Let me take a look at it," Parks said.

Marsha handed him the invitation and he looked it over and said, "Wait a minute. It says the marriage of Robyn Allison Fuchette and James Alan Weber."

"Yeah, so what?"

"So, when you get married, your name's going to be Robyn Allison Weber, right?"

"Officially, yes. But I'm still going to use Fuchette for work purposes and stuff. Jimmy and I talked about it and we both think it would be better that way."

There was a devilish grin on Parks' face and Robyn asked, "What?"

"So, Jimmy's initials are J.A.W and yours will be R.A.W. I'm going to start calling you two RawJaw. What happens between a man and woman behind closed doors is none of my business, but really, RawJaw? That sounds like something you might need to take antibiotics for."

"Did anybody ever tell you that you're sick, Parks?"

"Maybe so, but at least I don't have RawJaw."

"And you thought having dinner with us instead of your parents was going to be an escape," Marsha said.

"Trust me, I'd rather be sitting here with you guys than spending one more moment with my mother," Robyn assured her, then stuck her tongue out at Parks and said, "RawJaw and all."

The restaurant's door opened and three couples came in. The waitress started to show the newcomers to a seat next to the table

Big Lake Wedding

where the foursome was seated, when one of the women stopped her and whispered among her companions. Looking at Weber and his tablemates, the waitress rolled her eyes and then seated them on the opposite side of the room.

"What was that all about? Do they think we have cooties or something?"

"That's Elaine DeWitt," Robyn said. "They don't think we all have cooties. Just me."

"I know who she is," Marsha replied. "I never could stand that woman. The last time I talked to her was a few months ago at the grocery store. She told me that Parks and I were living in sin and that she was sure my mother would be rolling over in her grave if she were still alive. Holier than thou bitch."

"Just ignore them," Weber said.

"It's kind of hard to ignore somebody when they're glaring at you from across the room."

"No, it's not. I do it with Marsha all the time," Parks replied.

"Watch it, buddy," Marsha warned him. "You need to check yourself before you wreck yourself."

Before he could comply, Robyn's cell phone rang. She looked at the screen, shook her head, and pressed the button to answer. "Hello, Mother."

She listened for a moment, then said, "I told you we were having dinner with Parks and Marsha tonight."

Parks tore the wrapper from the end of his straw, then blew into the straw, sending the wrapper sailing across the table. Robyn waved it away and said, "I don't think you guys are going to go hungry, Mother. There's a refrigerator full of food."

She listened to her mother's reply and said. "That's ridiculous. What do you eat when you're at home? Well, I'm sorry there aren't any porkchops. I'll pick some up at the market." She paused a moment, then said, "No, Mother, I won't bring them right now. There's plenty of other stuff there. Help yourself."

She held the phone away from her ear and stared at it like the telephone itself was nagging her, and not the woman on the other end. Putting it back to her ear she said, "I don't know when I'll be home. Yes, Mother, I know that you and Daddy came up here to help me with the wedding, and I appreciate it very much. But I have things I have to do besides focus on the wedding, too. Just things, Mother."

Weber wasn't sure what his future mother-in-law said next, but obviously it was enough to exasperate Robyn past the point she could normally tolerate. "If you must know, Mother, after dinner Jimmy and I are going back to his cabin and we're going to do the nasty. So don't wait up, I might not make it home until morning."

Her mother was still talking when Robyn pushed the button to end the call. Her phone rang again almost immediately. She looked at it, shook her head, and turned it off.

"I can't believe you just said that to your mother," Weber said incredulously.

"She learned that sassy attitude from me," Marsha said with a big smile. "I have been such a good influence on you. I think my work here is done." With that she reached across the table to high-five Robyn.

Unaware that her last response to her mother had been loud enough to be heard by the people at the other table across the room, Robyn also did not see Elaine DeWitt shaking her head in disapproval as she whispered to the people seated with her. The gossip mongers of Big Lake would be titillated by this latest piece of news.

~*** ~

After dinner Weber and Robyn drove by the new house they had built on the site where Weber's boyhood home had once stood before an arsonist burned it to the ground. Walking through the empty house, admiring the huge fieldstone fireplace and big windows in the great room and the kitchen filled with the latest stainless steel appliances, Robyn smiled in spite of her troubles.

"I just can't believe this is going to be our home, Jimmy."

"It took a while to get everything done, but it looks pretty good, doesn't it?"

"It's beautiful. And it's going to look even better when we get furniture in it." She turned in a circle, taking it all in, and said, "I love this house, Jimmy. And I love you so much."

He wrapped her in his arms and kissed her forehead. "I love you, too. I'm not a wordsmith, so I don't know all the nice things to say to tell you how much I do. I'm not even sure there are enough words in the world to tell you how much."

He kissed her, a kiss that turned from gentle to passionate. When the kiss ended, Robyn smiled at him and took him by the hand, leading him up the stairs to the loft that would be their bedroom. Without saying a word she unbuttoned her blouse and took it off, then unfastened her belt.

"Really? Here? Now?"

"Yes, Jimmy, here and now. It's time we broke in this wonderful new house of ours."

"There's not even any carpet on the floor, let alone furniture."

"Well," she said as she pushed her pants down, "the good news is, we won't get rug burns, will we?"

Nick Russell

Chapter 13

Weber was a mile from the office the next morning when the dispatcher came over the radio.

"All units, there's a disturbance at Roberta Jensen's house on Zuni Lane. She says there's a man there threatening her."

Deputies Chad Summers and Dan Wright immediately responded, saying they were on their way. Weber keyed his microphone and asked, "Any other details on what's going on?"

"No, Sheriff. There was a lot of yelling in the background and she just said she needed help now, a man was threatening her. Then the line went dead."

"I'm on my way," Weber said, turning on his Explorer's roof lights and siren.

Roberta Jensen was a Big Lake native who had been blinded in a childhood accident and went on to graduate at the top of her class at law school at the University of Arizona and become an attorney. She operated a successful practice in Tucson for many years before growing tired of life in the big city and returning to her roots, opening an office in the home she bought two blocks from Main Street in Big Lake.

Siren screaming, Weber had to stomp on his brake pedal to avoid hitting Patrick McRae when the old man stepped off the curb directly in front of him. Oblivious to the fact that he had almost been run down, Patrick walked up to Weber's window and said, "Morning, Sheriff. When are you guys going to do something about those damn kids riding their skateboards up and down the sidewalks? I complain over and over and nothing ever gets done about it."

"No time to talk now," Weber said, "I've got an emergency."

"Well, you're going to have another one if one of those fool kids falls and breaks his skull. I'll tell you that right now. You need to do something about them." The sheriff didn't hear that last part. He was almost a block away by then.

Chad's patrol car and Dan's SUV had arrived on the scene ahead of him and both deputies were already inside the house when Weber got there. He called Dispatch to say he had arrived, then went inside. The sight that greeted him was appalling.

Papers, file folders, and assorted office supplies littered the floor of the living room, which had been converted into Roberta's office. A visitor's chair that was part of a pair that sat before her desk had been thrown across the room and its mate was upended. A computer monitor was on the floor. Drawers were hanging open from the two file cabinets along the wall and looked like someone had ransacked them. But the worst sight of all was Roberta herself.

Chad was just helping her to her feet, and when Weber saw the angry red welts on her face and the bright red blood that ran from her nose, the sheriff felt his blood boil.

"Are you all right, Roberta?"

"Who's that?"

"It's Jim Weber. Are you all right?"

"I think so. I don't know. My face hurts."

"I called for an ambulance," Chad said as he helped ease her down into the chair behind her desk while Dan, his weapon in hand, was clearing the rest of the house. Weber joined him and a quick check of the other rooms and closets showed that whoever had assaulted the woman was already gone. When he returned to the office Chad was handing Roberta a dampened washcloth to staunch the flow of blood from her nose.

"What happened here? Who did this to you?"

"It all happened so fast. I had just unlocked the office door when someone shoved it in and knocked me down with it. He started screaming at me, telling me I was going to die for interfering with his life, demanding to have any paperwork about him, and just... he was just crazy, Jimmy."

"Do you know who it was?"

"Yes. It was Donald MacGregor. Christine from SafeHaven brought his wife in yesterday so I could help her file for divorce. From the way the two of them talked, I could tell he was a bad guy. But I never expected this to happen!"

Weber keyed his microphone and called Dispatch. "I want an APB out for Donald MacGregor, white male, 6'2" tall and about 260 pounds. Tell any officers who encounter him to approach with caution. Felony burglary and assault suspect."

"10-4, Sheriff. Other officers are on the way."

"No need for them," Weber said. "We've got the situation in hand here. I want them out on the streets looking for MacGregor."

"10-4. Do you have any vehicle description?"

Weber looked at his deputies. Dan shook his head, but Chad said, "He usually drives a jacked up blue 4x4 Ford with a roll bar. That's what we had towed after he showed up at SafeHaven the other day."

Weber gave the dispatcher that information as he heard more sirens and vehicles stopping out front. Tommy Frost and Dolan Reed came in the door, along with two paramedics. Rusty Heinz, a stocky bald man with a goatee and a silver hoop in his left ear quickly began assessing Roberta's injuries.

"We've got things handled here. Dolan, I need you to get over to SafeHaven ASAP. There's a good chance MacGregor will show up there next. Tommy, get out on the road and see if you can find MacGregor. This just happened, so he can't be too far away." They started out the door and Weber keyed his microphone again and said, "Dispatch, call SafeHaven and tell Christine to lock the doors and be on the lookout for MacGregor. Tell her Dolan is on his way there to provide security."

Other deputies' voices came over the radio, acknowledging that they were out and searching for the man who had assaulted a helpless woman. A woman who happened to be dating one of their own. Within minutes, every deputy, including those who were off duty, joined in the search.

"Roberta? Where's Roberta? Is she okay?" A distressed Deputy Ted "Coop" Cooper came through the door dressed in blue jeans and a gray T-shirt.

"She got roughed up but she's okay, Coop."

"Coop? Is that you?"

"It's me," he said. Pat Price, the other paramedic on the scene, stepped out of the way to make room for Coop. He bent down to hug Roberta and assured her that everything was going to be okay. "Don't worry, honey, we're going to get you to the hospital real quick, okay?"

"I swear, Coop, that man was crazy. He just came through the door and went on the attack."

"It's okay, just relax. I'm here and I'm not going anywhere. You're safe now."

"I'm not worried about me," she said. "But I'm afraid he might try to hurt his wife and Christine. He was absolutely nuts."

"Dolan is almost there," Weber told her. "Don't worry, if MacGregor shows up there, he might wind up dead."

"It doesn't matter where he turns up, that son of a bitch is a dead man," Coop said. A former Army MP, Coop had joined the Big Lake Sheriff's Department after retiring from the military and was an excellent lawman with a lifetime of experience. Having been an MP himself during his Army days, Weber had felt an immediate kinship with the new deputy and they had quickly become good friends.

While Coop had always been professional in every way before this incident, the sheriff could tell by the rage in his eyes that he meant exactly what he said. He knew Coop would not leave Roberta's side until her injuries were treated and she was safe, and that was probably the best thing that could happen. Because in his present state of mind, Weber had no doubt that Coop would shoot Donald MacGregor on sight. He couldn't blame the man. If the situation were reversed and he was in his deputy's shoes, he knew he might do the same thing. As it was, nothing would bring him more pleasure at that moment than getting MacGregor in his gunsights.

"Roberta, we're going to transport you to the Medical Center, okay? I don't think you have any serious injuries, but we want to get you checked out just to be sure."

"Okay."

"We're going to bring a stretcher in and get you situated on it," Rusty continued. "Just hang on for a minute or two more."

"I can walk to the door if somebody will help me. Where's my cane?"

Weber spotted her white cane, broken in half amid the rubble on the floor. "It got broken, Roberta. I'm sorry."

"There's another one in the corner of my bedroom. Can somebody get it?"

"It's okay, we've got you, you don't need it," Pat Price said.

"I know, but I still want it," Roberta told him. "A blind person never wants their cane out of reach, just in case of an emergency."

Weber went to the bedroom and retrieved the cane while Roberta, with Coop and Rusty on each side of her, made her shaky way to the doorway, where they eased her down onto a stretcher.

"I worked until 1 a.m. and came home and got some sleep and was just getting out of the shower when I heard the first call go out," Coop said while the paramedics loaded the stretcher into the back of the ambulance. "Dammit, Jimmy, I should have been here."

"This isn't your fault, Coop. You know that. That idiot is totally out of control. He's always been an asshole, but he has to be crazy to pull something like this."

"If I'd have been here he would have never laid a finger on her."

Weber put his hand on his friend's shoulder and looked him in the eye. "Stop it, Coop. Don't let this eat you up. Nobody had any way of knowing this was going to happen. You can't be by Roberta's side to protect her 24 hours a day. And she wouldn't put up with it anyhow. You and I both know that, right? Right?"

"Yeah, I know you're right, Jimmy. I'm just so pissed off. So... I'm torn between wanting to stay by her side and wanting to get out there and find that bastard."

"You need to be with Roberta right now. That's what she needs. And the last thing *I* need is for you to be the one that finds MacGregor. We both know what would happen then. Leave it to us, buddy, we'll handle it. That's the same thing you would be telling me right now if I were in your shoes."

They started to close the ambulance doors and Coop said, "Hang on, I'm riding with her." He turned back to Weber and said, "Find him, Jimmy. Find him and put him down." Then he climbed into the back of the ambulance and the doors closed behind him.

Chapter 14

When they left Roberta's house, Weber, Dan Wright, and Chad drove directly to the suspect's, hoping he might be there. But the driveway was still empty. They pounded on the door, demanding anyone inside to open up.

"He ain't there. You guys need to stop harassing my son."

"Where is he, Sally?"

"I don't know. And if I did, I wouldn't tell you."

"Do you have a key to this place?"

"Yeah? So what?"

"Get it."

"You go to hell. You're not going in there without a search warrant."

"I said get the damn key, Sally."

"And I said no!"

Weber turned to Dan and said, "Kick it in!"

"Hey, you can't do that," the woman protested.

"Watch us," Weber said. "Do it, Dan."

The big deputy, who had been a high school and college football star, reared back and smashed his right foot into the door near the lock and it popped open. Drawing their weapons, they entered to the sound of Sally MacGregor cursing them from outside and threatening dire legal repercussions for what they were doing.

They entered through the living room, scanning in both directions to make sure there were no threats waiting for them. The room showed domestic touches that indicated a woman had lived there in the not-too-distant past; a crocheted afghan draped over the back of the couch, cheap prints of nature scenes hanging on the walls, and a wilted bouquet of wildflowers in a cheap glass vase on an end table. But there were also two hard-core adult magazines on the couch, empty beer cans on the coffee table, and a T-shirt discarded on the floor next to the couch.

"Sheriff's Department, MacGregor," Weber announced. "If you're here, show yourself with your hands up. If I see anything in your hands, you're a dead man."

They moved from room to room searching the house, but it was empty.

"I've called my lawyer. He says you guys have to get out of here right now. And somebody has to pay me for that door, too!"

Sally MacGregor was in the living room and her anger had reached a fever pitch.

"Get out of here," Weber told her.

"I own this place, I'm not going anywhere!"

"It's a crime scene. I'm not telling you again, get out."

"You go to hell."

"Cuff her, Dan. Then lock her in the back of one of the units."

"You can't do that to me!"

"You're under arrest for refusing a lawful order and obstruction of justice," Weber said.

The woman tried to struggle but was no match for the deputy. He easily stopped any resistance she attempted as he secured her wrists behind her, then took her out to the back of his vehicle.

"MacGregor's wife said he likes porn," Weber said. "I think that's an understatement, judging from this."

One bedroom had been made into a makeshift office. A piece of plywood laid on top of cinderblocks served as a desk, which held a computer, printer, and a stack of X-rated DVDs. The computer was on and the screen saver was a revolving slideshow of people engaged in various sexual acts.

"I want the computer and the DVDs and everything in here seized as evidence," Weber said.

"Don't we need a warrant for that, Jimmy?"

"Probably, but until Judge Ryman gets back to work, we're not going to get one. Take it all, we'll worry about the legalities later."

As Dan unplugged the computer, Chad called from the other bedroom. Weber joined him and his deputy said, "It looks like he's armed."

There was an open zippered handgun case on the unmade bed, along with a box of .357 magnum cartridges that had been spilled out on the sheet. A gun rack on the wall held a Marlin lever action .22 rifle and a Mossberg 12 gauge pump shotgun. A third spot on the rack was empty.

"I wonder what used to be there," Weber said.

"I don't know," Chad replied, "but a couple of weeks ago I was out at the cinder pit shooting and MacGregor was there with another guy. They were both shooting AK-47s."

Weber didn't like hearing that. The semi-automatic civilian clones of the Communist bloc Kalashnikov assault rifles were powerful weapons, capable of doing tremendous damage in the wrong hands. And if anybody's hands were the wrong ones, it was Donald MacGregor's.

Pressing the button on his microphone, Weber said, "Dispatch, amend the APB on MacGregor to say that he should be considered armed and extremely dangerous. It's possible he's in possession of a .357 handgun and an AK-47. If spotted, he should be approached with extreme caution."

~~***~~

Robyn called Weber on his cell phone while they were finishing up at MacGregor's house, asking what she could do to help.

"I know I'm suspended, or on leave, or whatever the hell they want to call it, Jimmy. But I can't just sit here with this going on."

"I know, and I appreciate it," he told her. "I can't have you on the street officially, but if you would go to SafeHaven to provide security for Christine and Cindy MacGregor, that would free up one more deputy to help in the search."

"You and I both know that if he shows up there, Christine will blow him away," Robyn said.

"I know. But I'd still feel better if she had some backup."

"I'm on my way."

"It's possible MacGregor has an AK and a .357 magnum," Weber told her. "Be sure you have your duty weapon with you, and your AR-15."

"You make it sound like it's gonna be the shootout at the OK Corral all over again, Jimmy."

"In the frame of mind he's in right now, anything could happen," he told her. "Don't take any chances, okay? If you see him anywhere around there, call for backup. And if you have to, don't hesitate to do whatever it takes to keep you and everybody else out there safe."

"Don't worry, Jimmy. He won't get past me."

The sheriff had no doubt about that. Robyn might be a petite woman, but she was a complete professional, and when things got physical, pound for pound she had more fight in her than any deputy he had ever worked with.

Weber and his deputies searched for hours, driving down every street in Big Lake, every dirt path leading off into the forest, any and every place where Donald MacGregor might be hiding. Their efforts were futile, he was nowhere to be found. Growing up in Big Lake, he knew every back road, every fire trail through the forest, every hole big enough for a man his size to hide out in. Weber knew it would take a full-scale manhunt with many more people than he had available to search the whole area, and there was still no guarantee of success. As far as he knew, MacGregor could be miles away by now.

But the sheriff suspected he wasn't. Donald MacGregor was big and mean, and stupid. He operated by some sort of primal instinct rather than thought much of the time. And Weber figured that right now, all of his instincts were telling MacGregor that he still needed to exact revenge on his wife for leaving him, and anybody foolish enough to help her escape their marriage. He was sure the suspect would turn up sooner or later, and when he did, he knew it was going to end in violence.

Nick Russell

Chapter 15

It was late in the day when Weber returned to the office, where he found a ruddy faced, burly man he didn't know seated at one of his deputies' desks.

"Sheriff, this is Captain Sweeney from the Department of Public Safety," Mary Caitlin said. "He's the investigator who's here to look into those fake pictures of Deputy Fuchette."

"Nice to meet you, Captain," he said, shaking the man's hand. "Jim Weber. I hope I haven't kept you waiting long. We had a situation come up and everybody has been looking for a suspect in an assault."

"No problem, Sheriff. Your assistant told me about it. Any luck finding the perp yet?"

"No, he's gone to ground somewhere. But I think it's only a matter of time until he shows up."

"How's your victim doing?"

"Coop just called a few minutes ago," Mary said. "No serious injuries, but the guy really roughed her up. She's pretty sore and will probably be even more so tomorrow. They're back at her house and Coop isn't going to leave her side."

"Good," the sheriff said. "If he comes across MacGregor, there's no telling what might happen. Meanwhile, Captain Sweeney, I appreciate you coming up to help us out with this other issue we have."

"I've been here about three hours already, Sheriff, so I've been able to get a head start. Mary has briefed me pretty thoroughly on what's going on. I've seen the pictures, and I've talked to Special Agent Parks. He tells me his people keep hitting roadblocks trying to track back the IP address of whoever's actually sending them."

"So, what do you want to do next, Captain?"

"Well, I'm already doing some of it. I want to pull those pictures up on a computer screen and show you something. How about we go in your office where there's a little more privacy in case a civilian comes in."

"Sounds good," Weber said leading the way into his private office. He waved his hand at his desk and said, "Help yourself."

Sweeney sat down in the chair Weber usually occupied and moved the mouse to open his computer screen. Weber pointed out the folder where the pictures were stored and he opened the first one. Zooming in on the picture of the woman standing in the forest, he said, "Looking at this, I don't see any evidence of photomanipulation whatsoever."

"I'm telling you, that's not Deputy Fuchette."

"I haven't met the woman, I've just seen her ID photo, but it looks like her to me."

The sheriff tried to hide his irritation when he said, "I don't care who it looks like, it's not her."

"I hear what you're saying. Don't get me wrong, I'm not saying I don't believe you. All I'm saying is that to the untrained eye, this woman looks like your deputy."

Weber started to reply and the other man held up his hand. "Let me finish, Sheriff. I said it looks like her, and that I don't see any evidence of photomanipulation. That doesn't mean it is her and it doesn't mean the photo isn't a fake. It just means that whoever did it did a damn good job of it. Which was their intention."

"So, we're looking for some kind of computer expert?"

Sweeney shook his head. "No, these days any high school kid could probably do it. I've got a twelve year old niece who taught herself how to write her own computer programs because she got bored with the games she found online. Girl is probably

Big Lake Wedding

going to be one of those dot-com millionaires by the time she's thirty."

"I don't care how old whoever is that is doing this," Weber said. "How do we find him?"

"I forwarded these down to our lab in Phoenix, and I've got a young woman named Valerie Carbanal working on them. When it comes to this kind of stuff, she's the best of the best. Let's leave that to her and let's focus on who might be doing this. Mary has briefed me on the suspects that you had originally, and she gave me the list of any guys that Deputy Fuchette dated in the past. What are your thoughts about any of them?"

"I don't think it's anybody she dated, to be honest with you," Weber replied.

"Based upon what?"

"Based upon what Robyn has said, I guess. She said she hadn't dated much and was pretty sure nobody from her past is involved."

"And what about people she's had to deal with on the job?"

"So far, my best guess would be Donald MacGregor."

"The same guy you're looking for that assaulted the blind woman?"

"That's him. The reason he attacked her this morning was because she does pro bono work for the women's shelter, and she handled the paperwork for his wife's petition for divorce. A fellow named Chuck Ferris serves legal papers like that, and he said when he showed up at MacGregor's house late last night to serve him with the divorce papers, the guy said that he was going to kill anybody who was helping Cindy, his wife."

"Did this Ferris guy report that threat?"

"No. We didn't find out about it until after he'd assaulted Miss Jensen."

"Why not? Maybe it would have prevented her from getting hurt."

"I'm pretty sure Donald MacGregor turned around and threatened to kill the doctor who smacked his ass when he was born," Weber said. "And he hasn't stopped threatening people since."

"Mary said he was a bully."

"That's putting it mildly."

"So why would MacGregor have it in for your deputy?"

"She got called out to their house several times when he was beating on his wife. When she left him, he decided that Robyn had encouraged her to do so."

"And did she?"

"Hell, Captain, everybody in town has encouraged her to get out of that mess. It's been going on for years."

"Anybody else you can think of that's not on one of the two lists that Mary gave me?"

"Not off the top of my head," Weber said. "But you've been a cop long enough to know that you can never tell who's holding a grudge over what may seem like a trivial matter to the rest of us."

"I'd like to talk to Deputy Fuchette. When can I do that?"

"I sent Archer out to take her place at SafeHaven," Mary said. "Let me give her a call and see if she can come in if you want to talk to her now."

"I know it's been a long day, but no time like the present," Sweeney said.

Mary left the room to make the call, and the DPS investigator looked to make sure she had closed the door behind her, then turned to Weber.

"Let me try to put this delicately, Sheriff. I understand that you and Deputy Fuchette have a romantic relationship and you're engaged. Is that correct?"

"Yeah, the wedding's in less than two weeks. And before you say anything, I know what you're thinking. Anyplace else in the country that would be inappropriate. But this is a small town and we do things a bit differently here in Big Lake. Archer Wingate, the deputy that Mary just mentioned sending out to SafeHaven, is the son of the man who was our mayor until he resigned recently. Lloyd Nelson, who runs the street department, is a cousin to one of the councilmembers. Cindy Oswald, our judge's court clerk, was married to another councilmember's son for a while before they got divorced. It's a small town with a small labor pool to draw from," Weber said

"Big Lake, home of nepotism," Sweeney said. "I guess if it works, what the hell. Anyway, like I said, I'm trying to be delicate, but I'm assuming that you have seen Deputy Fuchette naked. Look at this woman and knowing what you know about her body, are you convinced it's not her? I want you to answer that, setting aside your personal feelings. I'm just talking about evidence based upon your observations."

"It's not her."

"Again, Sheriff, is this based upon your feelings or…"

"Both," Weber told him.

"Could you elaborate on the latter, please?"

"First of all, Robyn got shot a while back. The bullet just grazed her hip, but it carved a furrow and left a scar. The woman in these pictures doesn't have that scar."

"From what I understand, one town councilmember said maybe that was because the photos were taken before she got shot. Anything else?"

"Yeah, if you must know."

"I'm not trying to be weird or a voyeur, Sheriff, but the more I know, the quicker we get to the bottom of this."

"I understand," Weber said, though he felt uncomfortable with the conversation and discussing anything personal about Robyn. But he knew that Sweeney was right, anything that might help needed to be put out in the open. "The nipples are wrong."

"The nipples?"

"Yeah. Robyn's are shaped differently. The skin around them, I forget what it's called, it's smaller on Robyn than on this woman."

"The areolas?"

"Yeah, that's it. Robyn's are smaller and they're darker than the ones on this woman in the picture."

"Okay, what else?"

"That's it for the physical part of it. But I know Robyn. She's a very modest woman. She would never do anything like this."

"I'm not arguing with you, Sheriff, not at all. But like you said, we've both been cops long enough that we can tell that you never know how somebody's going to react in a given situation. Maybe sometimes passion works the same way. Maybe she was being playful and did something totally out of character."

Weber thought back to the night before and their impromptu lovemaking in their newly built house. Yeah, Robyn surprised him sometimes by doing things that were totally out of character. But not this. "It's not her," he said evenly, trying to hide his irritation.

"Based upon what you've told me about your knowledge of her body, I believe you. I'm just saying we never really know people, do we?"

"I know Robyn. And I know she would never let anyone take any photographs of her like that."

"Okay, so we have this Donald MacGregor as a suspect, and you think he's our best bet at this point?"

"At this point I do, yeah."

Sweeney opened the folder and began reading through his notes.

"What can you tell me about Christopher Burton?"

"Chris Burton? I don't know much about him, really. He's a schoolteacher from Phoenix or Tucson or someplace like that. Comes up here and works for the Forest Service on the fire tower outside of town every summer. Why?"

"I see his name here on the list of people that Deputy Fuchette dated."

"Chris? I didn't know that?"

"What do you mean you didn't know? Are you saying that she hasn't been straightforward with you about other men who might be involved in this?"

"No, not at all," Weber said. "I purposely didn't want to see the list out of respect for her privacy, given our personal relationship."

"Even though that might lead you to the person behind these pictures?"

"I've got some very good deputies working with me. I left that part of the investigation in their hands. It just seemed like the right thing to do."

He wasn't sure if Sweeney understood where he was coming from with that, but a moment later Mary Caitlin knocked on the door and said, "Robyn will be here in five minutes."

Nick Russell

Chapter 16

Sweeney asked to interview Robyn privately, so Weber left them in his office and went out front to check with Mary.

"Anything new?"

She shook her head. "If Donald MacGregor's anywhere in town or near here, he's done a darn good job of hiding. I had to call some of the guys off because they need to get some rest before going on duty tonight. Sorry, Jimmy."

"No, that's all right. Some of those guys haven't slept since yesterday. I don't want them stumbling on him when they're so tired that they're not functioning at 100%. Speaking of which, you need to take off, too. By now Pete's going to be grumbling about dinner and wondering where you're at."

"That old fool can just wonder," Mary said. "Lord knows, I never had any idea when he was going to get home when he was sheriff. And I worked right here in the office with him!"

The phone rang and Mary answered it. She listened for a moment and then said, "Jimmy is right here, Christine, I'll let you talk to him."

She held the phone out to him and Weber took it. "What's up, Hillbilly?"

"I was just calling to see if you had any luck finding Donald MacGregor yet?"

"No. He's doing a good job of hiding, but we'll find him. Meanwhile, I still need you to be careful."

"We are, don't worry about that. And, we've got Archer here to protect us. How much safer could two women be?"

"As long as you don't get between Archer and a bowl of ice cream, it shouldn't be a problem," Weber told her.

Christine laughed and then said, "I just talked to Roberta. She said Coop helped her get her office cleaned up and put back together, and he's going to be spending the night there."

"I don't see MacGregor going back there for a repeat performance," Weber told her. "But then again, I didn't think he would do that in the first place." A thought crossed his mind and he added, "Hey, let me talk to Cindy for a minute."

"Sure, hang on. I'll get her."

When Cindy MacGregor came on the phone, Weber asked if she had any idea where her estranged husband might be hiding out.

"I don't know," she replied. "If he's not at home or his mother's place across the street, the only other place I can think of is his cousin Ed's."

"Ed? Ed MacGregor? Out on Sawyer Ranch Road?"

"Yeah. Him and Ed go way back."

"I used to see them around town together, but it's been a long time," Weber said.

"That's because they had a falling out a while back. Well, actually it wasn't so much Donald and Ed having a problem as it was Donald and Stacy. She got tired of him always dragging Ed off somewhere to get in trouble and put her foot down. They got into a real screaming match before it was over. I don't think Donald has been back there since. He was really mad about Stacy standing up to him like that, and madder yet that Ed wouldn't take his side. So I don't know if he would go there or not, but it's the only other place I can think of. Donald doesn't really have any friends."

"I know Mary called and asked you about Donald's guns earlier today. You said you know he has a handgun and the three long guns, right?"

"Yeah, the handgun is a Ruger Blackhawk single action, like a cowboy gun. I know about that one because I bought it for him for his birthday three years ago. The others I don't know much about. One of them had a long clip or magazine thing that went in from the bottom. He always liked to shoot that one the most."

Weber figured that would be the AK-47 which had once occupied the empty spot on MacGregor's gun rack. If the man was armed with that, the sheriff hoped his deputies got the drop on him before he could use it.

"While we were at the house looking for him today, we seized his computer and some DVDs," Weber told her.

"Yeah, and I can bet I know what those DVDs were of."

"Cindy, technically you and Donald are still married. Was that his computer or your computer, or did you both share it?"

"I'm not sure what you mean. Why would it make any difference whose computer it is?"

"Because if it belongs to the two of you, we can search it with your permission. If it's just Donald's computer, we're going to need a search warrant."

"Why would you need to search the computer? Donald's not the type to go online and book hotel reservations, if that's what you think."

"No, but it might tell us if he's the one sending those pictures that look like Deputy Fuchette."

"Do you still think he's the one doing it?"

"He's our best suspect at this point. So, does the computer belong to both of you or just to your husband?"

"I guess it belongs to both of us. But I use the laptop most of the time, that's what I have here with me."

"But do you use the desktop computer?"

"Once in a while to print out recipes or something like that, because the laptop isn't hooked to a printer. But he's the one that uses it mostly."

"Okay, but it's not like the laptop is yours and the desktop is his exclusively, right?"

"No, I guess not."

"Do you remember buying the computers?"

"Yeah. We ordered both of them online. We got the big one, the desktop first, and a year or so later got the laptop."

"How did you pay for them?"

"With our credit card."

"Is the card in both of your names?"

"Yeah."

"Great. So legally the computer is community property. Do I have your permission to go through it, looking for any pictures that might relate to the ones of Deputy Fuchette?"

"Ummm… let me think about that for a minute, okay?"

Weber wondered why she was hesitating, then the light dawned.

"Cindy, are there pictures of you on that computer?"

There was silence for a moment and he wasn't sure she was going to answer. Then she said, "Yeah, lots of them."

"I understand where you're coming from, and the last thing we want to do is cause you any pain or embarrassment, Cindy. But we really need to know if Donald is the one behind these pictures."

"Who all is going to be looking at them? I mean, it's a small town and everybody knows everybody. Every time I see one of your deputies I'm going to wonder if he saw them. Saw me that way."

"I can understand that," Weber told her. "What if the only people who look through the files are Deputy Fuchette and Mary Caitlin, my administrative assistant?"

Cindy seemed to think about that for a moment then said, "I'm not wild about anybody seeing them, but I understand that you need to look for those files. Yeah, I guess that's okay. I know Robyn and I know Mary. I know they won't blab anything to the rest of the town. I just hope they don't think I'm some kind of slut after they see them."

"Nobody's going to think that, Cindy. I promise you. So, do I have your permission to let them search the computer?"

"I guess so, if you promise it will only be Robyn and Mary. I know it has to be done."

"Thank you, Cindy. I promise you that it will be done with discretion and respect for your privacy."

He ended the call just as Robyn opened his office door and said, "Jimmy, you can come in now."

Sweeney was still sitting behind his desk, but he got up when Weber entered the office and moved to a chair next to the desk, beside where Robyn was seated.

"I have to be honest, guys, I'm not ruling anything out until my expert analyzes those pictures. That's not to say I don't believe you, but it's the way I work."

"I can respect that," Weber replied.

"I appreciate that, Sheriff. Here's the thing, I deal with facts when I'm investigating something. But we all know that facts have to be blended with experience, common sense, and sometimes, intuition. And while the jury is still out on the authenticity of these pictures, based upon my experience and my intuition, I don't feel that it is Deputy Fuchette in them."

Robyn breathed an audible sigh of relief. "Thank you."

"I'm not saying you're out of the woods yet, Deputy. But from what I've seen of you and heard about you from the sheriff and your coworkers, I believe somebody's doing this to hurt you. I'm going to do everything I can to help you get to the bottom of this and clear your name. But," he said, putting up a cautionary finger, "If it turns out I'm wrong and you haven't been honest with me about it not being you in those pictures, there's going to be hell to pay. I don't appreciate being lied to."

"I'm not lying," Robyn said with an edge to her voice.

"And like I said, I believe you. I'm just putting all the cards on the table."

"That's fair enough," Weber said. "What do we do next?"

Sweeney looked at his watch and said, "It's after six and your people have been on the go all day long because of the situation with the assault on the blind woman. And it's been a long day for me, too, driving all the way up here from Phoenix. How about we all get some rest, and tomorrow morning we roll up our sleeves and find the SOB that's doing this to this young woman?"

Nick Russell

Chapter 17

"Honestly, Robyn, I don't know why we are even up here. You disappear first thing in the morning and we don't hear from you all day long."

"You're here to help me with the wedding, Mother."

"How can we plan a wedding if you're never here to help me plan it?"

"I told you, Mother, something came up."

"Yes, something came up. *He* calls, and right away you're grabbing a rifle and running out the door with no explanation whatsoever, like you're Annie Oakley or something."

"It was police business, Mother. I told you that there was an emergency when I left."

"Yes, there was an emergency. An emergency requiring you to take off with a rifle. How do you think that makes me feel? How do you think it makes your father feel? We both sat here worried sick all day long, wondering if you were even alive."

"Stop being so dramatic, Renée. She's here and she's alive, isn't she?"

"Shut up, Bill. Maybe you can ignore the fact that this man is putting our daughter at risk every day, but I won't."

"He has a name, Mother."

"Yes, and apparently he has a name for me, too. We've already heard it."

"I apologize for that, Mrs. Fuchette. I was out of line."

"It was more than out of line, it was verbal abuse. And Robyn, you have to know that if he did it to me, he'll do it to you, too. And that's only the first step. It will get worse from there."

"Stop it, Mother. Jimmy has never been anything but a perfect gentleman to me. You're acting like he's some kind of monster who is going to abuse me the first chance he gets."

"It's only a matter of time," the other woman said primly. "Just know that when he does, your father and I will be there for you, to help you pick up the pieces. Who knows, Robyn? Maybe that's what needs to happen, God forbid. Maybe then you would finally open your eyes and see that you're throwing your life away up here with him and come back home where you belong. It's time to grow up and quit chasing this fantasy of being some kind of superhero with a badge."

"You know what, Mother? Jimmy was right. You *are* a bitch!"

At least Renée Fuchette didn't slap her daughter like she had Weber before she stormed off to the bedroom and slammed the door behind her.

The uncomfortable silence seemed to drag on for a long time before her father looked toward the ceiling and shook his head. "Well, that was awkward, wasn't it?"

~~***~~

"I can't believe I called my mother a bitch!"

"I've heard you call her that plenty of times before."

"Yes, but never to her face!"

They were sitting on the porch swing and Weber said, "So how did it feel?"

Robyn thought for a moment, then said, "Actually, it was surprisingly refreshing. It's been a long time coming."

The screen door opened and her father came out and sat in a rocking chair. He pulled his pipe out of one pocket and a tobacco pouch out of another and filled the bowl. Tamping the tobacco down with his finger, he struck a match and lit it, puffing out an aromatic cloud of smoke.

"Daddy, I know I shouldn't have said what I did, but I was just so angry."

"You're not the only one who was thinking it."

"Maybe so, but I can't believe you'd ever call Mother a name like that."

He puffed on the pipe again and then said, "Not out loud. She would smother me in my sleep with my own pillow. But don't think I haven't thought it more than once."

"I don't know how you have put up with it for so long. When I was little I used to pray that you two would get a divorce, so I could go live with you and get away from her. Did you ever think about that, Daddy?"

He shrugged his shoulders and said, "Not really. I come from a generation that believed that once you make your bed, you lie in it."

"But you deserve so much more, Daddy."

Her father puffed his pipe again and said, "The way I look at it, if she's busy making my life miserable, than some other poor slob out there doesn't have to put up with it. It's kind of like my service to the world in general."

"Don't you want to be happy?"

He smiled and looked at her fondly. "Robyn, I have a beautiful daughter who is intelligent and kind and loving, and she's doing what she wants with her life. Good work that makes a difference. And she's about to marry a wonderful man who I know loves her very much. What could make me happier?"

"Oh, Daddy." Robyn got off of the porch swing and went to his chair, bending over to kiss him on the cheek. "I love you so much."

He set the pipe on a table next to the rocking chair and pulled her into his lap and put his arms around her. "I love you, too, Pumpkin."

"And I love Mother, too. But sometimes she makes it so difficult."

"Welcome to my world, kiddo."

Her father held her for a while, then Robyn said, "I guess I'd better go check up on Mother and apologize."

She got up, kissed her father on his forehead, then went in the house. Bill picked up his pipe and relit it, then looked at the man who would soon be his son-in-law.

"Don't pay any attention to that bullshit of Renée's. I know how you feel about Robyn, and I know you would never put her in danger or abuse her in any way."

"I wouldn't," Weber said. "Besides, she has guns *and* pillows. I would never be able to sleep."

Bill laughed, and then his face turned serious as he said, "There's something else I need to say, Jimmy. Even up here in a little town like this, I know that police work can be dangerous. And while I know you wouldn't needlessly put Robyn in a dangerous situation, I also know that the reality is that it could happen. It's part of what you both do. Do I worry sometimes? Yes. Maybe even more after she got shot. That really brought it home, the possibility that something terrible could happen to her. But you need to know that if it ever did, heaven forbid, I wouldn't hold it against you."

"I appreciate that, Bill. Cops don't talk about it much, but we all know that it's possible. We take all the precautions we can, but there are some bad people out there."

"Like the one you dealt with today."

"Yeah, like him. They're not just in the big city. People like that are everywhere."

Bill nodded his head and said, "And that's why the world needs people like you and Robyn everywhere, to protect the sheep from the wolves. You're a good man, Jim Weber. My daughter is lucky to have found someone like you to share her life with."

Sitting there in the dark, just the two of them listening to the sounds of the night, Weber didn't reply. The lump in his throat would not allow him to.

Chapter 18

"We've searched everywhere, Jimmy. No sign of MacGregor anywhere."

"He's a big guy in a big ass truck. He didn't just disappear into thin air."

"I know, but wherever he's hiding out, he's done a good job of it. We've been watching his place and his mother's place, checking out empty cabins, although there aren't many of them, it being the middle of summer."

"What about campgrounds, Dolan?"

"Lots of flatlanders up here having fun, but nobody we've talked to has seen anyone that looks like MacGregor, or his truck."

"What about the cousin. Ed MacGregor? Any luck there?"

"Nope. I've talked to Ed and Stacy twice," Buz said. "Neither one of them have seen hide nor hair of him."

"Do you think Ed would lie to cover for him?"

"He might, I don't know. But Stacy damn sure wouldn't. She hates that guy with a passion."

"Yeah, I heard that she put an end to Ed and Donald running around together getting into trouble. She's not exactly his biggest fan."

"Apparently there's more to it than that, Jimmy."

"What do you mean?"

"According to Stacy, that wasn't the only problem she had with Donald. She said he tried to put the make on her a couple of times. And from the way she talked, he wasn't too subtle about it."

"Really? And Ed was okay with that?"

"I don't know, to tell you the truth. When she was telling me about it he just sat there and didn't say anything."

Mary Caitlin, sitting at the dispatch desk, was on the telephone. When she ended the call she turned and said, "The reason we can't find MacGregor is because he's nowhere around here."

"What do you mean?"

"That was the police department in Gallup, New Mexico, responding to our APB on him. Apparently sometime around 10 o'clock last night one of their officers spotted MacGregor in his Ford pickup and attempted to make a traffic stop. MacGregor fled with the officer in pursuit, but he was chasing him through an intersection when somebody failed to stop and T-boned the cop. At that time he was the only unit on the scene, and by the time others arrived MacGregor was gone. An hour later someone reported seeing a blue truck that matched the description of his driving recklessly on eastbound Interstate 40 just outside of Grants, New Mexico. Highway Patrol responded but couldn't find him."

"Is the Gallup cop okay?"

"Bumps and bruises, but nothing serious."

"Damn. I don't know how he got away from us, but he did it."

"The good news is that at least he seems to be headed away from here," Deputy Tommy Frost said. "Maybe Miss Jensen and Christine and his wife can breathe a little easier knowing that. And a guy like that, he can't stay out of trouble. He's going to turn up someplace and get busted sooner or later."

"Yeah, and let's just hope it's somewhere away from here, for everybody's sake," Weber said, though he had a strong suspicion they hadn't seen the last of Donald MacGregor yet.

"How's Miss Jensen doing?"

"I swung by her place this morning on my way to work," Weber said. "She's okay. A bit flustered maybe, but that's as much from Coop hovering over her like a mother hen as anything else. I told him to take a couple of days off, but Roberta jumped right in and said no, she was fine and he needed to get back to work. I guess they compromised and he's going to spend another day and night there and come back on duty tomorrow."

"In all the time I've known Coop, I've never seen him like he was yesterday, Jimmy. If he would have come upon MacGregor, that guy would be dead right now."

"No question about that, Chad. It wouldn't be any loss to the world, but if it comes down to that, I hope Coop's not the one that has to pull the trigger."

From the looks on his deputies' faces, Weber had a feeling that Donald MacGregor had stepped so far over the line that any of them would not have hesitated to take him out if push came to shove.

"Okay guys, those of you on duty, get out there and do your thing. And even though we know he's in New Mexico, or at least was in New Mexico, don't let your guard down. Just because he was there last night doesn't mean he hasn't circled back around and is headed our way again. The rest of you, get some sleep. I know we've all been hitting it hard looking for this guy."

"I just got off duty, I can stay out for another hour or two, just keeping an eye on things in case he does show up," Dolan said.

"Me, too," Dan Wright added.

"Guys, I appreciate it, but not too long, okay? You've got to get some rest sometime."

As the meeting was breaking up, Mary was back on the phone, saying, "I'll tell him. Yes, he'll be right there."

She turned to Weber and said, "You need to go to Town Hall. They've got a problem."

"Now what?"

"It seems that Chet Wingate is holding a sit-in in the mayor's office."

~***~

"He just walked in the door like he owned the place said hello to us, and then went in the mayor's office and closed the door behind him," Debbie Popovich told Weber. "At first I didn't even think about it, it was like any other day when he was mayor. Then it hit me, he's not the mayor anymore! So I went in and asked him what he was doing and he said he was doing his job and asked for the files on that new convenience store they want to build out by the ski lodge. He said he had to review them before next week's Town Council meeting. I didn't know what to do so I went and asked Rachel, and she went in the office and told him that he couldn't be there any more because he isn't the mayor. He refused to leave and told her he *is* the mayor and he just took a short leave of absence for medical reasons and now he's back." Debbie, a nervous young woman who had battled psoriasis since she was a teenager, wrung her red, irritated hands and paced back and forth like a caged animal. "I'm sorry. I tried to get him to leave, but he wouldn't go."

"I think he's lost his mind or something," Rachel Lucas, her coworker said. "He actually thinks he's still the mayor. I called the drugstore and told Kirby Templeton what was going on, and he wanted to talk to Chet on the phone. But Chet wouldn't take the call. He said he had work to do and didn't want to be interrupted again. That's when Kirby said to call you, and he would be on his way here as soon as he got Mrs. Dempsey's prescription filled. Apparently her IBS is kicking up big time again, poor thing. We saw her and her husband at the Roundup Friday night, and she had to leave the table and go to the ladies room three times."

As Rachel finished telling him about the other woman's digestive problems, the door opened and Kirby Templeton arrived.

"Is he still in there?"

"Yes, sir. He had me close the door behind him when I tried to get him to take your phone call, and he hasn't come out since."

"This is ridiculous." Kirby walked to the door to the mayor's office and tried to open it. When the knob wouldn't turn, he shook it, and pounded on the door. "Chet, open this door right now!"

"Go away, I'm working," the former mayor called from inside.

Kirby shook the knob again then pounded on the door once more. "Open the door, Chet. That's not your office anymore."

"Is too. I'm back from my leave of absence. Now go away, I've got work to do!"

"For the hundredth time, Chet, you didn't take a leave of absence, you resigned. Now open this door!"

There was no response and Weber said, "Let me try." He pounded on the door and said, "Chet, this is Sheriff Weber. You're trespassing. Now open this door before I kick it in."

"Don't kick it in yet, Jimmy. Let me focus my camera."

He wasn't sure when Paul Lewis had arrived on the scene. His friend preferred not to leave his newspaper office if he could avoid it, relying on people bringing routine stories about school functions and club meetings to him. But the man did have a nose for news when it was needed, and the town's former mayor taking over his old office and refusing to leave was news in Big Lake.

"Nobody needs to kick in the door," Kirby said, reaching in his pocket to pull out a key ring. He selected the right one and inserted it into the lock on the door knob and turned it. The door only opened three or four inches and then hit some sort of obstacle and stopped. Kirby tried to push it, with no success.

"Here, let me help you." Between the interim mayor and the sheriff, they were able to push the door open far enough that Weber could poke his head inside and see the four drawer filing cabinet and visitor's chair that Chet had pushed against the door to keep them out.

"Chet, move this crap right now."

"Go away."

"Come on, move it so we can get inside."

"I don't want you inside. This is my office and I've got work to do. Now go away like I told you to."

Weber swore under his breath and put his shoulder to the door, managing to force it open a bit at a time. Once inside, he jerked his thumb over his shoulder and said, "Okay, game's over. Out!"

"You can't come barging into my office like that!"

"It's not your office anymore," Kirby said.

"You're trying to steal my job, Kirby Templeton! I'm on to you."

"Chet, you resigned," Kirby said, pushing the frustration away and trying to explain something like he would to one of his petulant grandchildren. But the former mayor was more stubborn than a child. He had years of practice at it.

"I don't care what you say. I took a leave of absence, and now I'm back."

Kirby might have been able to control his frustration, but Weber, who was not known for his patience under the best of circumstances, had too much going on to waste any more time with Chet Wingate's stunts. "Okay, enough bullshit. Get out of here right now."

"No. You two get out of here."

"Dammit, Chet, you're really pissing me off. If you don't get out of that chair and out of this office right now, I'm going to arrest you for trespassing."

"How can I be trespassing if I'm in my own office?"

"It's not your office anymore," Kirby said. "How many times do I have to tell you that?"

Weber didn't wait for a response, instead he walked up to the desk and grabbed Chet by the arm and started to pull him to his feet.

"Get your hands off of me!"

"Last chance, Chet. One way or the other, you're leaving this office."

"I don't think so."

"Yeah? Well, you're wrong."

Weber tried to pull him to his feet and that's when he realized that removing the unpleasant little man from his former office might take more work than he had anticipated. Chet Wingate had handcuffed himself to the arm of the oak office chair behind the desk.

Nick Russell

Chapter 19

"Seriously? He handcuffed himself to the chair?"

"I'm as serious as a heart attack, Parks."

"And you rolled him and the chair out of Town Hall and all the way across the street here to your office and into a jail cell?"

"Yep, and he was raising hell all the way, threatening to have me fired and arrested for attacking a public official."

"I'd have paid money to see that, Jimmy."

"You'll see pictures of it in this week's paper."

"Where did he get the handcuffs? And please tell me him and that Gretchen woman don't have something kinky going on that requires them."

"I don't know what they do behind closed doors, and I don't want to know. That's none of my business," Weber said. "But I have a pretty good idea where the handcuffs came from."

As if on cue, Deputy Archer Wingate came through the door.

"Mary called and said you wanted to see me, Jimmy. And you wanted me to wear my uniform. It's my day off."

"I know that, Archer, but you do realize we've got a situation here with this crazy man running at large, right?"

"Yeah."

"And you know that all of the other deputies are out looking for him, even if they are off shift?"

"Yeah, I guess."

"But you don't feel any obligation to be out helping with the search?"

"I didn't really give it much thought, Jimmy. Kallie Jo's making lasagna for dinner."

"It's not even noon, Archer. Dinner won't be for hours."

"It's really good lasagna, Jimmy."

"I don't doubt it is."

"And garlic bread, too."

"Sounds delicious, Archer. But I didn't call you in here to talk about Kallie Jo's cooking. I actually wanted to do a quick inspection."

"An inspection?"

"Yes, Archer, an inspection. Don't you think it's important that all of our deputies are looking sharp for the public?"

"I guess so."

"Okay then. Let's have a look at you."

Weber had to admit that after Kallie Jo Phillips, Archer's mail order bride, had shown up in town there had been an improvement in the man's overall appearance, and even in his job performance. Not that the sheriff ever expected his chubby deputy to be a superstar in the annals of law enforcement, but at least it had been two or three months since a citizen had called to report that Archer had fallen asleep in his patrol car while on duty. That was an accomplishment in itself.

Kallie Joe, a tiny little woman who talked a mile a minute with her thick Georgia accent, always made sure that his uniform was clean and pressed and his shoes were polished before Archer left for work. After walking around his deputy, Weber said, "Let me see your weapon. Carefully, Archer. Carefully."

Archer drew his Glock Model 22 from its holster and handed it to the sheriff. Looking the pistol over and not seeing any rust on the magazine or smears of peanut butter on the polymer frame, he handed it back.

"Okay, let's see your handcuffs."

Archer put his hand on the nylon handcuff case on his duty belt and opened it, then looked confused.

"What's wrong, Deputy?"

"Huh?"

"What's wrong? Show me your handcuffs."

"Uh... I can't right now, Jimmy."

"Why not?"

"I don't know where they are."

"How can you not know where your handcuffs are, Archer?"

"I don't know."

"When did you use them last?"

"I'm not sure."

"Archer, did you handcuff a prisoner and forget all about him somewhere? Is there somebody wandering around Big Lake right now with your handcuffs on them, wondering how they're going to tie their shoes in the morning?"

"I don't think so. I haven't put handcuffs on anybody in a long time."

"And you never noticed they were gone?"

"I guess not."

"How is that possible, Archer? I mean every day you put on your belt with your weapon and your spare magazine pouch and your flashlight and all of your stuff, and you never noticed your handcuff pouch was empty?"

"No. Does this mean I have to buy new handcuffs, Jimmy?"

"Well, Archer, we do kind of like our deputies to have handcuffs with them. You know, just in case you arrest somebody who isn't willing to drive you back here to the jail and lock themselves in a cell."

"I'm kind of confused, Jimmy. Do I have to pay for new handcuffs or does the Department give them to me?"

Weber closed his eyes for a minute and pictured himself somewhere on a beach, drinking some kind of fruity concoction with an umbrella sticking out of it from a coconut and not having to deal with wife beaters and people who sent out fake photographs of women and most of all, not having to deal with Archer Wingate. It was a nice fantasy, but when he opened his eyes, Archer was still standing in front of him.

"No, Archer, you don't have to buy any new handcuffs. I found yours."

"You did? Where at?"

"Come with me, I'll show you."

Leading the way down the hall to the heavy door that separated the cellblock from the main office, Weber unlocked it and escorted Archer to the cell where his father was still sitting in the chair from the mayor's office.

"Daddy? What are you doing in there?"

"Apparently your father stole your handcuffs, Archer. Then today he went into the mayor's office and handcuffed himself to that chair. So how about you get your key out, I'm assuming you still have your handcuff key, right? That's good. So how about you unlock him."

"You didn't need me for that, Jimmy. All the keys fit the handcuffs the same."

Weber smiled and said, "I know that, Archer. But, they're your handcuffs and he's your father. And even though it's your day off, it's your mess. Go clean it up."

~~***~~

"Boy, Cindy MacGregor wasn't lying when she said her husband took a lot of pictures of her," Robyn said. "There must be a hundred or more of them."

"And if you'll notice, she's not smiling in even one of them," Mary Caitlin said. "It's pretty obvious to me it wasn't something she enjoyed doing."

"Is there anything that ties her husband to those pictures of you, Robyn."

"They're not me."

"I know that. I'm sorry. It's been a crazy day already. Are there any pictures that look like the ones that are being sent around? The same background, like they were taken in the same room, anything at all?"

"No. There's tons of stuff off the Internet that we haven't gotten to yet, but nothing so far."

Big Lake Wedding

Robyn's cell phone rang and she looked at it and shook her head, before swiping the screen to close the call without answering.

"Don't tell me. I bet that was your mother."

"Yes, she wants to go over the groomsmen's suits now."

"There are not going to be any groomsmen, unless something has changed that I don't know about. I thought it was just going to be you and me up there, with Parks and Marsha as our witnesses."

"You're right, but that doesn't mean she is willing to accept that. She thinks the deputies should all be in suits, too. And that I round up a bunch of women at the last minute to be my bridesmaids. I told her I didn't have that many friends up here, which right away turned into this big sermon about how if I still lived down in the Valley I would have plenty of friends who wanted to participate in my special day. The woman's like a pit bull, Jimmy. When she sets her mind to something, she just won't let go of it."

"If it would help you out, I'd be happy to be a bridesmaid for you," Mary said. "And I'm sure the dispatchers and Kallie Jo would, too. You do have friends here, Robyn. You know that, don't you?"

"Of course I do, Mary. And I appreciate the offer. But no matter how big a circus my mother wants to turn this into, we're going to keep it low-key. Or at least as low-key as possible. She has too much time on her hands, and I swear she spends it thinking up ways to irritate me. It wasn't bad enough that she arranged everything in my kitchen to make it more efficient, she also went through all of my dresser drawers, rearranging things there, too. I had to go rescue all of my girly underwear from the trash can. Seriously, I opened the drawer and all there were left were granny panties. She said thongs, or even bikini panties, are what prostitutes wear, and she didn't raise any prostitutes. I was really tempted to ask if she knew how I earned the money for my first car, but knowing my mother, after the paramedics resuscitated her, she would haul me up in front of a tribunal of preachers to confess my sins. She has absolutely no sense of humor."

"Well, at least you saved the thongs," Weber said. "So all is not lost."

"You're welcome, Jimmy."

"Hey, here's an idea. Since your mother doesn't have anything to do, and she keeps complaining that you two aren't spending enough time together, why don't you call her down here and ask her to help you go through the files on MacGregor's computer?"

"Are you kidding me? The paramedics would have to hook their paddles right up to the power line out in front to get enough juice to start her heart again. That's assuming they could find it in the first place."

Chapter 20

"Tell me you found out something," Weber said hopefully when Captain Sweeney arrived at the Sheriff's Office an hour later.

"I wish I did. I was on the phone most of the morning trying to salvage a case down in Globe that is going to go south. Cops down there busted a guy for a dozen different petty thefts and burglaries, and it turned out he is the brother-in-law to one of their guys. They caught him red-handed, then his wife put pressure on her brother, the cop, to do something. And the damn fool did. Suddenly a bunch of the evidence went missing. Evidence he had access to. They executed a search warrant at his house and found some of it there, but the chain of evidence has been broken and their case went out the window. So, it looks like Globe is out a cop and the original perp may walk."

"That sucks."

"Yes, it does. Meanwhile, on the situation here, I've talked to two of the possibilities, the ones you already ruled out. That guy named Bischoff and the other one, Wilder. Bischoff seems like a nice enough guy, but that Wilder's a piece of work. He's got a wise ass attitude. You'd think he was somebody important and not a bottom feeding thief. You said you didn't find a computer at his place, but I'm still not ready to cross him off my list. What about the third one, MacGregor? Is he still in the wind?"

"So far," Weber said, then told him about the sightings of the suspect in New Mexico. "We seized his computer and we're going through it now."

"Wait a minute. You seized his computer?"

"Yeah. His wife gave us permission to search it. It's community property."

"Sheriff, you didn't think maybe my people should be the ones doing that? Isn't that why you brought in an outside investigator?"

"There are extenuating circumstances, Captain."

"Such as?"

"MacGregor has a lot of photographs of his wife on the computer. Photographs that she wouldn't be comfortable with the whole world looking at."

"I've got to be honest with you, Sheriff Weber. I don't really care what makes his wife feel comfortable. Who's to say she's not covering for him?"

"I guarantee you she's not covering. She's done with him. That's why she's at the women's shelter."

"Who is looking at the files on that computer?"

"Mary Caitlin, my administrative assistant, and Deputy Fuchette."

"Are you freaking kidding me, Sheriff?" Sweeney did not try to hide the irritation in his voice. "You don't think that's a little bit out of line? The alleged victim searching the possible perpetrator's computer? Not to mention the fact that she's been suspended by the Town Council and shouldn't even be here?"

"She wasn't suspended, she's on paid administrative leave."

"Don't split hairs with me, Sheriff." The anger in the DPS investigator's voice was mirrored in his face. "I don't have time for that kind of nonsense."

"I'm not splitting hairs. I was trying to exercise discretion for the sake of Mrs. MacGregor."

"Okay, cards on the table time, Sheriff. You brought me up here to conduct an investigation so there wouldn't be any question of how things were handled, no matter how it shakes out. Now, either you and your people back off and you let me do my job my way, or I'm out of here and the ball's back in your court. Which is it going to be?"

"I'm not trying to undermine your investigation, Captain Sweeney. But this is a small town and..."

"I know it's a small town. I'm not blind. And I know how small towns work. I was born and raised in Willcox, down in Cochise County. That's no excuse for you trying to run a parallel investigation to mine. If anything, to an outsider it looks like you are trying to control the investigation. Do you have something to hide, Sheriff?"

"No, of course not," Weber said, feeling his anger building, but knowing that Sweeney was right. It was best for everybody concerned if they let the man do his job without help or interference from the Sheriff's Department unless it was requested. But he hated breaking his promise to Cindy MacGregor that nobody else would see any pictures of her that were on the computer they had seized.

"Look, Sheriff, I understand where you're coming from. No woman wants a bunch of strangers looking at intimate pictures of her. I get that. But sometimes there's collateral damage."

"Cindy MacGregor is not collateral damage. She's a victim. Just like Robyn is."

"There's a difference, Sheriff. If there are pictures of your deputy on that computer that somebody has faked, *she* is a victim. We have to assume that Mrs. MacGregor posed for any pictures her husband took of her. Big difference."

"Not if she was coerced into it," Weber argued.

Sweeney closed his eyes and exhaled and didn't reply for a moment. When he opened them again he said, "I'm sorry, Sheriff. I will see that every bit of discretion possible is exercised in reviewing the files on that computer. But it's my way or the highway. I've got over thirty open cases on my plate right now. And the reason I have so many cases is because I'm damned good at what I do. But I pushed them to the back burner to come here because it was a cop in trouble. So, either I do things as I see fit, or else I'll move on to the next case and leave you to figure out how to handle your little scandal here. Makes no difference to me."

Weber wanted to tell the man to go to hell and send him packing, but he knew that wasn't an option. The only way Robyn was going to keep her job and see her reputation restored in town was to prove those pictures weren't of her. And though Captain Sweeney might be somewhat abrasive, Weber couldn't deny that if he was in the man's shoes and felt like local authorities were muddying the waters of an investigation, he would react the same way.

"Fine," Weber said, relenting. "You win. We'll do it your way. What's the next step?"

"The next step is you get those two women away from that computer and shut it down. I'll take it back to my room with me and review the files tonight. Meanwhile, I want to talk to this Christopher Burton, guy that works at the fire tower that Deputy Fuchette dated at one time. I don't know the lay of the land around here. Can you take me there?"

"Uh… I guess so."

"Is there a problem, Sheriff Weber?"

"No. It's just that it might be kind of awkward, given the relationship that Robyn and I have now."

"Hey, you're the one that keeps telling me it's a small town. It's not like you're never going to see the guy, right?"

"Yeah, I guess so. Let's go."

Chapter 21

Two cow elk sauntered casually across their path as they bounced up the rough fire road that led to the Forest Service's lookout tower on Cat Mountain. One stopped in mid-stride and looked at them curiously before moving on. Having grown up in the mountains and seen hundreds, if not thousands, of big game animals over the years, it always amazed Weber how wildlife seemed to take humans for granted most of the year, but pull a disappearing act come hunting season.

Sweeney put his hand on the dashboard of Weber's Explorer to steady himself.

"Man, those are big animals. I've never seen an elk in the wild before."

"These mountains are full of them," Weber told him. "Along with mule deer, bear, and even the occasional mountain lion. Wait until you hear a bull elk bugling during rutting season. It's an eerie sound you'll never forget."

"No thanks. I'm a city boy. This is as far away from pavement as I ever want to get."

As he spoke, the Explorer's right front tire dropped into a particularly deep hole in the road and Weber felt a jolt from the steering wheel go up his arms to his shoulders.

"I'm glad we're in this thing. There's no way my unmarked Chevy would make it even part way up here. As it is, I think I bruised my kidneys on that last bump."

"Not much farther now," Weber told him. "Maybe a quarter-mile or so."

There was a green Dodge Forest Service pickup parked at the tower and Weber stopped his Explorer next to it. They got out and looked at the tall steel tower with its small structure perched on top. Weber was not a fan of heights and was not looking forward to climbing up there, but was saved when a voice called from above.

"Hello. Can I help you?"

"Christopher Burton?"

"What?"

"Are you Christopher Burton?"

"That's me."

"I'm Captain Sweeney with the Department of Public Safety, and this is Sheriff Weber from Big Lake. We need to talk to you."

"I'm sorry, I only got part of that," the man on the tower said. "Hang on, I'll come down."

They watched as he made his way down to ground level on the ladder welded to the tower as easily as anybody else would ride an escalator from the second floor of a shopping mall.

"Sorry, the wind at that level makes it hard to hear sometimes. What can I do for you gentlemen?"

Sweeney introduced himself and Weber again.

"Yeah, I've seen you around, Sheriff. Nice to meet you, Mr. Sweeney."

Burton was a slender man with a beard, who looked to be in his mid-30s. His dishwater blonde hair was pulled back in a ponytail. He was wearing a long-sleeved T-shirt with a picture of a bighorn sheep on it under the words Arizona Sonora Desert Museum. Weber noticed he had amazingly blue eyes, and when they shook hands, his grip was firm.

"We need to talk to you about Robyn Fuchette," Sweeney said.

"Robyn? Is she okay?"

"We understand that you and her dated for a while. Is that true?"

"Yeah," Burton said, concern on his face. "Did something happen to Robyn?"

"Not exactly."

"Not exactly? What does that mean?"

"It means she's okay physically, but something has come up."

"Something has come up? I don't know what that means."

"Mr. Burton, what was your relationship with Ms. Fuchette like?"

"Our relationship? It was fine, I guess."

"You guess? What do you mean by that?"

"We got along fine. She's a nice woman. I really cared about her."

"Cared, as in past tense? What changed that?"

"I just mean that when we were seeing each other I really liked her a lot. But after a while it became pretty obvious to both of us that it wasn't going anywhere."

"Why is that, do you think?"

He shrugged his shoulders. "I come up here to work the tower in the summer, and I teach school in Tucson the rest of the year. I wasn't looking to settle down with anybody, and neither was she. It was a casual thing, and at the end of the summer when it was time for me to go back to Tucson, we parted company."

"Would you say it was a friendly break up?"

"I don't know if you'd really call it a break up, because it was never that big of a thing," Burton replied. "We had dinner a few times, went to the movies in Show Low once, and on some hikes, that's about it. Like I said, it was casual."

"Did you maybe want it to be something more than that?"

"Not really, and neither did she. Look, guys, I don't know what's going on here, but I wish you'd tell me why you're asking me all these questions?"

"Mr. Burton, were you and Robyn ever intimate?"

"That's none of your business."

"Actually, it is." Sweeney pulled his phone from his pocket and opened the file with the photographs of the woman who looked like Robyn. "What can you tell me about these pictures?"

When the fire lookout saw what was on the screen of the phone, he looked away.

"Do those pictures bother you for some reason, Mr. Burton?"

"Yeah, they bother me. I don't know where you got them but it's not cool to be showing them to somebody like that."

"Why do you say that?"

"Because Robyn was my friend. I'd like to think we're still friends, and I don't appreciate it. Have some respect."

"Mr. Burton, did you ever take any pictures like this of Robyn?"

"What? Hell no!"

"Are you sure about that?"

"Yes, I'm sure. We never... you asked if we were ever intimate. No, we weren't. A few kisses and some cuddling a time or two, but that's about as far as it ever went."

"So she was holding out on you?"

"What? No! It wasn't a case of holding out. Our relationship wasn't like that. I mean, yeah, she's a beautiful woman, what guy wouldn't want to? But she was my friend more than anything. And she's not the type to sleep around. She made that plain going in, and there was no way I was going to mess up a friendship over sex."

"When's the last time you saw her?"

"I don't know. It's been a long time."

"Have you seen her since you two broke up?"

"I told you, there was never any breakup because it was not that serious of a relationship. I'm up here for the summer and then I go back to my life in Tucson. She was a dispatcher for the Sheriff's Department and wanted to become a deputy. Neither one of us was going to uproot our lives to be together."

"That doesn't answer my question."

"The last time I saw her... it was last summer, I know that. It must have been the middle of summer. My relief guy was watching the tower and I went to town to pick up my mail and some things at the store. I bumped into her in the parking lot. She was in uniform and driving a police car and we talked for a little bit. She told me that she was a deputy now and was involved with somebody and was going to be getting married."

"How did that make you feel?"

"I was happy for her."

"No jealousy?"

"No. Why should I be jealous?"

"Sir, would you take one more look at those pictures?"

"No, I won't."

"Why not?"

"I told you why. Because she was my friend and I respect her."

Sweeney looked at Weber and shrugged his shoulders.

"Mr. Burton, I'm not only the Sheriff in Big Lake, I'm also Robyn's fiancé. Somebody is sending emails with pictures that look like Robyn to people all over town. But they're not her. Somebody doctored them. That's why we're here, we're trying to find out who's doing that."

"And you think it was me?"

"We're just covering all the bases," Sweeney said.

"So, it's not Robyn in the pictures?"

"No, sir, it's not her," Weber told him.

"Okay, let me see."

He looked at the photographs and shook his head. "I don't know what to say. It looks like Robyn to me, but I never saw her naked. And I don't believe she would ever pose for pictures like that. But if you think I'm the one doing this, you're barking up the wrong tree."

"Do you have a computer here, Mr. Burton?"

"Yeah, my laptop. But there's no Internet access here. I have to go down by the ski lodge to get enough signal to send an email, and I only leave here every fifteen days when my relief comes and gives me a day off. You're welcome to look at my computer if you want to. I'll climb up and get it right now."

Sweeney looked at Weber again, who subtly shook his head.

"I don't think that will be necessary, Mr. Burton. Let me ask you one final question. Do you know of anybody who would want to do something like this, to hurt Ms. Fuchette? Did she ever mention having a problem with somebody that might have a grudge against her?"

He shook his head. "No. How could anybody have a problem with Robyn?"

"All right, thank you for your time, Mr. Burton. We'll let you get back to work."

"I hope you find the lowlife that's doing this. No woman deserves to have something like that happen. Especially not somebody as nice as Robyn."

They started to turn away and he added, "Sheriff Weber, congratulations. You're a lucky man. Robyn is a hell of a woman, and I wish you both lots of love and happiness. Please let her know I said that."

"I will," Weber promised him.

Chapter 22

"Please tell me that you're close to finding out who is sending those darned pictures," Marsha said that evening as they sat at a table at Mario's Pizzeria. "I'm tired of hearing all the gossip in town."

"At least people are talking to you," Robyn said. "Do you know that I was at the Dollar Store and saw Betty Conway and Trish Hansen, and neither one of them would even give me the time of day. I nodded and said hello to them and they both turned their heads like I was some kind of leper or something. Then as I was walking away, I heard them whispering behind my back."

"You just ignore those kind of people, honey," Christine said. "What they think about anybody ain't worth spit."

"I know what you're saying, but it still hurts," Robyn replied.

"I know it does, baby. But you know what I think? To hell with them! When this all clears up, and it will, they're gonna be the ones eating crow."

"Yeah, but in the meantime, everybody's acting like I'm a pariah."

"Not everybody, girlfriend," Marsha said. "You've still got me and Chris and Jimmy and Parks. What more do you need?"

"Seriously, you guys don't know how much it means to me to have you to lean on."

Christine hugged her and said, "We love you, girl. We've got your back. Now, let's talk about your honeymoon. Where are you guys going?"

"We have no idea," Robyn told her.

"What? Are you kidding me? What do you want to do, wait until you both say "I do" and then flip a coin to decide where you're going?"

"Pretty much," Robyn told her. "I think we're just going to leave it loosey-goosey and see what happens."

"Not on your honeymoon," Christine said incredulously. "That takes planning."

"Trust me, Christine, I've done enough planning to last me for the rest of my life. According to my mother, I should even plan what color sheets and pillowcases we're going to put on a bed so they complement the room, as she puts it."

"Hey, there's nothing wrong with doing things spur of the moment," Parks said.

"How about taking a cruise?" Marsha suggested.

"No, thank you," Christine replied. "I don't want anything to do with the ocean. I get seasick watching somebody fill up a glass with water."

"Yeah, but you're not planning to go on the honeymoon, too, are you?"

"I just might. It's not like I'm going to be going on one of my own anytime soon. Like never."

"Just remember, only two things swim in the ocean," Parks interjected, "sharks and shark food. And don't forget, the sperm whale isn't called a sperm whale for nothing. You don't want to go anywhere near the ocean."

"You were in the Navy, Parks. Don't tell me you haven't been on the ocean."

"I have, Jimmy. I'm speaking from experience here."

"Oh really? Tell us all about you and the sperm whale," Marsha said.

Before he could reply, the double doors to the kitchen opened. "Look at this," Salvatore Gattuccio said as he brought two large pizzas to the table. "All of my good friends here together. He placed the pizzas on wire racks and said, "Miss Robyn, how is the blushing bride to be this evening?"

"I've been better, Sal."

Sal, whose white apron stretched tightly over his belly, frowned and said, "I am so sorry this is happening to you, Miss Robyn," as he gently patted her shoulder with a meaty hand. "You are such a good woman and Sal cannot understand how anyone could treat you so mean. But you mark my words, the person doing this, they're going to regret it. Good follows good and bad follows bad. What is that word they talk about? Karma? Yes, karma. It is real, my sweet friend. And karma will take its price from them. Soon, I hope. Very soon."

Robyn reached up and put her small hand on his and said, "Thank you, Sal."

"Here, let me serve you a slice. Mama's pizza sauce will cure anything from pneumonia to a broken heart. I promise, one bite and you will forget your troubles, at least for a little bit."

"I know I will, Sal. Thank you."

"Now Sal, once you serve Robyn you sit down here and eat with us," Christine said.

"I will do that, my sweet. I promise. But first I must bring these ladies at the next table their pizza. Then, I turn it over to the young people and they can take care of the customers while I eat with my friends and my lovely lady."

He left the table and Marsha asked, "Is Sal all right?"

"What do you mean?"

"I don't know, Christine. He's got those dark bags under his eyes. I never noticed them before."

"I don't think he's sleeping well. I saw him yawning when I first came in."

"Well, lady, maybe you'll have to figure out some way to relax him," Marsha said with an mischievous grin. "I've got a book that might give you some ideas."

Christine laughed and said, "Well, you know what they say. Book learning isn't for everybody. Some of us are more hands on, if you know what I mean."

They were laughing when Sal came back from the kitchen, placing a pizza on a rack on the table next to them.

"There you go, my friends. Enjoy."

"Excuse me," Shirley Farmer said as he turned away.

"Yes, ma'am, how can I help you?"

She leaned forward and asked in a stage whisper, "Could we be moved to another table?"

"Another table? I'm sorry, is there a draft or something here?"

"No, it's not that. We would just prefer to be... away from that woman." She nodded her head not too subtly toward Robyn.

LeeAnn Reynolds, her sister-in-law, nodded. "If you don't mind. I don't know if you've heard about the pictures, but…"

The women might have thought their voices were low enough not to reach the neighboring table, but they were wrong. Robyn's face turned red and she hung her head. And while the women may have thought they were being discreet in their request to be moved, Salvatore Gattuccio's response was anything but discreet. Up until that moment, Weber had never heard the huge smiling man, who acted like he had never met a stranger, utter a harsh word about anybody. But now Sal's face darkened and he said, "You come into my restaurant and you talk that way about my friend? You help spread the gossip about her? No. No, no, no! I won't move you to another table, because you are not going to eat here. Not tonight, not tomorrow, not ever again."

With that he scooped up the pizza from their table with one hand and with the other he pointed at the door. "Out! Get out of my restaurant and never come back."

The women appeared stunned by his outburst at first, then LeeAnn said, "Well, if that's how you want to be, fine! There are plenty of other places that want our business."

"You go to those places," Sal told her. "You go anywhere you want. But you get out of my restaurant, now!"

The women got up and hustled out the door. A strained silence enveloped the restaurant. Robyn, never one who was comfortable with public attention, and even more so since the pictures had been circulating, started to get up. Christine laid a hand on her arm and said, "Uh uh. You're not going anywhere."

"I just…"

"You stay put," Christine told her. "You forget everything and everyone except right here at this table. The people that matter are sitting here with you, honey. To hell with the rest of the world."

After returning the pizza from the women's table to the kitchen, Sal returned and squatted down next to Robyn, an amazing feat in its own, given his bulk.

"Miss Robyn, I'm so sorry someone acted that way. And I'm sorry if I made it worse. But nobody treats my friends that way. Not in my restaurant."

Robyn wrapped her arms around his neck and hugged him, then kissed his cheek. "Thank you, Sal. But I hope this isn't going to cost you too much business."

"Hey, their money is not welcome here. Don't you worry about that. You just know that you are loved, my little Robyn bird."

"And I love you, too," Robyn said kissing his cheek again. "Now please get up, that can't be comfortable."

"No, but for you, it is worth it."

Putting his hand on the edge of the table and using it for leverage, he heaved himself to his feet and then took the chair next to Christine. She, too, hugged him and kissed him on the lips. "Look at you, being a knight in shining armor coming to the aid of a damsel in distress. No wonder I fell in love with you."

"That's why? And here Sal thought it was because of my cannoli."

"Cannoli? Is that what you guys call it? I call mine a thunder stick," Parks said.

They all laughed, lightening the mood. "No matter how uncomfortable something is, this man knows how to make it better for everybody," Marsha said, hugging her boyfriend's arm.

"I don't know about that," Parks said. "I know somebody who's going to be uncomfortable in a minute or two."

"What do you mean?"

"Those two women that were just here. The ones Sal threw out. They're standing out there on the sidewalk trying to decide which one of them is going to come back in and get the car keys and cell phone one of them left sitting there on the table."

~~***~~

"Do you want to come in?"

"Should we flip a coin first to see which one of us is going to piss off your mother and send her to the bedroom, slamming the door?"

Robyn laughed and said, "That would be funny if it wasn't so true."

"As much as I'd like to go a couple of rounds with her, I'd better pass tonight. Mary gave me a stack of reports that she says has to be signed and on her desk first thing in the morning."

"Chicken. That's just an excuse. Since when have you ever signed anything on time for her?"

"Here's an idea. We could go back to my place."

"As much as I'd love to, Jimmy, I probably shouldn't. I got the silent treatment the last time I was out overnight."

"I miss us sleeping together, Robyn. Not just the sex, I miss having you in bed beside me."

"I do, too. But it won't be long and we'll be together forever." They embraced and kissed, and then Robyn smiled impishly at him and said, "But you miss the sex, too, don't you?"

"I'd be lying if I said I didn't."

"Me, too."

"So, when's the last time you made out in a police car?"

"You should know," she told him. "You were there."

If either one of them thought things were going to go any further that night, they were proven wrong when the porch light flashed on and off twice, and then the door opened and Renée called out, "Do you plan to sit out there all night?"

Robyn sighed and looked at Weber. "Are you sure we can't just run off to Vegas and elope tonight?"

"That's not the worst idea you've had all day."

The porch light flashed again and her mother shouted, "Robyn, you do have parents here who would like to spend at least a little bit of time with you, if that's possible."

"How much time do you think I would get if I drowned my mother in the bathtub, Jimmy?"

"Believe me, no jury in the world would convict you."

"Robyn!"

"She's not going to shut up, is she?"

"Nope."

"Might as well get it over with." She kissed him, then opened the door and got out of the Explorer, trudging reluctantly across the yard to where her mother waited under the porch light, arms folded tightly across her chest in disapproval.

Nick Russell

Chapter 23

Three hours later, Weber had reviewed and signed the last of the reports Mary had given him and was just falling asleep when his phone rang. He looked at the display and saw Dispatch was calling. "Yeah, what's going on, Kate?"

"Sheriff, I hate to bother you, but there's a suspicious car parked on the road not far from SafeHaven."

Weber set up in bed "Tell me about it."

"Marlene Teague called in to report an SUV parked off the road just past SafeHaven. She said it's sitting at the entrance to the fire road that leads up to Settler's Ridge."

"Could she see who was in it?"

"No, it was too dark with just the moonlight coming through the clouds. All she could tell was that it was a big man. I'd send one of the deputies out, but Dan is working an accident out at the Y, and Chad is at the Antler Inn answering a disturbance call. I thought you should know."

"You did good, Kate. I'm on my way."

Pulling on jeans and a dark colored pullover shirt, Weber stuck his Kimber .45 semiautomatic pistol into his belt behind his hip. On the way out the door he picked up his short barreled Remington 870 tactical shotgun. If it was MacGregor staking out SafeHaven, the sheriff was going to put an end to that right now.

~~***~~

Parking 200 yards down the road, Weber eased out of the Explorer and carefully closed the door to make as little noise as possible. Whoever the mysterious man staking out SafeHaven was, he didn't want him to know he was coming. Keeping to the edge of the road so the shadows provided some concealment, he made his way to the suspicious vehicle, every sense on high alert for any sign of danger.

It was a dark blue Chevrolet Suburban and Weber knew he had seen it around town someplace, but he wasn't sure where. Approaching the big SUV, he saw the windows were down, which wasn't unexpected given the warm night. It was too dark to see who was behind the wheel, so he carefully made his way to just a few feet from the driver's window. Then he shouldered the shotgun with one hand and turned on his flashlight.

"Hands up! I want to see your hands right now. Don't do anything crazy or I'm gonna kill you."

"Don't shoot! It's me, don't shoot!"

Weber looked at the face of the frightened man behind the wheel and breathed a sigh of relief. Lowering the shotgun, he asked, "Sal, what the hell are you doing out here in the middle of the night?"

"Christine told me you're too shorthanded to have someone here all the time, but I'm scared for her. So I sit here every night. If that man comes back, the one that hurt Miss Jensen, Sal's not going to let him hurt his Christine or anybody at SafeHaven. "

"Sal, that's great of you, but the last we heard, Donald MacGregor was in New Mexico. I don't think he's headed back here. He'd be crazy to show his face anywhere around these parts.

"To do what he did to poor Miss Jensen, he is crazy," Sal said. "And don't forget, Sheriff Jimmy, the roads that go to New Mexico come back here, too."

"I really don't think he'll do that Sal. But even if he did, you need to let us handle it. MacGregor is a very dangerous man."

"I know. That's why I brought this." Sal held up a long-barreled revolver that was sitting on the dashboard in front of him.

Walking up to the window, Weber asked, "Where did you get that thing?"

It was an old .38 Colt Police Positive with a 6-inch barrel. Most of the bluing had worn off a long time ago.

"This was my grandfather's gun. He was a night watchman back in New York when my dad was a little boy. It got passed down to me."

"Have you even shot it, Sal?"

"Not since I was a teenager. My father took me out to the cinder pit and showed me how to shoot it. Then he put it back in the closet and told me to forget it was there. But now, with all this, I got it out."

"Go home, Sal. You don't need to be out here."

"No, Sheriff Jimmy, I do have to be here. I can't sleep at night anyway, worrying about Christine."

"Look, I appreciate what you're doing," Weber told him. "And I know that if Christine knew it, she would appreciate it, too."

"Oh no, Sheriff Jimmy, you must never tell her about this! Please, she would not like me doing this. You know Christine, she is how, I say...?"

He seemed at a loss for words and Weber suggested "Independent? Stubborn? Hardheaded?"

Sal smiled broadly and chuckled, and said "Yes, those things. But in a nice way, right, Sheriff Jimmy?"

Weber laughed with him and said "Oh, yeah, Sal, she's all those things in a nice way. But you go home and get some sleep. It's going to be okay. I have deputies driving by here all the time. And Christine is no slouch. You know that. She's got a .38, too, and she knows how to use it."

"Yes, but still, I worry. I think I stay here for a little bit longer, maybe. Just in case."

Weber sighed and asked, "Do you have coffee in there?"

"Yes," Sal replied, holding up a big stainless steel thermos.

"What the hell?" Weber walked around the front of the Suburban and opened the passenger door to slide in beside Sal. "I'll keep you company for a while."

Chapter 24

Weber was getting out of the Explorer in the parking lot of the Sheriff's Office the next morning when he heard someone call his name. He paused to see a man wearing a shirt and tie walking across the parking lot toward him from the street.

"Good morning, Sheriff."

"Hello, Reverend Collier. How are you this morning?"

"I'm all right. But we need to have a talk."

"Okay, come on in."

"Actually, this won't take long. Listen, Sheriff, I don't quite know how to say this…"

"Say what?"

"Well, there's been… this is very uncomfortable."

"Whatever it is, just say it."

"It's about those pictures. The ones of Robyn."

"They're not Robyn. Somebody is faking them."

"Be that as it may, it puts me in an untenable position."

"What are you saying, Reverend?"

The man looked away and swallowed twice, obviously trying to figure out some way to put the news he was bringing in a better light. "It's just that… with those pictures circulating around town, I'm getting a lot of pressure from my congregation."

"What kind of pressure?" Weber asked warily.

"Well… I don't how to say this, Sheriff."

"Just say it and get it over with."

The other man took a deep breath, then said, "I'm sorry, but we're not going to be able to accommodate your wedding."

"What do you mean?"

"Just that, Sheriff. I'm sorry."

"Seriously? Someone is sending fake pictures out to embarrass Robyn, and even though I've told you they're not real, suddenly you don't want her in your church? And you come up with this, what, how many days before the wedding?"

"Please understand, Sheriff. It's nothing personal toward you or Robyn. But I have a responsibility to my congregation."

"You said you're getting a lot of pressure from your congregation. Would that by any chance be LeeAnn Reynolds and Shirley Farmer? Because I know they attend services at your church, and I know Sal Gattuccio threw them both out of his restaurant last night when they were acting rude to Robyn."

"I'd prefer not to name names."

"You don't have to name them, I already know," Weber said. "Both are Sunday School teachers and Joe and Natalie Farmer give big bucks to your church. When Natalie heard what happened at the pizza place, she wasn't going to let anyone treat her daughter like that. This is payback."

"I'm sorry, Sheriff. Like I said, it's nothing personal."

"Yeah, right. Nothing personal. It's just our wedding. A wedding that you suddenly don't want to happen in your church, even though we made the arrangements six months ago and paid a deposit."

"You'll be getting your deposit back, I assure you."

"It's not about the damn deposit," Weber said angrily. "How dare you call yourself a man of God when you judge somebody like this? How dare you? I could walk into that church of yours any Sunday morning and point out people who spent Saturday night getting drunk. People who spent it sleeping with someone they're not married to. People who would cheat you out of a nickel in a business deal if they thought they could get away with it. Dopers, wife beaters, and shoplifters sitting right there in the pews looking holier than thou. They're welcome in your church."

"Jesus tells us to love the sinner, not the sin."

"But apparently if someone's *not* a sinner, if they are someone who is being attacked, you'll turn your back on them in a heartbeat."

"I have the reputation of the church to take into consideration. With the scandal hanging over Robyn…"

"Isn't there something in that Bible of yours about judging not, lest you be judged?"

"Sheriff, please don't make this any more uncomfortable than it has to be."

"Oh, I'm sorry. I didn't realize I was making you *uncomfortable*. I can't imagine how that would feel."

"Sheriff, once this is all over with…"

"I don't know about the rest of it, but our conversation is over with right now," Weber told him. "Get out of my sight, you hypocrite."

He turned on his heel and stormed through the office door, leaving the preacher standing in the parking lot alone.

~~***~~

"Here, you look like you need this," Mary said, extending a cup of coffee toward him when she saw the look on his face. "What did Robyn's mother do now?"

"Nothing that I know of. But that doesn't mean she's not out spreading cheer and love among the community," he replied, taking the cup from her.

"What's wrong, Jimmy?"

"We lost the church?"

"You lost the church? How could you lose a whole church?"

"We lost the church for the wedding. Stephen Collier just stopped me in the parking lot to tell me that they couldn't accommodate us, as he put it, because of those damn pictures."

"You're kidding me," Mary said incredulously. "He can't do that!"

"Well, apparently he can, because he just did."

"I can't believe that. That is so asinine of him."

Weber didn't reply. His jaw was set and there was fire in his eyes. Mary knew that look. She had seen it before and it was never a good thing.

"Look, Jimmy, I know this is bad, but we'll figure out something."

"How, Mary? The wedding is in just a few days now. How are we going to reserve a church and get everything set up for it someplace else at this point?"

"You leave it to me. I'll handle it."

"I swear, if that sanctimonious jerk hadn't been a preacher, I would have knocked him on his ass. And I'm still tempted to go back out and do it."

"You just relax. I've got this, Jimmy."

~~***~~

An hour later, Mary knocked and came into his office with a glum look on her face. "I don't have this. I've called around, and the Baptist Church isn't available because they've got a crew coming in to paint the inside for the three days starting the day before your wedding. The Presbyterian Church has a women's worship week scheduled, so that's out. Mike Goldhatch at the Lutheran Church said he hated to say no, but they have Buster O'Brien's funeral scheduled the same day. The ministers at the Pentecostal and Methodist churches both had the same line of crap that Stephen Collier did; they just wouldn't be comfortable hosting the service given those pictures. I'm sorry, Jimmy. I tried."

Weber knew from her expression that Mary was taking her failure personally. He tried to assuage her feelings a bit by saying, "It's not your fault. Thanks for trying."

"Have you told Robyn about it yet?"

"No, and I'm dreading it. She said last night that we should just run off to Vegas and elope, and I'm beginning to think she's right."

There was a knock on the door, and when Weber called for whoever it was to come in, Dispatcher Kate Copeland poked her head through.

"I'm sorry, Sheriff, but I think you need to see this."

"What is it now?"

"You'll have to see."

Weber and Mary followed her to the outer office and she pointed her hand toward the door. "They're out there. I sent Archer out to tell them to leave, but they ignored him."

Weber walked to the door and looked out into the parking lot, then turned back to Mary with a stunned look on his face. "This can't be happening."

But it was happening. A dozen women, including LeeAnn Reynolds and Shirley Farmer, along with Natalie, Shirley's mother, were standing in the parking lot holding signs and chanting "Harlots Must Go, Fire Her Today."

Weber started to push the door open and Mary grabbed his arm. "Don't go out there, Jimmy!"

"Bullshit. I'm not going to stay in here while they're out there doing that."

"I know it sucks, but the law says they have the right to picket as long as they do it peacefully."

"They can stick that law up their ass, along with their signs."

"Kate, call Bob Bennett," Mary directed the dispatcher. "Tell him what's going on and that we need him over here ASAP."

When Kate hurried away to do her task, Mary led Weber away from the door and said, "Jimmy, I know you're pissed off, and you have every reason to be. But trust me on this, if you go out there, you're going to make it worse for yourself, and for Robyn."

He knew she was right, but his fists were still balled in anger and he really felt the desire to punch somebody. He thought it was probably fortunate that Reverend Collier had already left.

"He's on his way," Kate called from the dispatch desk. "But we've got more trouble. There's a news crew out there."

"No way. How could they get up here from Phoenix so fast?"

"They had to have known in advance," Kate said. "I don't think this is a spur of the moment protest. I bet somebody tipped them off last night."

Weber walked to the door and looked out again. Heather Barthel was holding a sign that said "No Whores With Badges" and talking to a reporter from Channel 8. Weber was tempted to go outside and remind the woman that a year earlier he had caught her married daughter in flagrante delicto in the backseat of Jim Younger's SUV, exposing an affair with her much older, also married boss that resulted in the breakup of both of their marriages. Before he could act on that impulse, Bob Bennett made his way through the crowd and in the door.

"Are you seeing that shit out there?"

"Yes, Jimmy, I'm seeing it. And you are *not* to go out that door, do you understand me?"

"I'm just supposed to sit here with my thumb up my ass while they trash Robyn's name like that?"

"I'm sorry. I know this sucks big time. But legally, they have a right to do what they're doing."

"What about Robyn's rights, Bob? What happened to her rights?"

"Jimmy, you have to trust me on this. Kirby is on his way over and we're going to talk to them, okay?"

"I've got a thing or two I want to say to them!"

"I know you do, and you're not going to."

"Why not? You're talking about people's rights. Don't I have a right to free speech anymore?"

"Jimmy, I'm telling you this as your friend and from my position as the Town's Attorney, don't do it! I know how you're feeling right now, but…"

"Do you, Bob? Do you really know how I am feeling? Is it your wife that someone is sending pictures of? Is it your wife that they're whispering about? Do you know that Sal Gattuccio threw two of those women out of his restaurant last night because they were insulting Robyn? Do you know that the other day two women she has known ever since she moved to town shunned her at the grocery store? Do you know how many people whisper to each other when they see her? Has your wife experienced all of that? Because if she hasn't, you have no freaking idea how I feel!"

"Okay, take a deep breath, Jimmy. You're right, I don't know how you feel. But I know how *I* feel. I'm enraged that people who should know better are treating a good woman like Robyn the way they are. I'm enraged that some jerk is getting his jollies off ruining her reputation. I'm enraged that this town that I thought I knew better is turning its back on somebody of her caliber. And knowing the rage I feel about that, I can only imagine what you're feeling right now. But we have to set our feelings aside and be professional. Trust me, it's the only way to do this."

Weber knew his friend was right. He didn't have to like it, but his going out there and confronting the picketers would only make matters worse for Robyn.

Nick Russell

Chapter 25

Weber fumed while Bob Bennett and Kirby Templeton addressed the crowd picketing outside the sheriff's office. He watched through the window as more people gathered to see what the hubbub was about.

"Don't keep staring out there, Jimmy. You're just making it worse for yourself," Mary said.

"What am I supposed to do, Mary?"

"You might want to give Robyn a call and give her a heads up about everything that's happened this morning."

"I really don't want to do that."

"I know you don't, but you need to before she hears about it from somebody else."

Weber nodded, knowing that she was right. He headed back for his office and Mary stopped him and said, "There's more bad news, Jimmy."

"Now what?"

"Have you checked your email this morning?"

He looked at her and said, "Please don't tell me there's not another one."

Mary nodded her head sadly and said "I'm sorry. It came in while you were talking to Bob Bennett. Do you want to look at it?"

"No, I don't. I've had enough bad news for one morning."

He went into his office to call Robyn.

"Hey, what's up?"

"You sound chipper today. Things must be going well there for a change."

"As good as can be. We're trying to figure out what we're going to do about a limo, since we lost the one we had scheduled. There are not many of them anywhere around here."

"I guess there's not all that much of a demand in a small town."

"How are things at the office? Has everybody forgotten all about me by now?"

"No, you'd be pretty hard to forget. But I'm afraid I've got more bad news."

"What, Jimmy?" He could hear the dread in her voice. "Please tell me that more pictures didn't show up?"

"I'm afraid so. But that's not the worst of it."

"What do you mean?"

He told her about the church and there was silence at the other end of the line for so long that he thought he had lost the connection.

"Are you still there, Robyn?"

"Yeah, I'm here. Now what do we do, Jimmy?"

"I don't know. Mary's been calling around, but every church in town has something going on or they don't want anything to do with this."

"Vegas is looking better all the time, isn't it?"

"Yeah, it is," he admitted. "And, there's more. And I really don't know how to tell you this."

"God, Jimmy, I don't know how much more I can take."

"I know. I'm sorry."

"What is it?"

"There's a crowd of protesters and a news crew in the parking lot here at the office."

"Protesters? What are they protesting?"

"You, Robyn."

More silence.

"I know this seems terrible, but…"

"No Jimmy, it doesn't *seem*, terrible. It *is* terrible! When will this ever end?"

"I don't know," he admitted. "I really don't. Once we figure out who is sending the pictures, that's going to finally let people know that this was all an attack on you."

"Will it, Jimmy? You and I both know that there are a lot of people that don't care about facts once their minds are already made up. No matter what the truth is and no matter how it's proven, there are always going to be some that will be looking at me and whispering behind my back. You and I both know that."

"I don't know what to say."

"I don't, either. I just want to leave here and never come back. I'm so sick of this pettiness."

Weber took a deep breath and said, "If that's what you want, that's what we'll do."

There was a pause for a moment, then Robyn asked, "What do you mean, Jimmy?"

"I mean, if you want to leave and start someplace else, we'll do it. We don't have to be in Big Lake. There are lots of other places in this country we can be."

"Wait a minute. You're saying you'd leave here because of me?"

"It's a town, Robyn. Just a town. There are lots of towns in this country, big and small. Neither one of us would have a problem getting on with a department somewhere else."

"You can't do that, Jimmy. This is your home. Your family's been a part of Big Lake forever."

"Yeah, and I couldn't wait to get away when I was a kid. I only came back because of my family obligations. But now I don't have any family left here, Robyn. You're my family. You're all that matters. And if you're not going to be happy here, neither am I."

"No, Jimmy. God, I love you for being willing to do that, and I know you mean it. I really do. But no. Big Lake is your home, and you *do* have family here. Maybe not blood, but Mary and Pete, they're family. I feel closer to them than I do to my own family. And Marsha, and Hillbilly and Parks, and the rest of the guys on the department, the dispatchers, Paul at the newspaper, everybody in town. They're your family, Jimmy. I can't ask you to do that."

"You didn't ask me to do it, Robyn. I volunteered. If you're not going to be happy here after all of this, we'll start over someplace else. You're the only thing in the world that matters to me."

"Start over someplace else? You're the sheriff. Are you really going to be happy just being a regular cop working under somebody else? You're used to being the big fish in a small pond."

"Look at the bright side; I wouldn't have nearly as much paperwork to deal with."

"Oh Jimmy, I love you so much. And I appreciate that. I really do. But no, you're not going anywhere. And neither am I. As long as I've got you by my side, screw the rest of the world. They can all go to hell."

Weber was just ending his call with Robyn when Bob Bennett and Kirby Templeton finished with the crowd and came back inside the office.

"I'll tell you what," Bennett said. "For church people, they have sure got a hateful attitude about them."

"How long are they going to be out there, Bob?"

"I don't know, Jimmy. Until they get tired of it, I guess."

"And we're supposed to just let them stay there?"

"That's exactly what we're supposed to do, and that's exactly what we are going to do," Kirby Templeton said. "I know this is pissing you off, Jimmy. All of it. And I can't blame you. But we've got to ride it out."

"Do you know that a new picture came today?"

"Yeah, I got it just as I was leaving to come over here," Kirby said. Bob Bennett nodded his head again to indicate that he had also received the latest picture from the secret messenger.

"How is Robyn handling things, Jimmy?"

"About as good as you could expect. Better than I am, probably."

"She's a strong woman, she'll get through this. Both of you will."

"Yeah, but when? How long is this going to continue?"

"It's going to continue until you can figure out who is doing it. Has that guy from the Department of Public Safety made any headway yet?"

"Not that I know of," Weber replied. "He's talked to people, we've talked to people, nobody seems to know anything about who's behind this bullshit."

"Well, I don't know that we changed any minds out there in that crowd," Kirby said. "But at least we made it very clear to that reporter that those pictures are fake and that someone's doing it to discredit Robyn."

"Do you think she believed you?"

Bennett shrugged his shoulders and shook his head. "I really don't know, to be honest with you, Jimmy. You know how those people like a sleazy story, whether it's true or not."

"Okay, we've got to get out of here," Kirby said. "Listen to me, Jimmy. *Do not* go out and engage those people. That's the last thing we need. Especially with a news crew out there. Do you understand me?"

"Is that an order, Kirby?"

"How many times did you tell Chet Wingate that the mayor can't give you an order unilaterally?"

"More than once."

"That's right. So, no, it's not an order. But it's a strong suggestion that you really need to follow." He saw the look on Weber's face and added, "Remember, Jimmy, we're on the same side here. We want to find out who's doing this and we want to put an end to it. And we want Robyn back on the job with her reputation restored. And it's going to happen."

Those words were little comfort to the sheriff, but he nodded his head.

When they left, Mary hugged Weber and said, "It's going to be okay, Jimmy. I promise."

"People keep telling me that, but I'm beginning to wonder if it's true or not."

"I know. How is Robyn taking all this?"

"She wants to either elope to Vegas or pack her bags and leave Big Lake forever. I told her that if she did that, I'd go with her."

Mary looked at him with love and concern in her eyes and said "I hope that doesn't happen. You belong in Big Lake, and this town needs you. It needs you and it needs Robyn."

"It needs me, does it? What does it need me for, Mary?" He looked out the window to the picketers and the crowd their activities had drawn to the parking lot. There were at least a hundred people out there. "Does the town need me to protect those people who turned their backs on me and Robyn both? A bunch of ingrates that think they're so much better than anybody else? I'll be honest with you, the way I feel right now, this town can go to hell, and take everybody in it, too, present company excluded."

Chapter 26

A grim faced Captain Sweeney came into Weber's office and said tersely, "We've got to talk, Sheriff Weber."

"What's up?"

"What's up is that your fiancée hasn't been completely honest with us."

"What do you mean?"

"Have you seen the list of guys that Deputy Fuchette says that she was involved with?"

"No. I told you I preferred not to look at that out of respect for her privacy. The only one I know of is Christopher Burton, the guy at the fire lookout tower we talked to the other day."

"Well, you need to take a look at this list," Sweeney said.

"I really don't want to."

"Sheriff, it's not a request."

He laid a single sheet of paper on Weber's desk. The sheriff picked it up and read four names. Matthew Tibbetts, Reggie Arnold, Christopher Burton, and James Hightower.

"Besides the guy from the fire tower, are any of those names familiar to you?"

"No, not really. Why?"

"Do you know who Jack DeFray is?"

"Defray? The DPS officer? Yeah, I know him. He works out of the Springerville substation. What about him?"

"His name's not on the list."

"Okay. Should it be?"

"This is supposed to be the list of men that Deputy Fuchette dated at one time or another."

"And?"

"And DeFray's name isn't on the list."

"You're saying that they dated?"

"Yeah, they dated. From what I hear, they were going at it pretty hot and heavy for a while. You didn't know anything about that?"

"No, I didn't."

"And you don't think that's a problem?"

"Whatever Robyn did in her personal life before we were together is none of my business," Weber said.

"But it is *my* business, for the purposes of this investigation. Do you have any idea why she didn't list him?"

Weber shrugged his shoulders. "Not really. Maybe she forgot?"

"Come on, Sheriff. She remembered four guys that she dated, all but three of them casually, but she forgets DeFray completely, and they were an item?"

"I don't know what you mean by an item."

"I mean just what I said before. They were spending a lot of nights together, even took off for a couple of weekend trips."

"Who told you this?"

"I got that information from Andy Blanchard. You know him, right?"

"Of course I know Andy. He patrols the highway around here. We've worked together for years."

"According to him, he and DeFray were roommates for over a year. During that time, DeFray and Robyn were seeing each other regularly. He said there were a lot of sleepovers."

"I had no idea," Weber said.

"So why is she holding out on us?"

"I don't know."

"I don't either, Sheriff, but I'm telling you this right now. Given this new information, everything that Deputy Fuchette told me is suspect, as far as I'm concerned."

"That's bullshit," Weber said. "I don't know where Andy got that information, but it's not true."

"Like I said, him and DeFray were roommates while it was happening, Sheriff. He seems pretty sure of it."

"I don't care what he's sure of, he's wrong. When did he tell you this? How did him or DeFray become part of this investigation, anyway?"

"Blanchard and I have been friends for ten years. I gave him a call when I got to town and we said we would get together for lunch or something. We just did, and that's when he told me about Robyn and DeFray."

"I don't believe it."

"Sheriff, I've never known Andy Blanchard to be less than truthful about anything. Why would he lie to me about something like that?"

"I don't know, but I want to talk to him myself."

"I'm not sure that's a good idea. You had no knowledge of Deputy Fuchette and DeFray having a relationship?"

"No! This is the first I've heard of it."

"Why do you think Deputy Fuchette didn't tell anybody about her affair with DeFray?"

"You keep asking me that and I keep telling you, I don't know. I don't believe there was a relationship in the first place."

"Why do you seem so insistent about that, Sheriff?"

"Because Robyn's not that way. She doesn't sleep around."

"Not to be rude, but you two sleep together, right?"

"That's not the same thing at all!"

"Why not? You guys hooked up and it seemed like the right thing to do and you started a relationship right? So why is it so hard to accept the fact that before you were in the picture, she had a relationship with somebody else? There's a difference between sleeping around, as you call it, and being in a relationship with a man, isn't there?"

"Yeah, I get your point," Weber said. "But I just don't see it happening that way."

"Why not?"

"For one thing, Robyn doesn't like DeFray, that's why?"

"And why do you think that is?"

"I don't know. The guy's kind of a jerk. Have you met him?"

"No, can't say that I have. Not yet, anyway. Why do you say he's a jerk?"

"He just has that typical attitude that some cops have. You know what I mean. The badge and gun are real heavy on them."

"I ran a background check on DeFray. Started out with the Cottonwood Police Department and spent three years with them before coming to DPS. I didn't see anything indicating that he's ever been involved in any kind of problem. There have been the usual complaints when he gave someone a ticket that they didn't feel they deserved, but overall his record seems pretty damn good to me."

"What happens now?"

"I'm going to interview him."

"I want to be there."

"That's not going to happen, Sheriff."

"Why not?"

"Because it's not. This is my investigation and I'm going to do things my way."

"Do you think DeFray could be the one sending those pictures?"

"Anything's possible. That's why I want to talk to him."

"And why don't you want me there when you interview him?"

"Because I'm not sure how much you can separate your personal feelings from the investigation. That's why."

"Or maybe you think it's possible he is the guy behind all this, and you want to protect your agency's reputation?"

Sweeney's face darkened and when he spoke it was obvious to Weber that he had stepped over a line. "You listen to me, Sheriff, and you listen good. I don't care if it was my own brother or father sending those pictures. If I caught them, I would hang their ass out to dry. If you think there's some kind of brother officer bullshit going on and I'm trying to cover for DeFray, you and I have a problem. A big problem."

Big Lake Wedding

Weber knew he was wrong to question the man's integrity and he apologized. "I'm sorry, Captain Sweeney. This thing is just tearing this whole town apart. Have you seen that circus out there in the parking lot?"

"Yeah, I saw it. I can imagine how you and Deputy Fuchette must be feeling. But I will find out who's doing this, and I am going to find out why Deputy Fuchette has been holding out on us."

"*If* she's been holding out. I still don't believe it."

"You're a stubborn man, Sheriff.'

"No, I just know Robyn well enough to know that she's not a liar."

"Again, why would Officer Blanchard tell me about it if it wasn't true? Have you or Deputy Fuchette ever had a problem with him?"

"No, not at all. We've always gotten along fine. He's backed us up when we needed it, and we've backed him up."

"What about DeFray?"

"I know who the guy is, we've worked a couple of accidents together, but that's about it. I wouldn't call us friends."

"Why is that?"

"I don't know," Weber said. "Like I said, he's got an attitude. I'm just not impressed with him."

"Let me ask you this, Sheriff. I know you're saying that Deputy Fuchette isn't holding out on us about her relationship with DeFray, but let's assume just for a minute that what Blanchard told me is true. Based on what you know about him, is DeFray the kind of guy that would do something like this to Deputy Fuchette? And if so, why?"

"I don't know," Weber admitted. "Like I said, I don't know the man that well. But he's got a big ego. If there was something going on between the two of them, which I still don't believe, maybe she hurt his pride when it ended. You and I both know that some guys aren't willing to accept the fact that something is over. We've both seen it more than once in our work."

"True."

"You said you want to talk to Robyn, too?"

"Yes, I plan to talk to her before I talk to DeFray. Do you know if she's home now?"

"Yeah, I just talked to her. Could you talk to her here instead of at her house?"

"Actually, I'd prefer that. But is there a reason why you don't want me to go to her house?"

"Her mother and father are there, and her mother is, how do I put it... she's a bitch. I think it would be better for Robyn if you talk to her somewhere away from them."

"Fine, call and ask her to come in."

Chapter 27

90 minutes later, when Sweeney walked out of the interview room, he shook his head and said, "Somebody's lying to me, and I don't appreciate it."

"What do you mean?"

"Deputy Fuchette insists that she's never had a relationship with Officer DeFray. In fact, she seems to really dislike the man very much. Why do you think that is, Sheriff?"

"I don't know. You tell me."

"We've talked about how when relationships go south there can be hurt feelings. Maybe it ended badly on both their parts."

"Or, there never was a relationship. Which I told you before, and which I'm sure Robyn told you just now."

"How about you go back in there with me and see if you can get anything more out of her?"

"You want me to interrogate my fiancée about another man?"

"No, Sheriff Weber, I want you to help me interview your deputy so we can help figure out where these pictures are coming from. Now, shall we?" He waved his hand to indicate the hall leading to the interview room.

Robyn looked less than happy when they sat down across the table from her.

"Usually I'm on that side of the table. It feels weird being over here."

"I'm sure it does, Deputy Fuchette. Listen, we need to get on the same page here. You do understand that lying to me during the course of a criminal investigation is a felony, right? It could cost you your badge, and even wind up with you going to jail."

"Wait a minute," Weber interrupted. "Robyn is the victim here. You even said you don't believe those pictures are real."

"I don't," Sweeney said. "But just because she's the victim of whoever is sending these fake photos doesn't mean she can lie to me."

"I'm not lying," Robyn shouted, rising out of her chair. "I keep telling you, I never had an affair with Jack DeFray!"

"Sit down, Deputy."

She did as instructed, but Weber could tell she was teetering on the edge of an outburst that would not help her position at all. Sweeney gave her a moment to get her emotions under control, then said, "You keep insisting that you never had any kind of relationship with Jack DeFray. But I have information from a reliable source that you and DeFray had an affair that lasted most of a year. What do you have to say about that?"

"I don't know who your reliable source is, but he's not all that reliable," Robyn said. "I didn't have an affair with Jack DeFray at any time. Not for a day, or a week, or a year. Not ever!"

"What if I told you the person giving me that information was a police officer?"

"I would say he is either lying to you or is sadly mistaken," Robyn replied.

"Why would my source lie to me?"

"I have no idea," Robyn said. "But I know that he's not telling you the truth."

Sweeney looked at Weber and Robyn and said, "How about I should leave you two alone for a few minutes? Maybe there's something you need to clear the air about."

"You don't need to go anywhere as far as I'm concerned," Weber told him. "If Robyn said she never had an affair with DeFray, she didn't have one."

"Maybe so, maybe not. You guys talk."

Sweeney left the room, closing the door behind him.

Robyn looked at Weber and asked, "What the hell is going on here, Jimmy?"

"I don't know," he told her. "Sweeney came in and said that Andy Blanchard told him that he was living with DeFray for about a year, and during that time you two were having an affair."

"Why would Blanchard say that? I thought he was my friend."

"I don't know why, Robyn. I don't have an answer for you. I wish I did. All I can say is, Sweeney believes Blanchard, for whatever reason. He says they go back a long way."

"This is ridiculous," Robyn said, the frustration straining her voice. She was fidgety in her seat. Weber reached across the table to place a comforting hand over hers. She looked at him with tears in her beautiful almond shaped eyes. Eyes that Weber had gotten lost in more than once.

"Jimmy, I swear to you, I never had any kind of affair with Jack DeFray. Never. If I was going to have an affair with anybody, I can assure you it wouldn't be him!"

"Why is that, Robyn?"

"What do you mean?"

"He seems like a nice enough guy. Kind of cocky, but not bad looking."

"You should know me well enough by now to know that what a person looks like doesn't mean a thing to me, Jimmy."

"I'm not sure how I feel about that, based on the fact that we're engaged," he said, trying to lighten the mood and failing.

"Besides, I wouldn't care if he was movie star handsome. Jack DeFray is an asshole."

"Why do you say that?"

"Besides the fact that he thinks he's God's gift to women? And the fact that he won't take no for an answer?"

"What do you mean by that, Robyn?"

She looked away, then back at him. "It was a long time ago. Back when I was still working Dispatch. He brought in a drunk driver one night, and after he booked him he hung around for a while making small talk. Just like the deputies do on a slow night. I didn't think anything of it at first. But I got up to go to the bathroom, and when I came back he put his arm around me and tried to kiss me. I turned my head and pushed him away, and said no. He just kind of laughed it off and said he was sorry, but I couldn't blame a guy for trying. When I sat back down to take a call, he came up behind me and started massaging my shoulders while I was on the phone. I tried pushing him away, and he dropped his hands down and put them on my boobs. As soon as the call was over I jumped up and told him to get the hell out and never come back."

"Did he leave?"

"Yeah, he kind of just laughed it off like it was all a joke and said if I ever changed my mind or got lonely, he was just a phone call away."

"Can I ask why you never told me about this before?"

"Because it wasn't that big of a deal to me. He's not the first guy who ever made a pass at me. And it happened a long time before we were together."

"Did he ever give you any more trouble?"

"No, he stayed away for a long time, and when I did see him again, it was all business."

"When was the last time you saw him, Robyn? Did he act okay toward you then?"

She thought for a minute, then said, "It's been a while. I think it was that bad accident out on the highway last summer, the one where the tourists hit that elk out on the highway. Do you remember that one? Two fatalities on the scene, and two more airlifted to a trauma center."

"Yeah, I remember. It was a bad one."

"DeFray was the first to respond, and me and Tommy went out to help with traffic control."

"And there weren't any problems with him?"

"No, not at all. Strictly professional. Do you think he's the one behind the pictures, Jimmy?"

"I don't know," Weber said, with a hard tone in his voice. "If it is, he's going to pay. I promise you that. Meanwhile, there was another picture in the email this morning."

"No!"

"I'm afraid so, and this time he took it to another level."

"Let me see."

He pulled out his phone and handed it to her. She opened the photo file to the latest picture and said "Oh, my God!"

In the picture, the woman was standing in the street in front of the Big Lake Brewpub with her shirt pulled open to reveal her bare breasts.

"Jimmy, that's not me. You know I'd never do something like that!"

"I know that, Robyn. We just need to find out who is doing this so we can put a stop to it."

He went to the door and called for Sweeney to come back in. As the DPS captain sat down, Weber said, "Robyn has something to tell you."

When she was done repeating the story of her encounter with DeFray, Sweeney asked, "Why didn't you tell me about this before?"

"Like I told Jimmy, it was just a guy hitting on a woman. It's not like he tried to force himself on me or anything. He was a little slow to get the message that I wasn't interested, but he did. I didn't want to ruin his career over it."

"It was conduct unbecoming an officer," Sweeney said crossly.

"Yes, it was. But let's be honest. Things like that happen. We were both single, he tried and I shot him down. No harm, no foul. If I had to blame DeFray for anything, it would be for having poor people skills."

"A lot of women would have filed charges against him and tried to get him fired," Sweeney said.

Robyn looked the investigator in the eyes and said, "Maybe so. And maybe they'd be right. But I'm not a lot of women. I'm just me."

Nick Russell

Chapter 28

"I'm so sorry about the church and the picketers," Marsha said that evening as they gathered at her house for dinner. "I can't believe how hypocritical those women are."

"Yeah, me, too. Do you know that I had to sneak in the back door of the office, through the cellblock, today? It was either that or run the gauntlet of those women in the parking lot."

"Don't worry, honey, this can't go on forever."

"It sure seems like it," Robyn replied gloomily.

"Well, maybe this will cheer you up," Parks said. "I have news."

"What is it? Please tell me you've figured out who's doing this."

"We're not that far yet, Robyn. If I knew who it was, Jimmy and I would be out hunting them down right now. But we're getting closer."

"What did you find out?"

"Just before you showed up, I got a phone call from my friends down in Phoenix. The trace on the IP address where the emails with the pictures are coming from led them down a bunch of blind alleys, but they have made some progress."

"Blind alleys? What do you mean?"

"It's confusing to explain," Parks told her, "and I'm not a techno-wiz. But let me try. Whoever is behind this set up the account to go through a series of redirects, which means that the email went from one place to another place to another place every time they sent out a new picture. And with each redirect down a different path, it gets a new IP address automatically."

"Speak English," Marsha said. "I don't understand any of this computer stuff. I get confused by where the decimal point goes when I'm using a calculator."

"IP stands for Internet Protocol," Parks explained. "It's a series of numbers and decimal points that is unique to each computer. So, for the sake of simplicity, let's say the IP address of my laptop is 123.4.567.89 or whatever. Think of it as the computer's phone number."

"And every computer has one of them? An IP address?"

"Not just computers. Also tablets and smartphones. Anything that can connect to the internet has an IP address."

"So if you find out the IP address, you can find the person doing this to Robyn?"

"Unfortunately, it's not quite that easy. Because part of that IP address is the network you're connecting to the Internet through. Let's say I'm at the office and I log on to the Internet through the Wi-Fi there. Part of my IP address is going to reflect that. But later on if I go to a coffee shop that has Wi-Fi, and I get on the Internet there, the IP address changes. And when I come home and log onto the Internet through your cable modem, it changes again."

"Then how in the world can you trace something backwards like you're talking about?"

"It takes time. Especially because some of the emails were routed through Peru and Venezuela and Panama, and a couple of them went through Luxembourg. One even came through Russia."

"Geez, Parks, you're making this all sound like some kind of international conspiracy," Robyn said.

"It is, in its simplest terms," he replied. "And darn near as complicated. The point is, if you follow things back far enough, eventually you'll get somewhere. It just takes time. And believe me, they've put a lot of time into this. And through all the mazes created by the redirects back and forth like a ball bouncing around inside a pinball machine, if they follow it far enough, it all comes right back here to Big Lake."

"You're kidding me?"

"Nope. It's only a matter of time now before we catch this dickhead."

Robyn was bouncing in her seat with excitement as Parks spoke, the most animated Weber had seen her since the first picture appeared.

"I love you, Parks," she said, jumping out of her chair to throw her arms around the FBI agent's neck. "I take back every bad thing I ever thought or said about you!"

"Now hold on, girlfriend," Marsha said. "Don't go jumping the gun. A lot of that stuff you thought and said was well deserved."

"I don't care," Robyn told her with a happy smile. "Right now, he's my hero!"

"Keep that in mind for later when you hear the details of what's going to happen at Jimmy's bachelor party."

"I appreciate the offer," Weber said. "but I already told you I don't need a bachelor party."

"Doesn't matter, you're getting one. It's my duty as your best man."

"Besides, it will keep you guys out from under foot while we have Robyn's bachelorette party."

"Forget it, Marsha. That's a bad idea."

"Why is it a bad idea, Robyn?"

"For starters, the way things are in town right now, nobody would come."

"Are you kidding me? You're having a party. I'll be there, and Christine, and Mary, and Judy, the dispatcher. Not to mention all of the deputies' wives. And don't forget, your mom's going to be there."

"Oh, that's going to be fun. Can you see my mother at a bachelorette party? Especially one put on by you and Christine? Please don't tell me some male stripper is going to show up."

"We tried to make that happen," Marsha told her. "The only problem is, we can't find anybody we can afford. Paul from the newspaper backed out because he can't find his G-string and Chet Wingate is too busy trying to take over the mayor's office again to be there. I don't know who else to ask."

"I know the problem," Parks said. "Try finding a decent looking gal to shake her boobs in Jimmy's face at his party."

"Not that I'd be looking," Weber assured Robyn.

"If you didn't look, you'd be dead."

"If I *did* look I might wind up dead, too."

"Come on, Jimmy, I'm past all of that jealousy nonsense."

They could joke about it now, but there was a time when her jealousy had threatened to drive a wedge between them.

"I never understood the whole jealousy thing," Marsha said. "If some woman wants to flash Parks here, I'm fine with it."

"Seriously, that wouldn't bother you?"

"Heck no! Not as long as he comes home to me all turned on and ready to go. That means half of my job is done for me already. Anyway, what do you say, girlfriend? Are we going to have us a bachelorette party or not?"

"What good is bachelorette party if we can't find a church to get married in?"

"Maybe if they wrap this investigation up fast enough and people realize that you're not the one in those pictures, somebody will change their mind."

"I'm not holding my breath on that," Robyn told her.

"Here's a crazy thought. Why do you have to get married in a church?"

"What do you mean?"

"Just that. Why do you have to get married in a church? A couple of times now you've said something about eloping to Vegas."

"Believe me, Marsha, sometimes I think it would be the easiest thing to do."

"But that wouldn't be in a church, it would be in a wedding chapel, right?"

"I guess so."

"So, if you are going to get married in a wedding chapel in Las Vegas, why not get married at the courthouse right here in

Big Lake Wedding

Big Lake? I'm sure Judge Ryman would be happy to marry you two. And you guys know him better than you know any of the preachers in town."

~~***~~

"Absolutely not! I won't have it."

"Mother..."

"Forget it, Robyn. It's not going to happen!"

"If you'll just listen to reason..."

"No daughter of mine is getting married in a courthouse like a... like a commoner."

"A commoner? Who do you think we are, Mother, some kind of royalty? Just because Daddy used to call me his little princess doesn't make it true. I'm a civil servant and I spend a lot of time at the courthouse as it is. I think it's a good place for Jimmy and I to get married."

"Robyn, you're only going to have one wedding. "Don't you want it to be something you can look back on with pride?"

"Really, mother? Just one wedding? How many times have you told me that this thing between Jimmy and me isn't going to last? Just the other night you told me that the sooner it was over and I found somebody decent and respectable to marry, the better. How about we save the big church wedding for then, okay?"

"Why do you insist on being such a petulant child, Robyn?"

"Maybe because I'm not a child, Mother. Did you ever think about that? I'm a grown woman, whether you want to believe it or not. And I can make my own decisions, whether you think so or not. And Jimmy and I are going to get married at the courthouse, whether you like it or not. You're welcome to be there, and I really hope you'll come, but I'm done listening to your crap. I don't tell you how to live your life, and you're not going to tell me how to live mine."

"You! I blame you for all of this," Renée said, pointing an accusing finger at Weber. "She was never like this until she met you."

"Put a sock in it," her husband said, then turned to Robyn and said. "Honey, I don't care if it's a church here, or the biggest cathedral in the country, or the courthouse. This is your wedding. You and Jim do it the way you want to. And wherever it is, you just know that I'm going to be there walking you down the aisle, okay?"

Following her typical pattern, Renée Fuchette stormed out of the kitchen and down the hallway, slamming the bedroom door behind her. Weber couldn't help thinking to himself that she must have a supply of bottled water, beef jerky, and Snickers bars hidden away under the bed to sustain herself after her daily temper tantrums.

Chapter 29

Weber was pulling into the parking lot of the courthouse to talk to Judge Ryman about officiating at the wedding ceremony when he noticed a Department of Public Safety car parked there. He slipped in the back of the courtroom to see Andy Blanchard testifying in the trial of a man he had arrested for driving under the influence.

Even though Blanchard's dash and body cameras showed the defendant's car weaving across the centerline of the highway, and then him pulling so far onto the shoulder that he almost went in the ditch when the red lights of the police car came on behind him, the driver insisted that he had had nothing to drink that day. The body camera footage of him failing every roadside test administered by Blanchard, and the fact that he had blown almost twice the legal limit for alcohol on the breathalyzer, but the man still insisted it was all a mistake and he had not touched a drop of alcohol or taken any medications that day. No matter what the evidence was, he was innocent.

Judge Ryman, a man of good humor but also one who did not suffer fools well, was unmoved by his protests. After hearing both sides of the story, he said, "Sir, I find you guilty of the charge against you of driving while under the influence. I also find it very offensive that, besides endangering your life and the lives of everybody else on the highway that day, you come into my courtroom and lie to my face. You have wasted this officer's time, and my time, and yours, too. If you would have been honest with me and told me you made a mistake, I might be inclined to be more lenient. But since you chose not to take that route, I'm sentencing you to thirty days in jail, $1,500 in fines, and I'm suspending your license for one year from this date." He rapped his gavel to end the session.

"Do you have a moment, Andy? I need to talk to you about something," Weber said as Blanchard handcuffed the convicted man and led him out of the courtroom.

"Sure. I'm taking this gentleman over to your jail right now until I can call the Navajo County Jail in Holbrook and arrange for him to do his time there. Can we talk after I do that?"

"Yeah, no problem. I need to talk to Judge Ryman about something anyway. I'll see you back at the office."

He called out to the judge as he was stepping away from the bench and asked, "Sir, can I have a minute of your time?"

"What's up, Sheriff?"

Weber approached and they shook hands.

"Are you feeling any better?"

"I do now that I got that kidney stone passed. Trust me on this, Sheriff, if you have the option to do that or not, don't. It felt like I had a tumbleweed going through there."

Weber laughed and said, "I'll keep that in mind."

"So, what can I do for you except offer such noteworthy advice, Sheriff?"

"It's about our wedding, Judge. You know about those pictures that are going around that are supposed to be Robyn, don't you?"

"I do," Judge Ryman said, shaking his head solemnly. "For the record, I don't believe for one minute that they are her, either."

"I appreciate that," Weber told him. "And I know Robyn does, too. Here's the thing, Judge. The church where we were going to get married suddenly decided they don't want us there."

"You're kidding me? Why?"

Big Lake Wedding

"Because apparently a couple of the old biddies that go there took offense to the idea of a fallen woman like Robyn being married at their church."

"That's ridiculous. Do you want me to call Stephen Collier and have a word with him about it?"

"I appreciate that, sir. But actually, we were talking last night about maybe having the wedding here at the courtroom and having you officiate."

The judge looked at him and smiled as he said, "Jimmy, I would be honored. I truly would. You tell me when you want this wedding to happen and I will have my clerk clear the docket that day completely. How's that?"

Weber shook his hand and said "That's wonderful, Judge. I can't tell you how much I appreciate this."

"I can't tell you how much this town appreciates you and Robyn, my friend. I know things are rough right now, but this too shall pass. You tell Robyn that I am proud of her as a person, as a woman, and as a deputy. And tell her I'm very proud to be the one to officiate at your wedding."

~~***~~

"I know what you want to talk to me about," Andy Blanchard said as he sat down in the chair next to Weber's desk. "I don't want to cause Robyn any trouble and I wish I hadn't said anything to Sweeney at all about it. The whole thing with her and Jack DeFray was none of my business and it happened before you two got together, so it wouldn't be right to bring it up. Let's face it, Jimmy, you got around, too."

"I did, no question about that. I just don't see Robyn and DeFray together."

"Well, they were."

"Robyn insists that nothing ever happened between the two of them."

Blanchard wrinkled his brow and said, "I don't know what to tell you, Jimmy. I've always had a lot of respect for Robyn. And you, too. You know that. But I know what I know."

"You actually saw them together?"

Andy thought for a moment or two and then said, "You know, I'm not sure."

"What do you mean you're not sure, Andy? You just told me they had something going on before Robyn and I got together. That's the same thing you told Sweeney. How did he say you put it? That they were going at it hot and heavy?"

"Yeah, that's what I told him."

"You said there were some sleepovers while you and DeFray were roommates. Now you're saying you're not sure you ever saw them together. What the hell is going on, Andy?"

"Look, the reason I said anything at all was because Robyn's in trouble and I wondered if there was a possibility that DeFray is the one sending those pictures of her to everyone."

"Do you think he would do something like that?"

"To be honest with you, Jimmy, I don't know. DeFray is a horn dog. He's always bragging about some woman he got to bed. But sending the pictures of Robyn? I just can't say one way or the other."

"If he did, why do you think he would do that, Andy?"

"I don't know. To try to destroy her reputation and get her fired?"

"If they did have a relationship of some kind, which she insists never happened, would he be that petty?"

"I'd like to think not, but I couldn't swear to it, Jimmy. But the more I'm thinking about it, when you asked if I ever saw them together, I realized that I don't know that I ever did. I really don't remember ever seeing them together."

"Then why did you tell Sweeney they had an affair?"

"Because DeFray was always bragging about it. Sandra and I split up and I needed a place to stay and he had an extra room. You know how that goes."

Weber did know. More than one deputy had camped out at his place over the years when the demands of the job caused marital strife.

"Jack was spending a lot of time gone," Blanchard continued. "Sometimes he would take off for a few hours, sometimes overnight. A couple of times I didn't see him for two or three days at a time when he was off-duty. If I asked him where he had been, just in passing, he'd tell me that he was with Robyn."

"You said you were roommates for about a year? And this was going on all during that time?"

"Pretty much, yeah."

"When did it end?"

"I don't know. Sandra and I patched things up and got back together, so I didn't see as much of DeFray, except on the job."

"I hope things are better for you two now."

"We're working on it. We're seeing a marriage counselor, and it's been rough, there's no question about that. A lot of it was my fault, not hers. You know how it is, Jimmy. A cop works a lot of hours, and sometimes the job takes over your whole life. It can be hard to take off the gun belt and the badge at night and just become a civilian. I brought a lot of things into the house that I should have left at the door at the end of the day."

"What's your relationship with DeFray like these days?"

"I don't know that we have a relationship outside of the job."

"Why is that?"

"You know what they say about how you never really get to know somebody unless you live with them? That's pretty true. I didn't like the way DeFray talked about women. You know the type. To hear him tell it, every woman around was pulling off her panties and throwing them at him. It didn't matter if it was the waitress at the burger joint or the woman working behind the checkout counter at Safeway. If she was over 18 and under 200 pounds, according to Jack, he had been to bed with her. It got tiresome. And when he would go into detail about things between him and Robyn, that didn't set well with me at all. It was disrespectful."

"Andy, Robyn says there was never an affair, and I believe her."

"I don't know what to tell you, Jimmy. If I had to believe one of the two of them, she's a lot more credible than DeFray."

"Something did happen between the two of them, but it's been a long time ago," Weber said, then told him about the incident when DeFray had made advances towards Robyn while she was still working as a dispatcher.

"Now that I can believe," Andy said. "That's classic Jack DeFray all the way. More than once I saw him step over the line with some woman, maybe a waitress at lunch or something like that, and then he'd laugh it off like it was all a big joke if she shot him down. But the minute she came back to the table he was right back at it again."

"Based on knowing that he tried and didn't get anywhere with Robyn, do you think he would do something like sending those pictures?"

"I really don't know. You said it was a long time ago. And while the guy's got a big ego, I'm not sure I see him holding a grudge for that long. But I'll tell you this right now, Jimmy. If DeFray is the one doing this crap, I will do everything I can to help you and Sweeney hang his ass out to dry."

Chapter 30

Mary was waiting for Weber when Blanchard left his office. "You're not gonna like this, Jimmy, but he's at it again.?
"Who's at it again, Mary?"
"Chet Wingate."
"Now what?"
"Apparently he is taking a clue from the women who were here yesterday protesting about Robyn, because now he's standing in front of City Hall with a protest sign saying that they are unfair to him."
"You're kidding me? I don't have time for this shit."
"Normally I wouldn't bother you with it. Just like those witches who were here yesterday, he's got a right to protest," Mary told him.
"Then why are we talking about this?"
"Because he's not just standing there with his sign. He's blocking the sidewalk, and when anyone walks by he hands them a flyer, whether they want it or not. He's calling the Town Council members liars and thieves and cheats and creating a general disturbance. I sent Archer over there to try to handle things, but you can guess how that went."
"Archer's as worthless as tits on a bull. Especially when it comes to his father. I'm surprised he still had his handcuffs when he came back."

"I know, Jimmy. You're preaching to the choir. Meanwhile, Chet's creating a scene and blocking the sidewalk, and that *is* against the law."

Weber sighed as he heaved himself out of his chair. "I'll handle it. If you hear gunshots, send an ambulance."

"Tell me you're not going to shoot him," Mary said.

"The way I feel right now, I might shoot myself."

~~***~~

"Go away, Sheriff. I have a right to be here. The Constitution says I have the right to express my opinions."

"You do, Chet. But you don't have the right to block the sidewalk. And you don't have the right to accost people like you're doing."

"All's fair in love and war, Sheriff."

"No, Chet, it's not. You can stand here with your silly little sign if you want to, and you can offer people a flyer as they walk past if you want to. But you can't stop people on the sidewalk and demand they listen to you. You can't call people names. Basically, Chet, you can't act childish. If you want to keep this up, you have to at least pretend to be an adult. I know that's a stretch for you, but what's the chance that you might be able to pull it off?"

"You have always hated me, haven't you Sheriff?"

"Chet, Chet, Chet. No, I don't hate you. You're not worth that much effort on my part, okay? I think you're a pain in the ass. I think you're two tacos short of a combination plate. But I don't hate you. Right now, I'm so fed up with you that I'm not gonna put up with any more crap. Either you play by the rules or you're going back to jail. But this time you're not going to walk out. If I have to take you in, you're going to be formally charged and you're going to have to go see the judge.

"For what?"

"Do I have to explain it to you again, Chet? You're breaking the law by blocking the sidewalk and you're disturbing the peace.

That's it. End of story. Settle down or go to jail. Which is it going to be?"

Weber would never know how that might have ended, because a moment later he heard tires squealing and a crashing noise. He turned his head in time to see Mary Ellen Gardner behind the steering wheel of her Hyundai Sonata, looking dazed. Weber ran into the street, stopping a car coming from the other direction, and opened the woman's door.

"Are you all right, Mrs. Gardner?"

"I… I don't know. What happened?"

Weber looked at the back of the Ford pickup truck that she had rear-ended. It didn't seem to show any damage at all, as opposed to the crumpled front end of her Hyundai.

"You sit right there, okay?"

"Don't leave me. I'm not sure what's happening."

"You'll be all right," he assured her, "I need to go check on the other driver."

He ran to the cab of the pickup, where Wayne Morgan was just opening the door to get out. "I don't know what the hell happened, Sheriff. I stopped because a car was pulling out into the street from the curb and the next thing I know, somebody hit me."

"It's okay. Are you injured at all, Wayne?"

"No, I'm fine. Is that Mrs. Gardner? Is she all right?"

"Sit tight. I think she's going to be okay."

Weber went back to check on the elderly woman, and called dispatch, "I need EMTs on Main Street in front of Town Hall, and somebody to help with traffic control. Traffic accident, possible minor injuries. And I need a tow truck."

"10-4, Sheriff, on the way."

Mary Ellen Gardner was 82 years old, half blind, and should not be behind the wheel of a car. She lived with her daughter, Elizabeth, who had taken the car keys away from her more than once. But Mary Ellen was not ready to completely give up her independence, and the minute Elizabeth's back was turned she was sneaking out of the house to drive, like a rebellious teenager.

Weber had known it was only a matter of time before something like this happened, and was grateful that nobody seemed to be seriously injured. He checked the woman's vital signs and everything seemed to be okay.

"I just don't understand what happened, Sheriff. He stopped right in front of me. I was trying to push on the brake pedal but I think I hit the gas instead."

"Yeah, I think you did, too," he told her. "That's all right, so long as nobody's hurt bad, the rest doesn't matter."

"Is that Wayne from the roofing company I hit?"

"Yes, ma'am."

"Please tell me that he's all right."

"He's just fine, Mrs. Gardner."

"But what about my poor car?"

Weber looked at the buckled hood and crushed front end of the Hyundai, which was leaking radiator fluid onto the pavement, and thought it might be the best thing that ever happened to the town if Mary Ellen never got her car repaired and tried to drive it again.

~~***~~

An hour later Weber was just finishing his report on the traffic accident when Captain Sweeney stormed into his office without knocking.

"I don't appreciate you going behind my back and interviewing Andy Blanchard, Sheriff. I told you before, this is my investigation."

"I understand, and I wasn't trying to go behind your back. I ran into him at the courthouse and I just wanted to find out…"

"You wanted to find out something more than what I had already told you," Sweeney said, cutting him off. "If that's not going behind my back, Sheriff, what is?"

"This may be your investigation, but Robyn Fuchette is *my* deputy."

"And your girlfriend. Would you be doing the same thing if it were any of your other deputies?"

"You bet your ass I would," Weber told him. "I would still be feeling the same way if it was any one of my deputies being accused of something that could impact their whole career. And if you have a problem with me caring about my people, tough shit. This isn't the big city, Captain Sweeney, and I'm not somebody who sits on his ass at his desk all day long. I work side by side with my deputies every day. You have to understand that these people are my family."

"What I understand, Sheriff, is that you're not able to stand back and take an unbiased look at this problem. That's what I told you going in. You're too close to the investigation."

"Hey guys, could you keep it down? We can hear you loud and clear out in the main office," Mary said from the door.

Neither man had realized they were shouting and both looked chagrined.

"Sorry, Mary," Weber said.

She looked at both of them like a teacher might two rowdy schoolboys, then closed the door.

Weber sighed. "Maybe you're right. Maybe I am too close. But I'm not a guy that can just sit around and twiddle my thumbs while something like this is happening. I'm sorry. I wasn't trying to interfere. I had no intention of seeking Andy Blanchard out, I just ran into him at the courthouse and asked if we could talk."

"Okay, just don't do it again, Sheriff."

"What about what he said about him never seeing DeFray and Robyn together that he can remember?"

"Actually, he never told me that," Sweeney admitted. But that doesn't mean it didn't happen, Sheriff."

"I understand. But couldn't it also mean that it really didn't happen? Did you ever think about that?"

"What? You're saying that DeFray made up the whole thing about him having an affair with Deputy Fuchette? And he continued telling that story for a year? Why would he do that?"

"I don't know," Weber admitted. "Some guys just like to brag, I guess. According to Andy, DeFray is always going on about some women he slept with."

"And you're thinking that if he would lie about that, maybe he's the one behind the pictures too, is that right?"

"Maybe. Have you talked to him yet?"

"No, not yet. He was testifying in court in St. John's today. I left messages for him on his phone and at the substation, but he hasn't gotten back to me yet."

"I really would like to be there when you talk to him."

"I told you before, that's not a good idea."

"Let me ask you the same question you just asked me, Captain Sweeney. If it were one of my other deputies would you tell me not to sit in on the interview?"

Sweeney look at him long and hard, as if trying to make up his mind. Finally, he said, "If I decide to let you sit in on, and that's a big if at this point, Sheriff, I need your word that that's exactly what you'll do. Sit there with your mouth shut unless I indicate it's time for you to say something. Do you understand me?"

"I promise," Weber told him

"All right. I'll think about it and get back to you."

Chapter 31

The next three days seemed to drag by at a snail's pace, even though it was summer and the town was filled with tourists and seasonal residents who came to the mountains to escape the heat of the desert. Weber and his deputies wrote tickets for speeding, broke up the occasional fight between people that had too much to drink and not enough common sense, answered two calls for visitors who were suffering from altitude sickness in the thin mountain air, and listen to the old-timers grouse about how things used to be back in the good old days before Big Lake got discovered and the mountains became covered with summer cabins and lodges. They were old complaints, and having grown up in Big Lake and seen how the community had changed since his youth, Weber knew there was some validity to them.

On the afternoon of the third day, Captain Sweeney called Weber and said, "I haven't forgotten you. I had to testify in a case in Kingman and it took longer than I thought. But I heard back from Officer DeFray and we're going to get together tomorrow."

"Can I come along?"

There was silence on the other end of the phone for a long time, and then Sweeney said, "You might hear some things you don't want to hear, Sheriff. Can I trust you to control yourself?"

"You can," Weber told him. "I give you my word."

~~***~~

"Okay, Sheriff Weber, I'm trusting you to be on your best behavior," Captain Sweeney reminded him the next morning. "I brought you along as a professional courtesy. Don't make me regret it."

"I understand," Weber told him, getting out of the unmarked DPS car. "I gave you my word."

Department of Public Safety Officer Jack DeFray could have been on a recruiting poster for the perfect police officer. He was a handsome man with dark hair and eyes, and a chiseled chin. His shoes, gun belt, and other leather were polished to a high gloss. Weber had never much cared for the man, based upon his attitude, but now found it even harder to tolerate being in his presence, knowing the things he said about Robyn. He still didn't believe that they had ever had an affair, but now he wanted to know why DeFray claimed they did and had gone into such detail about it with Andy Blanchard.

"Have a seat, Officer DeFray. I'm Captain Sweeney, and this is Sheriff Weber. I think you know him."

"Yeah, I do. How you doing, Sheriff?"

"Hanging in there. How about you, DeFray?"

"Can't complain. Nobody listens anyway, right?"

If DeFray wondered why a high ranking investigator from headquarters and the sheriff of Big Lake had summoned him to the DPS substation in Springerville, he did not show it. His demeanor was cool and confident. Weber had to resist the urge to reach across the table and throttle the man."

"So, do you have any idea why I asked you to meet with us today?"

"No, sir, I don't. How can I help you?"

"Some allegations have come up that we would like to talk to you about."

"Allegations? What allegations, sir?"

"How well do you know Deputy Robyn Fuchette?"

DeFray shrugged his shoulders and said, "I know her. Not all that well, but we've worked together a few times. She seems like a competent officer."

"What do you think about her honesty?"

"Her honesty, sir? As far as I know, she's very honest. I've never heard anything bad about her."

"Do you think that Deputy Fuchette would lie to me during the course of an investigation?"

"Again, sir, I don't know her all that well. But from what I do know of her, I'd say no, she wouldn't."

"Do you think she's someone I can trust?"

"I don't see why not," DeFray said.

"Are you aware that compromising photographs of Deputy Fuchette, or a woman looking very much like Deputy Fuchette, have been sent to different people?"

"I've heard some rumors, but that's about it, sir."

"These are the photographs I'm talking about, Officer DeFray," Sweeney said as he laid prints of the pictures on the table. "Do these look familiar to you?"

"They look like Deputy Fuchette. I have to say that I'm a little surprised seeing her in pictures like this."

"Yeah. We were, too," Sweeney told him.

They sat in silence for a moment, then DeFray asked, "Is Deputy Fuchette under investigation because of these pictures?"

"She's been suspended pending the outcome of my investigation into them," Sweeney replied.

"That's too bad. I'm disappointed to hear that."

"Why is that?"

"Why is what, sir?"

"Why are you disappointed to hear that?"

"I don't know. I just hate to see another officer get in trouble for anything."

"But what if they've done something that merits getting in trouble for, Officer DeFray? Do you think they should just be allowed to skate if they break the rules and do something out of line? Especially something this egregious?"

"No, sir, that's not what I meant. I just mean that I hate to see another officer do something to get in trouble, assuming that they did it in the first place.?"

"Look at the pictures again, Officer DeFray. Do you still think those are of Deputy Fuchette? Could they be another woman that looks like her? Or could the photos have been manipulated somehow to put her face onto those pictures? What do you think?"

DeFray looked at the pictures and shook his head. "I don't know what to tell you, sir. They look like Deputy Fuchette to me."

"Deputy Fuchette insists that it's not her in those pictures."

"I'm not an expert on things like that, so I don't know what to say, sir."

"But you think those photographs are of Deputy Fuchette. Isn't that what you said?"

"With all due respect to Sheriff Weber, since I know they have a relationship, to me they look like they are Deputy Fuchette. I'm sorry, Sheriff."

"So, do you think she's lying to us?"

"Again, with all due respect, sir, I don't know the details of the investigation, so I don't know that I can really comment on that."

"All right. Aside from denying that this is her in these pictures, do you think she's an honest woman?"

"Like I said before, sir, as far as I know, yes."

"So then, if Deputy Fuchette said that you did something inappropriate to her, should I believe her or not?"

Watching DeFray, Weber thought that the man must have been one hell of a poker player. He didn't blink or twitch or show anything to indicate that the question rattled him in the least. Which made Weber want to strangle him even more.

DeFray took a deep breath and said, "So that's what this is about. Yes, sir, I did something really stupid a while back. It was before you and Deputy Fuchette got together, Sheriff."

"What happened between you two?"

"I was at the Sheriff's Office in Big Lake one night, it's been a couple of years ago at least. I couldn't tell you the exact date. Deputy Fuchette was working the night shift as a dispatcher at the time. We got to talking and teasing and flirting, you know, like people do. I guess I misread the signals and I tried to kiss her. That was my bad. I'm sorry, Sheriff Weber. Like I said, it was before you two were together."

"You tried to kiss her? How did she respond to that?"

"I don't remember exactly, sir."

"It would be in your best interest to remember, Officer DeFray."

"Let me think... as I recall, she turned her head away and said no."

"And what happened after that?"

"Sir, it's been a long time. I'm not really sure."

"That's interesting, because Deputy Fuchette seems to remember it all very well."

"I don't think anything happened after that, we talked a few more minutes and she seemed like she was okay. I thought we parted as friends. I've seen her a few times since then and it never came up, so I just figured it was one of those things that happen between a man and a woman and forgot about it. Apparently she didn't."

"Did you at any time put your hands on Deputy Fuchette's breasts, Officer? And before you reply, keep in mind that if you lie to me, it's going to cost you your badge."

Weber had interviewed a lot of people in his time as a police officer and he was pretty good at telling when someone was lying, and when someone was trying to figure out the best way to reply to a question and still keep themselves out of trouble. Now there was a tiny flicker in DeFray's right eye and his hands seemed restless on the tabletop. He dropped them into his lap and said, "As I recall, she was rolling her head around like her neck was stiff and I started rubbing her shoulders and the back of her neck. My hands might have bumped onto her breasts or come in contact with them at that point. But sir, if that's what happened, it was wholly unintentional."

"And how did Deputy Fuchette react to that?"

"I think she told me to keep my hands to myself, or something like that. I told her it was an accident and we both kind of shrugged it off, to the best of my recollection. I'm really sorry if this has caused her any kind of problems or if she resents me over what happened. I apologized to her back then, and I would apologize to her again in a heartbeat if that would help."

"Since that incident, have you and Deputy Fuchette come into contact with each other, either on or off the job?"

"We worked a couple of accidents together, sir, and I saw her at the Safeway in Eagar one time and said hi. We talked for a minute or so. That's about it."

"Were there any problems those times that you were working together or when you ran into her at the store?"

"No, sir. That's why I'm kind of surprised she's bringing this up after so long. I'd done something stupid and apologized for it. I thought we were good. Like I said before, I'd be happy to apologize to her again if that would help."

"Thank you for being candid with us about that," Sweeney said, his tone switching from that of an interrogator to that of just another guy shooting the bull. "Sheriff Weber and I both understand that things like that happen sometimes. Hell, I bet we've both misread a woman's signal a time or two, haven't we Sheriff? At least I know I have. It's not the end of the world."

Weber nodded in agreement. He had to hand it to Sweeney. The man knew how to handle an interview. He would not have wanted to sit down at a card table with either of them if money was at stake. DeFray was back to being casual, his body language more relaxed.

In the same relaxed demeanor, Sweeney asked, "By the way, have you heard that Andy Blanchard is up for a promotion?"

"I saw he made the list. Good for him. He deserves it."

"You know we run pretty extensive background checks on new recruits, right?"

"Yes, sir. Of course."

"We also take a long look at someone when they start advancing up through the ranks. Just to make sure there's nothing we missed, or that something hasn't come up since then."

"That makes sense, sir," DeFray said.

"What do you think of Blanchard?"

"He's a fine officer, sir."

"How is he to work with?"

"Great. He's a professional all the way, sir."

"Do you two get along pretty well?'

"Yes, sir. I would say so."

"Do you consider yourself friends?"

"Yes sir, I do. I would trust Andy with my life. I have more than once on the job."

"What about Blanchard's honesty? Do you think he's an honest man?"

"Yes sir, I do. Absolutely."

"I understand that you and Blanchard get along so well that a while back you offered to let him stay with you? What was that all about?"

"Him and his wife were having some problems and he needed a place to crash for a while. I have an extra room at my place and I told him he was welcome to stay there. But his problems at home never interfered with his job performance, sir."

"How did you two get along while he was staying there?"

"Fine, sir. A lot of times he was working days and I was working nights or the other way around, so we didn't hang around a lot together. But I'd have him back as a roommate again anytime. He's a good guy."

"So, you're telling me that Andy Blanchard is a good guy and an honest man. Is that right?"

"Yes, sir, that's what I'm saying."

"Well then, do you have any idea why Blanchard would tell me that you and Deputy Fuchette had an affair that lasted for more than a year? Because you're telling me that you haven't had much contact with her, and the way he tells it, you guys were quite an item for a while."

In spite of himself, De Fray did a double take. It was clear that the question was from out of left field and had taken him by surprise. There was no denying the deer in the headlights look on DeFray's face.

"In fact," Sweeney continued, and the no nonsense interrogator was back, "Blanchard said that when he was staying with you, you and Deputy Fuchette spent quite a few nights together and even went out of town together a time or two. He was also quite detailed about the things you told him the two of you did together. So, somebody's lying to me, Officer DeFray. It's either you or Andy Blanchard."

Defray was quiet for a long moment, then he looked toward the door and Weber wondered if he would actually try to make a run for it. Could the man really be that stupid? Finally, he opened his mouth to speak and when he did Sweeney held up a cautionary finger and said, "Keep in mind, Officer, if you lie to me I'm going to have your badge. Understood?"

The little twitch in DeFray's eye was now much more evident. He looked at the door again, licked his lips and swallowed, and looked at the two men sitting across the table from him and asked, "Does what I tell you stay in this room?"

"It depends on what you tell us," Sweeney replied.

"Sir, do I need some kind of legal representation?"

"That's entirely up to you, Officer. But the longer you jerk me around instead of telling me what I need to know, the harder it's going to be on you."

DeFray looked at the door one last time, then back at the two men and hung his head. "I was having an affair, but it wasn't with Deputy Fuchette."

"Okay, who was it?"

Defray said something that they couldn't understand.

"Speak up, I can't hear you."

"It was with Sandra." There was a look of misery on DeFray's face, and Weber didn't know if it was because he knew his back was to the wall and he had no other options or if he really regretted what he was telling them.

"Sandra? Sandra who?"

With a noticeable tremor in his jaw, DeFray said, "Sandra Blanchard."

"Sandra Blanchard? Andy Blanchard's wife?"

"Yes sir," DeFray replied, nodding his head. "I feel terrible about it."

"Really? You feel terrible? You're screwing your fellow officer's wife behind his back, while the man is staying with you, and you feel terrible about it?"

"Neither one of us meant it to happen," DeFray said, and now there were tears in his eyes. Again, Weber didn't know if they were tears of guilt or were brought on by his getting caught. "They were having some problems and they broke up. Andy needed a place to stay, so I offered him my spare room."

"And in return you took his wife to bed. I'm not sure how Blanchard would feel about that trade off."

"Like I said, neither one of us planned it. It just happened."

"Thunderstorms just happen," Sweeney said, working to keep his voice even. "Winter just happens, summer just happens, and snow just happens. But I've never heard of sex between a man and woman just happening. How did it *just happen*? Did you bump into her at the grocery store and your penis fell into her vagina all on its own? Is that the way it just happened?"

"Look, sir, Andy's a great guy. And Sandra is a wonderful woman. They were on the outs and it looked like they weren't going to get back together."

"So you took advantage of the situation. Is that what you're telling me?"

"No, sir. I went over there one night when Andy was working to pick up some paperwork that I needed for court the next day. Sandra had had a couple of drinks. She wasn't drunk, but she had a couple of drinks and she was feeling sorry for herself and needed someone to talk to. We talked for a while. When I got ready to go I hugged her, just like I would any friend. And then we wound up kissing. Next thing I know, it happened."

"And it continued to happen for a while, apparently," Sweeney said, with bitterness in his voice.

"Yes, sir, it did."

"Are you two still involved?"

"No, sir. We were seeing each other for a while and we both realized it wasn't going anywhere. And I could tell that Andy and Sandra really loved each other. I guess I kind of encouraged them both to start talking and see if they could work out their problems."

"Well, that's damned noble of you, Officer," Sweeney said sarcastically. "I guess we should start calling you the Marriage Fixer, shouldn't we?"

"Sir, I know what I did was wrong. It happened. And I don't have any excuse for it. But it's over with, and I've been kicking my own ass ever since."

"Let me see. You make a pass at a woman dispatcher and then you grope her when she says no to your kiss. And you know it was wrong. Then you sleep with the vulnerable wife of another officer, but again, you know it was wrong. You have an amazing sense of right and wrong, don't you, Officer DeFray? Tell me, why does it only kick in after the fact?"

"I don't know what to say, sir."

"It doesn't matter what you say, I don't want to hear it," Sweeney snapped.

The only sounds in the room were DeFRay's sobbing and the ticking of the wall clock.

"Why did you tell Andy Blanchard you had something going on with Deputy Fuchette?"

"I don't want this to sound bad, but Sandra is kind of wild in bed…"

"Spare us the locker room talk, De Fray."

"I don't mean it that way, sir. I'm just trying to explain. One time she left a big hickey on my neck. Andy saw it and commented on it and asked me who the lucky woman was. What was I going to do? I couldn't tell him it was his wife, could I?"

"So instead you said it was Robyn?"

The other two men in the room looked at him, and Weber realized he was shouting when he asked the question.

"I'm sorry, Sheriff. It just... The whole thing caught me by surprise. It was the day that I bumped into Robyn at Safeway, and when Andy asked me who gave me the hickey, she just came to mind. After that it was, I don't know, convenient to say I was seeing her. I know that makes me sound like a real asshole."

"Is that what you call it when you smear a woman's reputation? Being an asshole?"

"Sheriff," Sweeney cautioned.

Weber forced himself to sit back in the seat and keep his hands on top of the table.

"What do you know about these pictures of Deputy Fuchette?"

"Nothing, sir. I never saw them until today. I swear."

"Why should I believe you, Officer?"

"Because I'm telling the truth! I would never do something like that!" DeFray looked miserable when he asked, "Is this going to cost me my job?"

"I should rip that badge off of you right now and kick your ass," Sweeney told him. "Or better yet, let Sheriff Weber, here, kick it for me. Because you certainly deserve it. The only reason you're not up on charges right this minute is because of my respect and affection for Andy and Sandra Blanchard, and for what this could do to their marriage if it got out. As far as what happened between you and Deputy Fuchette, if she decides to press charges against you, I'm going to back her all the way. But right now, as much as I hate to say it, you still have a job. My suggestion to you is to resign while you can. And my promise to you is that if you don't, I'm going to find the hottest, most remote, most miserable place in the state and see that you are stationed there permanently. Hopefully someplace where your only companions are rattlesnakes and tarantulas. And once you get there, I'm going to make sure that you never get a positive evaluation, you never get a promotion, and you get every shit assignment I can send your way. Do I make myself clear, Officer DeFray?"

"Yes, sir. Are you going to tell Andy about this?"

"No, and neither are you. Those two were high school sweethearts and they are trying to make their marriage work. That's the only reason that I won't tell him. But if Sandra decides to, I wouldn't blame Blanchard if he hunted you down and kicked your ass. Or worse. That's why it's in both of your interests for you to turn in your badge or get transferred out. And believe me, DeFray, if it wasn't for that, I would have you up on charges right this minute. You're a disgrace to your badge, you're a disgrace to your fellow officers, and you're a disgrace to humanity."

DeFray hung his head and didn't respond.

"Do you have a personal computer?"

"A computer? Yes, sir, I've got a laptop."

"I'm seizing it, and your Department issued laptop, along with your cell phone. If I find any pictures of Deputy Fuchette on any of them, not only will I take your badge and throw your ass in a jail cell, I'll give Sheriff Weber here a key to that cell and go out for a long lunch. Do we understand each other?"

"Yes, sir."

There was no question about it, DeFray's voice was that of a man who was watching his entire world collapsing around him. Weber felt no sympathy for him at all.

~~***~~

"Well, did you find anything out?" Mary asked when they got back to the Sheriff's Office in Big Lake.

"I found out Jack DeFray is an even bigger jerk than I thought he was," Weber told her. "He made up the whole story about him and Robyn having an affair."

"Why would he do that? I mean, I know guys brag about stuff and make crap up, but why go into all that detail?"

Weber couldn't tell her the real reason for DeFRay's lies, so he just said, "I guess some people have a pretty wild fantasy life."

"Does Robyn know yet?"

"Yeah, I called her on my cell before we left Springerville."

"I bet she was upset. Or maybe relieved that the truth about that came out."

"A little of both, I think. I'm going to head over to her place in a few minutes."

Sweeney was on the telephone, and he interrupted, saying, "Sheriff, I need to put this on speaker phone. You're going to want to hear this."

Nick Russell

Chapter 32

Excitement shot through Weber's body like electricity when Kirby Templeton called the executive session of the Town Council to order the next day. He had been awake all night, going over the information in his head that had been revealed the previous afternoon when he and Sweeney returned to Big Lake after interviewing DeFray. When Kirby called him to the podium to speak, he spent a long time laying out what they knew about the source of the pictures, referring to his notes to make sure he got everything right.

When he was done, there was silence for a moment, and then Adam Hirsch spoke up. "Do you really expect us to believe this cockamamie story? Russians? South America? That there's some kind of worldwide conspiracy to fake those pictures of Deputy Fuchette and send them to everybody? I think you have been watching way too much TV, Sheriff Weber."

"I didn't say people in those places were doing anything that had a part in this, Councilman Hirsch," Weber said. "The way Special Agent Parks explains it, it's like going through a maze following the trail the emails took to throw us off the path of whoever is sending them."

"I've heard enough," the councilman said. "Whatever you and Deputy Fuchette think you can dream up to get her out of this, it isn't going to work. You have had over a week to investigate this and nothing's happened. We need to stop wasting money paying someone who's on suspension. I make a motion that Deputy Fuchette be dismissed right this minute."

"Hold on, Adam," Kirby Templeton said. "I'm not a technical person myself, and all this computer stuff just confuses me. But Special Agent Parks is a smart man and he knows his business. With other FBI people providing this information to him, I don't think we can just dismiss it out of hand."

"Why do you keep defending this woman? This needs to be over and done with," Councilwoman Gretchen Smith-Abbot said.

"Because she's a good person. Because she's a faithful Town employee. And because she is not the type of person to do the things that we are seeing in those pictures. We need to know what's happening. And until we do find out, we're not going to be firing anybody."

Adam Hirsch immediately chimed in. "I agree with Gretchen. At least we shouldn't be paying Deputy Fuchette for the time she's on suspension."

"If you people would all just forget your little petty grievances and deal with the issues and the facts, that would be real nice," Councilman Frank Gauger said, with irritation in his voice.

"The facts are we have a deputy who obviously has no morals. Who seems to get a thrill out of showing her body off and ruining this community's good name."

"That's enough, Gretchen," Kirby said. "We don't know what's going on here. Based upon Deputy Fuchette's reputation, on her testimony, and on this new information from Special Agent Parks, we're not going to punish her for something I'm convinced she had nothing to do with. That's not the way we do things here."

"Well, maybe it's time we change the way we do things," Gretchen snapped.

"I beg your pardon?"

"When Chet Wingate was the mayor this would not have been a question. It would have been settled by now."

"Chet's no longer the mayor, Gretchen. Don't start that."

"He was on temporary leave and you stole the mayor's job from him," she shouted.

"That's enough," Councilman Gauger said. "We're not here to play these games, Gretchen. The topic for tonight is an update on the situation with Deputy Fuchette. Does anyone else have anything to add?"

The councilwoman frowned but didn't say anything.

"We're working on it," Weber said. "Captain Sweeney from the Department of Public Safety has interviewed several people, and for the record, he doesn't believe the photographs are of Robyn either."

Adam scowled at the sheriff. "I know what this is. It's cops taking care of each other. We all know about the thin blue line, don't we, Sheriff?"

"No, Adam, that's not what it is. Captain Sweeney is here, and he has something that he wants to show you folks that will prove the woman in those pictures is not Deputy Fuchette."

"Proof? What kind of proof?" From the tone of his voice, it was obvious Hirsch was not prepared to believe anything that might clear Robyn's name.

"How about you keep quiet and let the man tell us, Adam? Captain Sweeney, we'd like to hear what you have for us," Kirby said.

Sweeney walked up to the projector screen set up on a side wall and turned it on, and then clicked a button on his laptop computer. An image of a woman came on the screen.

"Ladies and gentlemen, this is Valerie Carbanal from DPS headquarters in Phoenix," Sweeney said. "Ms. Carbanal is an expert in photomanipulation and I have asked her to take part in this live videoconference so she can hear you and you can hear her. Valerie, thank you for joining us this afternoon."

"My pleasure, Captain Sweeney. Hello folks."

There were nods and a couple of murmurs from the Town Council.

"Valerie, can you explain to us what you found out in your research of the pictures that have been circulating around here?"

"Wait a minute," Gretchen said. "Before we listen to whatever this woman has to say, what are her qualifications?"

"That's a good question," Valerie said. "I have a BA from the University of Arizona in computer sciences, and a Masters in computer forensics from Arizona State University. I've been employed by the Department of Public Safety's computer forensics unit for the last nine years, and I have been the supervisor of that unit for four years. Before that, I spent three years with the Phoenix Police Department as a forensic computer analyst."

"Sounds like she knows what she's talking about to me," Kirby Templeton said. "Please continue, Ms. Carbanal."

"I'm going to present a PowerPoint display," Valerie said "and I apologize for the content of these pictures, though I know you've all seen them before. Let me show you something."

The image of the first picture that had been received, the woman standing in the forest with her shirt open, came on one side of the screen and a picture of Robyn was on the other side. "I'm going to zoom in on these two pictures to demonstrate to you why I can tell that they have been altered."

"Hold on a minute if you would," Councilman Gauger said. "What you're telling us is that these pictures have been Photoshopped?"

"Photoshop is a generic term, just like Xerox is for a copy machine." Valerie said. "Photoshop is an excellent program for working with photographs, but it's not the only one in existence. So technically, the pictures have been manipulated, whether or not the person doing so used Photoshop or some other program."

"Thank you," Gauger said. "Please continue."

"Okay, as I was saying, I want to show you something."

A new image came on the screen, this time a closeup of just the woman's face and neck on one side of the screen, and of Robyn's on the other side.

"If you look here, Valerie said, "you will notice the difference between the skin tone between these two pictures." A pointer moved on the screen between the necks of the two women in the pictures.

Big Lake Wedding

"This is ridiculous," Gretchen Smith-Abbot said. "I can't tell any difference at all. These are just a bit closer."

Valerie did something from her office and the pictures zoomed in closer.

"It's subtle, but if you look carefully, the woman on the left has a definite line of discoloration here." She positioned the pointer at the neck of the woman standing in the forest. "You don't see that on Deputy Fuchette's neck over here." The pointer moved Robyn's neck. "Deputy Fuchette's skin is a shade darker. It's not much, and you wouldn't see it in the overall picture. But this is where the photo was manipulated. Where Deputy Fuchette's face was put onto this woman's body."

"I can see it," Gauger said. "Anybody else?"

"I can see it, too, Councilman Mel Walker said.

"I can't see anything," Hirsch snapped. "This is a waste of time."

"Settle down, Adam," Kirby Templeton said. "Please proceed, Ms. Carbanal."

"Next, I'm going to zoom in a little bit further now. Do you see these little squares that the photo is breaking down to? Those little squares are called pixels, which are what makes up any electronic image, whether it be a photograph, a graphic image like a company logo, or a video from your cable TV. You'll notice on Deputy Fuchette's neck, the pixels are smooth. Now, going over here to the woman standing in the woods, notice that the pixels are irregular around the neck and face."

"Which means they were pasted in," Kirby said.

"Exactly. Whoever did it did a good job. But I can tell you, this is an altered image."

"Can you move Deputy Fuchette's face back off, so we can see the woman's real face?"

"Not with this image. After it was manipulated it was saved as a JPG, which is a standard photo file. I'd have to have access to the original manipulated picture before it was saved to be able to access the layers and do that."

"I'm not buying any of this," Gretchen Smith-Abbot said. "You're telling me that someone cut Deputy Fuchette's head off and pasted it on some other woman. That makes no sense to me. Why would anyone go to all the trouble to do that?"

"They didn't cut her head off literally," Valerie replied. "Let me show you something." She moved to another image of the two women. "Here is a rough step by step of how it's done." A dashed line appeared around Robyn's head and neck. The next picture showed Robyn's face being moved onto the neck of the woman standing in the forest. The next picture was zoomed back out, showing the picture they had received in their email. "See what I mean?"

"No, I don't see what you mean," Gretchen said. "This is all mumbo-jumbo."

"It's not mumbo-jumbo," Valerie replied. "It's computer science. Let's move on to the next picture."

She went through every picture in the series and with each one, she was able to zoom in and show subtle differences between the picture of Robyn and pictures of the nude woman.

"As you can see, sometimes there's a difference in skin tone. It's more pronounced in some of the pictures than in others, but it's there in all of them. So are those irregular pixels I showed you before. Also, look at this photo in the bedroom that shows the woman looking back over her shoulder." The image of the woman on her hands and knees came on the screen. "If you zoom in on the neck and head only, like I'm doing here, you'll see the head is turned in a different direction than the neck. Which means the picture of Deputy Fuchette's face was taken straight on, face forward, not at the angle this woman was posing in."

"You're wasting our time with this nonsense," Adam said.

"It's real simple to prove to yourself. Captain Sweeney, would you mind leaning forward and try looking over your shoulder, like the woman in this picture is doing?"

Sweeney did as she asked. Several of the councilmembers left their seats to move closer to him and looked from different angles."

"I see what you're talking about," Mel Walker said.

"I'm sorry, I'm still not convinced," Gretchen said stubbornly."

"Well, I *am* convinced, Kirby Templeton said. "Who else now thinks that these photos have been manipulated?"

"Not me," Adam Hirsch said. "These are real pictures, they haven't been changed in any way at all."

"Adam, I don't know if you're blind, or just blinded by your animosity toward Sheriff Weber and Deputy Fuchette," Mel Walker said, "but I can see it."

"So can I," Frank Gauger agreed.

"Ms. Carbanal, let me ask you a question," Kirby Templeton said. "Are you absolutely sure these photographs have been manipulated? There's no question in your mind that Deputy Fuchette is not the person in these pictures?"

"Sir, I would stake my reputation on it. I'm prepared to testify to that in any court in the country. But just to be sure, I've had two other forensic computer photo specialists look at each picture. They are Marcus Harper, from the Department of Public Safety, and Sebastian Barabas, from the Phoenix Police Department. They concur completely with my findings. Here, I'll show you."

The screen changed again, this time with two letters from the other forensic analysts, both agreeing with Valerie's assessment.

"There you go," Captain Sweeney said. "No question about it, the pictures are fake."

"Which is what I've said all along," Weber said. "I've said it and Robyn said it. Now do you believe it?"

"Captain Sweeney, Ms. Carbanal, thank you very much for your time and efforts in this case," Kirby said. "It is very much appreciated."

"You're welcome," Valerie replied. "Do you need anything else from me?"

"No, I think we have what we need."

"I will be sending my full report and a copy of this presentation to the Sheriff's Office," Valerie said. "And if you have any further questions, please don't hesitate to reach out to me."

The screen went blank, and Kirby looked at the other councilmembers and then said, "Deputy Fuchette, would you please stand for a moment?"

Robyn stood up, and Kirby said, "Deputy, this whole Council owes you an apology. In fact, this whole town owes you one. There is no question that whoever is sending these pictures did it maliciously and that you are an innocent victim. I make a motion right now that Deputy Fuchette be returned to duty with all the benefits and respect she deserves."

"I second that," Mel Walker said immediately.

"This is ridiculous. We haven't proven anything."

"We have a motion and a second," Kirby said, ignoring Adam. "All those in favor of returning Deputy Fuchette to her former status, please say aye."

There were five ayes, only Adam Hirsch and Gretchen Smith-Abbott dissenting. Kirby rapped his gravel and said. "Motion is passed. Deputy Fuchette, I know this has been very hard on you, and I know it's not over just because you're back on the job. If it's any consolation to you, I'm going to write a formal letter of apology, reinstating you to full active duty status, and I'm going to ask Paul Lewis at the newspaper to put it in the next edition."

"I'd be honored to sign that letter, too," Frank Gauger added. Every other councilmember except Gretchen and Adam said the same thing.

"Deputy, I know there are still a lot of small minds around here," with that, Kirby looked toward where Gretchen and Adam sat. "All I can tell you is that given time, hopefully, people will realize how wrong they've been about you. And I sincerely hope that some members of this Council," again he looked toward Adam and Gretchen, "will someday admit they were wrong. Welcome back."

"Thank you, sir," Robyn said. "And thank you to the other members of the Council who stood behind me. I appreciate you more than I can ever say."

She sat down and wiped tears from her eyes.

Big Lake Wedding

Kirby asked, "Captain Sweeney, now we know for sure that the photos are fake. But do we know who is sending them?"

"No, but we're closing in on whoever it is right now. Special Agent Parks from the FBI is here and he can tell you a little bit more about that."

"Special Agent Parks, what can you tell us?"

Parks stood up and said, "As Sheriff Weber said earlier, people from the FBI office in Phoenix have been able to trace back the IP address through a series of reroutes. Some of them go to other countries and back again. It's been a bit of a chore to find where everything originates from, but it all comes back to the same thing. The emails started right here in Big Lake."

"When did this become an FBI investigation, Special Agent Parks? I don't remember anybody calling in the FBI, Adam Hirsch said.

"This is not an official FBI investigation," Parks told him. "My co-workers down at the Phoenix office agreed to look into this as a favor to me."

"If it's not an official investigation, how can your results be official? How do we know you even know what you're talking about? Maybe your friendship with Sheriff Weber has skewed your thinking. Is that possible, Special Agent?"

Weber had known Parks a long time and had never seen his friend get angry before. Parks was always the easy-going farm boy from Oklahoma who went to the big city and made it as an FBI agent. But now there was no question, Parks was riled when he replied.

"Councilman Hirsch, are you calling me a liar?"

"What I'm saying is…"

"I get what you're saying. You're saying I'm a liar. You're saying that my friendship with Jimmy and Robyn gave me cause to come in here and lie in an official statement to this body. If You really believe that, I encourage you to file an official complaint against me. I'd be happy to give you the number of the Special Agent in Charge of the Phoenix office."

"All I'm saying…"

"I heard what you're saying," Parks told him. "Now you hear me. I did not lie about anything in this investigation and I resent you inferring that I did. So, either put up or shut up, sir." Parks wrote the number of the Special Agent in Charge on the back of one of his business cards and offered it to Hirsch. When the councilman would not take it, Parks dropped it on the dais in front of him. Then he turned to the rest of the Town Council and asked, "Does anybody else here care to question my integrity?"

"Absolutely not, Special Agent Parks," Kirby said. "I apologize for my fellow councilmember's lack of respect. We are grateful for what you've done to help us get to the bottom of all this. Please keep up the good work. Now, I think we're done here. I make a motion to adjourn this meeting."

Frank Gauger seconded the motion and a show of hands ended the meeting. Kirby rapped his gavel, then came down off the dais to hug Robyn and shake hands with Weber, Parks, and Sweeney.

Chapter 33

"Well, look who the cat dragged in," Mary Caitlin said the next morning when Robyn came into the Sheriff's Office in her uniform.

"And right through the front door like I belong here," Robyn replied. "No more sneaking in the back like some kind of cat burglar."

Mary hugged the younger woman and said, "It's so good to see you back here, Robyn. I told you it was going to happen, didn't I?"

"You did," Robyn agreed. "I just wish it happened sooner."

"We all do, honey," Mary assured her. "But you're here now, and that's all that matters."

Every deputy on duty made it a point to hug Robyn and welcome her back.

"Now we just need to find the bastard behind this and nail his ass to the wall," Dolan Reed said.

"You get the nails and I'll bring the hammer," Buz told him.

"When do you think we'll find him?"

"We're getting closer all the time, Robyn," Weber assured her. "Trust me, we're going to get him."

"In the meantime, lock up the women and the children," Larry Parks said. "We've going to have us a bachelor party!"

"I told you, I really don't care about a bachelor party," Weber said.

"My mama told me to always wear clean underwear in case I got in an accident," Parks replied. "But the fact is, I wear my skivvies at least two days in a row. Of course, I turn them inside out every morning."

"You are a sick man, Larry Parks," Weber said. "Do you know that?"

"I do. And if you found out I was wearing your skivvies once in a while, too, you'd think I was even sicker."

The office door opened and Captain Sweeney came in. "Is this a private party or is anyone welcome?"

"I don't know about just anybody, but you sure are," Robyn told him, crossing the room to give him an unprofessional hug. If he was uncomfortable with her physical display of gratitude, Sweeney didn't show it. "I can't tell you how much I appreciate what you did for me, Captain. You're my hero."

"Happy to do it, Deputy. But we're not done yet. We're going to find this guy. I promise you."

"Hey, I thought I was your hero," Parks said.

"Not anymore, Parks. Now it's Captain Sweeney."

"Are you seeing this, Jimmy? You can't trust these women," Parks said, with a sorrowful look on his face. "One day you're a hero and the next day you're a has been."

"Bite me, Parks."

"Bite you? That's the thanks I get for enlisting the full force of the Federal Bureau of Investigation to help you? Bite you, Robyn?"

"Well, there are other things I could say, but I'm a lady," Robyn said impishly. "Now, I just want to get back in my car and out on the street doing my job. What do you want me to do today, Sheriff?"

"Well, I was thinking about giving you another day off so you can spend it with your mother."

"Hey, you know how I just told Parks to bite me? There was something else I was going to tell him, but I'll reserve it for you. I've had more than enough of that woman in the last few days, thank you very much!"

Big Lake Wedding

"How about you take a run out to SafeHaven and check in with Christine and make sure things are okay there, and then patrol that side of town."

"10-4, Sheriff," Robyn said, with a big smile on her face as she went out the door.

"Did she just skip out of here?"

"I believe she did, Chad," Mary said. "Our girl is back!"

Getting back to business," Chad said, "There are four security cameras along Main Street by the Brewpub. I've looked at the video on all of them, Unfortunately, none of them cover out into the street where that picture was taken from."

"It was worth a try," Weber said.

"Nothing shows on the street, but does anything show on the sidewalk leading up to where the last picture was taken?"

"No, sir, Captain Sweeney," Chad said. "I looked at everything around. No such luck. Big Lake hasn't gotten to the point where people have all that many security cameras."

"Well, it was worth a shot."

The phone rang and Mary picked it up, and when she hung up there was a strained look on her face."

"What is it, Mary?"

"That was the Highway Patrol in New Mexico. An officer in Lordsburg stopped a blue Ford pickup last night. The computer system was down and the dispatcher wasn't able to run the plate for him. By the time she did, it was too late. The officer was dead."

"Please don't tell me it was MacGregor."

"The plate came back to him, Jimmy."

The joy everyone felt at Robyn's return to duty was quickly erased by the sad news of the death of a fellow officer. Especially since the person suspected in taking that officer's life was someone from Big Lake that they had had in their custody at one point.

"Do they have any idea where he's headed?"

"No, they don't. But every cop in the country is looking for him now." Mary said. "Somebody will get him sooner or later."

"Let's hope it's sooner rather than later," Weber said.

~~***~~

"How are you doing with everything, Coop?"

"To be honest, Jimmy, I don't know," his deputy said as he stirred powdered creamer into his coffee.

"Is Roberta okay?"

"Yeah, she's handling it better than I am. She's just accepted the fact that there are bad people in the world and sometimes you have to deal with them. Me, I wish I was doing as well as she is. I mean, I've dealt with bad people throughout my career. But when it hits this close to home, it's not that easy to just let go of. One minute I want to go rogue and hunt MacGregor down and blow him away, then the next I know I have to trust the system to do its job."

"That's what separates the professionals from the rest of the world," Weber told him.

"All I can say is, part of me wishes MacGregor is heading back this direction because I would love to get my hands on him. And part of me hopes he doesn't ever show up around here again, just because I'd love to get my hands on him. I don't know that I could remain professional if I did come face to face with him, to be honest with you. Does that make me a bad cop?"

"No, Coop, it doesn't," Weber assured him. "It makes you a good man that has seen someone they care about abused and is struggling with how to handle it. And I'm confident that if MacGregor does show his face here, the cop in you will do things appropriately."

"Then you have more confidence in me than I do right now. I never thought I'd feel this way about somebody, Jimmy. Especially not at this stage in my life. I just figured I was an old dog who was better at being alone than being in a relationship. Boy, she sure proved me wrong about that!"

"Yeah, I hear you. That's the way it was with me and Robyn. Neither one of us was looking to get into a relationship. But Mary told me something quite a while back. She said that sometimes you find what you're looking for when you don't even know you're looking. I think that applies to both of us."

"Yeah, I guess you're right."

"Shoot, Coop, we both know I'm not right very often. Those are Mary's words, and we both know she's always right, don't we?"

His deputy laughed and said, "And if she ever *is* wrong, I don't have the balls to tell her. Do you?"

"Me? Oh, hell no! My momma didn't raise any fools."

~~***~~

"Mother, we've been through this a thousand times. It's all settled, we're having the wedding at the courthouse."

"If you would just listen to reason…"

"I'm done listening to anything you have to say," Robyn said. "I told you before, I would love for you and Daddy to be there. But it's *my* wedding, not yours. And we're doing it our way. If you can't handle that, maybe it's best for both of us if you just go home right now."

Her mother stared at her, lips tightly clenched as if holding back whatever it was she wanted to say. That surprised Weber, because Robyn's mother *always* expressed her opinion, no matter whose feelings were hurt in the process.

"Would you just please stop, René," her husband said. "You keep saying you want this to be a special day for Robyn. Okay, cut the crap and let her have *her* special day, not the special day you think she should have. Why is that so hard for you to get through your head?"

Weber was surprised by Renée's response. He expected her to fly down the hall and slam the bedroom door behind her as she had so many times in the past. Instead she chose a new route, collapsing into tears. He didn't know how to react to that, Robyn and her father, having been down that road with her before, were unmoved by her histrionics.

"All I want is the best for my baby! Why is it so hard to understand?" She sobbed and kept her face buried in her hands for what seemed a long time. Eventually realizing she wasn't getting any response, she looked up and said, "Fine! Do it your way. Someday you will look back and you will wish you had listened to your mother, Robyn. You mark my words, someday you will!"

With that she got up from the table and began preparing dinner, rattling pots and pans in the process, but not saying anything else. Weber decided he liked the sounds of the noisy pots and pans more than he did his future mother-in-law's voice.

Chapter 34

Department of Public Safety Captain Edward Sweeney bustled into the Sheriff's Office two days after the Town Council meeting and said, "We've got him!"

"What?"

"We've got him, Sheriff. We know who's been sending those pictures."

"You do?"

"I do. And so do you."

"Who?"

"I want to show you something."

Sweeney opened his laptop computer, waited until it connected with the Sheriff's Department's Wi-Fi signal, entered the password Weber had given him when he first arrived to begin his investigation, and used the mouse to click on something. An icon revolved on the screen for a moment and then it opened to reveal Valerie Carbanal sitting in her office at the DPS crime lab in Phoenix.

"Valerie, can you hear me?"

"Yes, sir."

"I've got Sheriff Weber and some of his people here, and I know they're going to want to see what you showed me a little while ago."

Weber, Mary, Robyn, and several deputies crowded around the desk the laptop was sitting on and peered at the screen.

"It's your show, Valerie."

"Hello, ladies and gentlemen. First, I want to apologize for not seeing this before. I was so busy trying to ascertain if the pictures had been manipulated that I completely overlooked it until just a little while ago when I was reviewing the files to get ready to send to Sheriff Weber. Then when I saw it, it stuck out like a sore thumb. I don't know how I missed it up until now."

"What?" Robyn asked.

"Let me show you something," Valerie said. The screen switched to the picture of the woman who looked like Robyn standing in front of the Big Lake Brewpub, the same heavy black lines covering her breasts that Valerie had added to the pictures before putting on the presentation for the Town Council. "I know you've all seen this before, but I found something this morning that just blew me away. Does anybody notice something in this picture?"

"No, I don't see anything different than I did before," Weber told her. "A woman holding her blouse open and showing her boobs."

"One of the primary rules in photography or any other visual art is perspective," Valerie said. "For example, if you see a picture of a bride and groom, that's what you see, the bride and groom. They're the main point of the photograph, right?"

"Yeah, I guess so." Weber said

"Now, in this picture, the woman showing her breasts is what everybody looks at," Valerie continued. "Right?"

"Yeah, I guess so."

"That's what we all saw at first," Valerie said. "But look here."

A pointer appeared on screen and moved to the window of the Brewpub in the background. Do you see something here?"

"No, what are we supposed to see?"

"Here, let me zoom in. And when I do, and you're going to see it too."

The screen changed as she zoomed in on the picture, and the pointer moved back to the window again. "Now do you see it?"

"I'll be damned," Chad exclaimed. "Is that..."

"That's exactly who it is," Weber said. "I'll be a son of the bitch!" Then, as if remembering who he was talking to, the sheriff corrected himself and said, "Excuse my French, ma'am."

"No problem, Sheriff. Not being from Big Lake, I didn't know who that was, but Captain Sweeney did right away."

"I can't believe it," Mary Caitlin said.

"I can," Weber said. "And now we're going to put an end to this crap once and for all. Valerie, can you send me that picture?"

"I just sent it to your email, Sheriff."

"I can't tell you how much we appreciate this," Weber told her.

"You have no idea," Robyn added. "Thank you, thank you, thank you!"

"Happy to help," Valerie said. "Now you can prove to the whole town that they've been wrong about you all along Deputy Fuchette."

"Yes I can, and I'm looking forward to it," Robyn told her. "You have no idea how much I'm looking forward to this!"

~~***~~

"Can somebody please tell me why we're here? We just had a meeting the other day," Councilwoman Gretchen Smith-Abbott said.

"Because Sheriff Weber said we all needed to be here. He said it was important," Kirby Templeton said.

"Sheriff Weber is always saying something," Councilman Adam Hirsch said. "And most of it isn't worth listening to."

"Trust me, this one's worth being here for," Weber said. "We have a break in the case and we know where the pictures are coming from."

"What is it now, Transylvania? Or maybe the planet Neptune?"

Weber ignored the peevish tone of Councilwoman Smith-Abbott's voice and said, "I've asked Paul Lewis from the newspaper to be here, also."

"This is highly irregular, Sheriff," Kirby Templeton said. "Personnel matters are supposed to be discussed in closed session."

"I know that, sir. But since Deputy Fuchette is the person we're discussing, she agreed that she wanted him here. But, this isn't a personnel matter anymore," Weber said. "This is about wrapping up a criminal investigation. And I want the press here to cover it."

"Then let's have at it, Sheriff."

"Captain Sweeney, would you do the honors, please?"

"Tell me it's not going to be another slideshow," Adam Hirsch said. "I've got better things to do than look at the same pictures over and over. I believe we've all seen more than enough of Deputy Fuchette."

"Agreed," Gretchen added.

"We've already established that the photographs are not of Deputy Fuchette," Councilman Mel Walker corrected him, then added, "please continue, gentlemen."

"Don't worry, you're not going to have to sit through a whole slideshow," Weber assured the assembled body. "There's just one thing you need to see. Captain, if you would."

Sweeney did his magic with the mouse and the picture of the woman who looked like Robyn standing in front of the Brewpub came on the screen.

"This is nothing new," Gretchen Smith-Abbott said. "We've seen this before. We've seen all of them before, Sheriff."

"Yes, ma'am, so have I. But when Valerie Carbanal down at the DPS lab was getting ready to send these to me, she noticed something that none of us saw before. Something she hadn't even seen."

"And just what is that?"

Weber nodded his head to Sweeney, who zoomed in on the picture and moved the mouse so that the glass window of the Brewpub showed. There were gasps from several members of the Town Council.

"Ladies and gentlemen, that's the person who has been sending the pictures out. He was real good at faking the photos, but I guess he never thought about what's in the background. Even if the background is a window that clearly shows his reflection taking this picture with his cell phone. But there he is. Any questions?"

"Why in the hell would you do something like that, Adam?" Kirby Templeton demanded.

"That's not me," Adam Hirsch protested,

"It most definitely is," Councilwoman Janet McGill said. "I can't believe you would do something like that, Adam!"

"Adam Hirsch, you are under arrest for video stalking, distributing revenge porn, sending obscene materials by electronic means, and any other charges that we can figure out," Weber said. "Deputy Fuchette, would you do the honors?"

"With pleasure," Robyn said, approaching the dais and pulling her pink handcuffs from the pouch on her uniform belt. "Stand up and turn around, sir."

"I didn't do this! This is all something the sheriff drummed up to make me look bad," Adam protested.

"Councilman Hirsch, I'm not going to tell you a third time, stand up and turn around," Robyn ordered.

The man looked toward his one faithful supporter on the town Council, Gretchen Smith-Abbott, but she turned away from him, shaking her head in disgust.

Finally he stood and allowed himself to be handcuffed, and then Weber patted him down. Meanwhile, Paul Lewis was taking pictures of what was taking place. One of Robyn handcuffing the councilman would be front and center on the front page of the next issue of his newspaper.

"Why, Councilman? Why would you do this to me?" Robyn asked.

"It wasn't about you, you silly twit," Hirsch snarled. "You're nobody. Just one more woman in Weber's long line of women. You aren't the first and you won't be the last. It was all about him! About bringing him down. He's strutted around this town like some kind of peacock since we were kids and somebody needed to do something about it."

"Adam, you sorry excuse for a human being," Kirby Templeton said, enraged. "How dare you try to ruin the reputation of a fine woman like Deputy Fuchette? And why? Because some girl in high school shunned you and went out with Jimmy? My God man, is your life so pathetic that that's all you have been able to think about for all these years? I'd tell you to grow up, but it's obvious that it's way past time for that! You are a disgrace to this Town Council, to this community, and to everything we stand for. Get him out of here, Sheriff, before I do something I'll regret later!"

~~***~~

"Just once," Robyn said. "Just let me go in there and kick him in the nuts one time, Jimmy. You let me do that, and I promise you I will never ask you for anything else the rest of my life!"

"Don't think I wouldn't like to see that," the sheriff told her. "And don't think I don't want to do it myself, either. But we both know I can't, and neither can you."

"Now don't waste your time with that kind of nonsense," Parks said. "Save all that energy for your honeymoon and put it to use then doing the horizontal hula, or whatever position you prefer. Marsha did give you that copy of the Kama Sutra, didn't she?"

"Yes, she did, Parks," Robyn said. "And I must say, my mother was very surprised to find it in my nightstand. We had a conversation about that."

"Don't blame me for that. When my kinfolk come to town I put them up in a hotel. I don't want them poking around in my business."

The door of the interview room opened and Captain Sweeney and another investigator from the Department of Public Safety walked down the hall.

"That is one warped puppy," Sweeney said, shaking his head. "I can't believe this crap started over some girl way back in high school that shot him down."

"The crazy thing is, I don't even remember who she was," Weber said.

"Maybe you don't, but Hirsch does," Sweeney told him. "Deborah Lawrence."

"Yeah, now I remember her," Weber said. "She moved away and I never gave it another thought."

"Well, he sure did. It humiliated him and he's lived with it ever since, letting it fester inside of him. It was bad enough that you left town and then came back and became sheriff, but people were always talking about how much they respected you. And just like back in high school, he was part of the wallpaper that nobody ever noticed. And now with you and Robyn getting married, he wanted to find some way to ruin it for you."

"I'd have had more respect for him if he would've challenged me to my face," Weber said, "instead of doing something like this to hurt Robyn just to get at me."

"The man's a worm," Mary said. "He doesn't have the backbone to stand up to anybody, so he does crap like this."

"But how did he even get the pictures of me? I don't remember him ever taking my picture," Robyn said.

"Probably with a telephoto lens and you never knew it," Sweeney told her. "He could be a block away and zoom in on your face and you wouldn't be aware of it."

"Unbelievable. Just unbelievable."

"We seized his computer and found the original images that he manipulated," Sweeney said. "And Valerie Carbanal will have no problem using them in court to make a case that's foolproof."

"I still want to kick him in the balls," Robyn said.

"Do we know who the other woman was?"

"Yeah, her name is Celeste Fortner. She's a wannabe model and part-time hooker from Phoenix that Hirsch found online. We found her contact information at Hirsch's house and talked to her. She's willing to testify that he paid her to pose for him, but she swears up and down that she had no idea what he was doing with the pictures. I tend to believe her about that part of it. She didn't seem to like him very much. And following the leads that Special Agent Parks and his people tracked down, we've actually got security video of Hirsch using the Wi-Fi at the Mountaintop Café that ties in within about five minutes of when one of the pictures was sent. And the lady at the library keeps track of who uses the Wi-Fi there, and we can prove that Hirsch signed onto it twice when pictures were sent. It's all over."

"We appreciate all of your help, Captain," Weber said. "We really do." But looking at Robyn as he said it, he knew that Sweeney was wrong. Despite every bit of proof in the world that Robyn was not the woman in the pictures, he knew that in the small minds of the local gossip mongers, she would still be a tainted woman for a long, long time.

Chapter 35

"Okay everybody," Parks said. "Welcome to Jimmy's home and his bachelor party. We're here to have fun, drink a little bit, and laugh a lot. And please, whatever you do, don't trash the place. I'm the one stuck with cleanup duty."

The men assembled for the party laughed and Parks said. "Hey, y'all think that's funny, but I've been cleaning up after this guy since the day we met."

"Then why stop now?" Dolan asked. "Seems like when you find something you're good at, you should stick with it."

Parks waited until the laughter died down and turned to Weber, who he had seated in a wooden chair brought in from the kitchen, and said, "Jimmy, me and these guys have put our heads together to share our collective wisdom."

"Your collective wisdom is about three steps below a gerbil," Weber said.

"Now, be nice."

"I'm always nice, Parks. And believe me, there are times when being nice to you is a real chore."

"Well, be that as it may, us men with more experience with the fairer sex just want to give you some advice to help ensure you lots of matrimonial harmony."

"Isn't that kind of like the Pope giving birth control advice?"

After another round of laughter, Parks said, "So here's the first thing you need to understand Jimmy. All women are bi.

That's right, they are. As a husband or boyfriend, our job is to figure out if it's bisexual or bipolar. It's been my experience that there are a lot more of the polar kind than there are of the sexual ones."

"Oh, wait until Marsha hears you said that," Chad said.

"Hey, as long as she takes her meds every morning, I don't care what you tell her. She's in the zone," Parks replied.

"I've got a word of advice for you, Jimmy."

"What's that, Dolan?"

"Don't do it!"

Laughter filled the room, and when it finally died down it was time for Buz to put his two cents in. "Just remember this, Jimmy. When a woman says 'Correct me if I'm wrong' Do Not under any circumstances do it!"

"Something else," Chad added, "When she says 'Just do whatever you want,' Do Not do whatever you want! I bought and sold a new bass boat in one week because I forgot that rule."

"I haven't been married as long as these guys," Jordan said, "but when I got married my dad told me two things I've never forgotten - happy wife, happy life. Dad also said that anytime we get into an argument a guy has two choices. He can be right, or he can be happy."

"Amen to that," somebody said.

"My old man told me never go to bed mad," Dolan said. "Not only does it keep you from getting a good night's sleep, but if you're mad, she's mad, too. And don't forget, Robyn has guns and knows how to use them!"

"Robyn isn't the type to shoot a man in his sleep," Chad said.

"Hell, no. She'd wake him up and look him in the eyes as she put a bullet right between them," Parks agreed.

"Stop it, you guys are scaring me," Weber said with a laugh.

"I don't have any advice for you," retired Sheriff Pete Caitlin said.

"Really, a man that's been married as long as you have and you don't have any advice? I find that hard to believe," Parks said.

"Hey, don't blame me. Mary was busy getting ready for the bachelorette party and didn't tell me what I'm supposed to think," the old man said with a twinkle in his eyes.

"You know, if you were married to any other woman in the world, I might not believe that," Weber told him, drawing guffaws from the other men.

"Enough of this bullshit," Pete replied. "Where are the women?"

"The only women we know are at Marsha's place having a bachelorette party for Robyn," Parks told him. "And the ones we don't know would probably get us in a lot of trouble if they did show up."

"No boobs at a party like this? That's unacceptable. I want to see boobs," Pete said indignantly. "This is like waking up Christmas morning and finding a bunch of presents under the tree and then opening them and finding out that they're a bunch of empty boxes."

"Pete, look around this room," Weber said. "Have you ever seen such a collection of boobs in your life?"

"Well, you got a point there," Pete admitted. "but I still think this is all wrong. I've been looking at the same boobs on the same woman for over 40 years. I was hoping for some variety."

There was a twinkle in Pete's eyes to match the one in Parks' and Weber knew something was coming. Sure enough, the next thing that happened proved him right.

"Okay, you want boobs, you got boobs," Parks said. He turned toward the back of the house and called out, "Hey Pauline, bring those boobs out here!"

Somebody pushed a button on their smart phone and stripper music began to play as Paul Lewis from the newspaper came prancing into the room wearing bright pink short shorts over red fishnet stockings and the biggest red brassiere Weber had ever seen on a person. It wasn't just big, it was huge. He was pretty sure he could have parked a Toyota pickup in each cup. And not the small Tacoma, the full-size Tundra.

Paul sashayed into the room, wearing a lascivious grin on his face and heavy makeup on his eyes, doing a dance as he approached the sheriff. It wasn't a graceful dance, because a 300 pound man wearing high heels and giant falsies can't be graceful in the best of circumstances. Weber could hardly hear his falsetto voice singing off key over the raucous laughter of every man in the room.

"You have got to be kidding me!"

"Oh, no. You sit down and enjoy this," Parks said when Weber started to rise from his chair. "In fact, I insist," he added, pushing hard on his friend's right shoulder as Chad did the same on the left to hold him in place as Paul bumped and ground his way around the room, running his bright red fingernails down each man's cheek and whipping a feather boa around his neck when he approached the kitchen chair where Weber was seated. He licked his heavily painted lips and cooed, "Oh my, what have you boys brought for me?"

"Don't even think about it," Weber warned, laughing hard.

"Oh, I'm not going to just think about it, I'm going to do it," Paul trilled, turning around and wiggling his ample rump at the sheriff as he said with a seductive leer, "You're about to get the lap dance of all lap dances, sweetheart."

Weber hoped that someday he would forget the memory of his portly friend bending over and dancing for him. He was sure there were men in prison who might appreciate the show after 30 or 40 years behind bars, but then again, maybe they would just prefer to wait until the walls fell down and they had a better opportunity.

When the dance finally ended, Paul wrapped the boa around Weber's neck and kissed his forehead, leaving a crimson souvenir before prancing back out of the room.

"I'd ask if anyone wants pizza, but I think I lost my appetite," Dolan Reed said.

"You know what? Forget what I said before," Pete said, wiping tears from his eyes and holding his ribs, which ached from laughing. "That old woman I got at home ain't never looked so good to me in all the years we've been together."

After another round of drinks and banter, Parks stood up and said, "Okay, guys, now it's time for the serious part of the evening. We've had a lot of fun, and it's not over yet, but before anybody gets so drunk they can't remember why they're here, I just want to make a toast to my best friend, Jim Weber. Bubba, we've had us some good times and some bad times over the years, but I want you to know that I feel closer to you than I do either of my brothers. I mean that, man. And now you're going to marry the love of your life, and I couldn't be happier for you. I wish you and Robyn a lifetime of love, and joy, and happiness. I love you, brother."

"Here, here," Chad said, standing up when Parks sat down and saying, "I coached this kid when he was in Little League, if you can believe that. That tells you how old I am!" There was a round of laughter from the assembled men, and when it quieted down, Chad continued, "And now you're my boss. Go figure. I know I'm speaking for every deputy in this room when I say, you're more than just a boss. You have been a true friend and a brother to all of us. And I couldn't be happier to see you and Robyn getting married. It's been a long time coming."

Dolan, Buz, and the other deputies all had good words for the Sheriff and his bride to be, Coop ending his tribute by saying, "When I was in the Army I saw a lot of places in this world, some of them good and some not so good. I was looking for a place to finally call home when I retired, and when I found Big Lake, and met Jimmy, I knew I was there. But I will have to say, if I'd have seen whatever the hell that was that came in here and gave you a lap dance way back then, I think I'd still be driving fast and looking in my rearview mirror to be sure it wasn't catching up to me!"

Paul Lewis, who had changed into regular clothes and tried to scrape the heavy makeup and lipstick off of his face, with only a certain degree of success, blew Coop a kiss amid the laughter of the men. Then he stood up and said, "I've known this guy since both of us were kids playing marbles in the dirt. Now, I know that some will claim that I lost my marbles along the way, and that may be true. But the one thing I never lost was my love and my respect for this man here. Jimmy, I couldn't ask for a better friend in this world, and I couldn't ask for a better woman than Robyn for you to share your life with. Congratulations."

Weber couldn't help brushing a tear away as everyone else clapped their hands, patted him on the back, shook his hand, or hugged him. When Robyn had talked about wanting to leave Big Lake, and he had agreed to go with her to make a new start someplace else. At the time, he thought he could do that. Now he realized that that could never happen. Robyn had been right when she said that this was his home and these people were his family. And he loved them just as much as they loved him.

Chapter 36

On his last morning as a bachelor Weber was just getting out of bed when his cell phone rang. He answered and asked, "What's up, Judy?"

"Sheriff, Don MacGregor's pickup was spotted five minutes ago just outside of town."

"You're kidding? Where?"

"He was headed toward SafeHaven. I already called Christine and told her to lock all the doors, and I've got two units headed there now."

"Good work. I'm on my way. Tell the responding units to approach with extreme caution. We know that MacGregor has already killed one police officer. I don't want there to be any more."

"10-4, Sheriff. Should I call the other deputies who are off duty?"

"All except those that worked night shift. They need to rest. I want everybody else on the street, and tell them I want them locked and loaded. Warn them that if they see MacGregor, don't give him a chance to get the drop on them, because he won't hesitate to shoot."

Weber ended the call before she could respond. Dressing quickly, he grabbed his shotgun and AR-15 on the way out the door. He peeled out of the driveway in a shower of gravel and dust, siren screaming as he headed toward town. A thought came to him and he picked up his microphone and call Dispatch.

"Is Coop on duty?"

"No, sir. I was just getting ready to call him."

"Tell him not to, I repeat *not*, to come out on the road. Tell him I want him at Miss Jensen's house in case MacGregor comes back to finish what he started there."

Weber hoped with all his being that it was a false alarm and that the wanted man had not returned to town. But if he had, Weber hoped he wasn't headed toward Roberta's house for everyone's safety. He knew if the man showed up there it was going to end badly for everybody involved.

He was rolling through town with his siren splitting the mountain morning and red and blue lights flashing when Dolan and Jordan radioed to say that they had arrived at SafeHaven and everything was secure.

"Jordan, you stay there," Weber ordered. "Dolan, get back out on the street."

Robyn's voice came over the radio, asking, "Where do you want me at, Jimmy?"

"I want you to stay right there at home," he told her. "This wedding's happening today one way or the other."

"No, I'm already on the road. Tell me what to do."

Weber knew he wasn't going to change her mind. "Make a run past the boat ramp and then past the schools," he replied, then added. "I'm serious, everybody. If any of you see this guy, don't approach him alone. Call for backup immediately. I don't want this man walking away this time. You all have a green light to do whatever you have to do to take him down."

In saying that, Weber knew that he might well have issued Donald MacGregor's death warrant. While he placed a high value on human life, he believed that if it came to it, MacGregor's was one that the world would not miss.

An hour later the search had turned futile. MacGregor could not be found anywhere near SafeHaven, Roberta Jensen's house, or his own and his mother's homes.

"I don't know if it's a false alarm or what," Chad said over the radio. "None of us can find him."

"Keep looking, guys," Weber said. "I've got a feeling he's not that far away."

After yet another hour of searching, they realized that there was nothing to be found. Four blue pickups had been spotted, but none of them were Donald MacGregor's.

Weber had cruised past the man's house and his mother's twice and didn't see anybody. He decided he would check it out, just to be sure. He called two deputies to back him up. When they pulled into Sally MacGregor's yard she came out onto the porch and shouted, "You get the hell out of here. You ain't got any right to be on my property!"

"Have you seen your son?"

"No, and if I did I wouldn't tell you."

"Look in the garage," Weber ordered. Chad and Dan Wright approached the garage, pistols in their hands.

"What are they doing? You get out of there," Sally said.

"Listen, Sally, if he's here we're going to find him. It would go better for everybody if you tell us where he's at."

"I told you, I don't know where he's at. I haven't seen him since you run him out of town!"

Dolan Reed called on the radio and said "Sheriff, someone broke into a cabin up here on Antler Ridge. But it looks like it's old and there's nobody around."

"All right, keep looking," Weber said. He turned back to MacGregor's mother and said, "If I find out that your son's anywhere around here and you've been lying to us and are helping him, you're going to jail for harboring a fugitive. Do you understand that?"

"I understand that my son ain't done nothing, but you people keep hassling him for no reason. That's what I understand!"

"Lady, your son killed a highway patrolman in New Mexico," Weber told her with frustration. "Wake up, will you? We're going to find him sooner or later."

"I don't believe that for a minute," Sally said. "But if he did, he had a good reason for it."

"A good reason for murdering someone? Christ, you're as bad as he is. That cop's blood is on your hands, too, lady. If you would have been a real mother and made him own up to all the crap he did as a kid and dealt with it back then, that cop might be alive today."

"You go straight to hell, Sheriff!"

"I just may do that someday," Weber told her. "And if I do, I know I'll see you both there."

~~***~~

Another hour of searching convinced Weber that if MacGregor was indeed back in Big Lake he had gone to ground somewhere where they were not going to find him. He drove to SafeHaven to check in with Christine and Jordan.

"I don't know if it was a false alarm or what, but we haven't been able to find anything at all," he told Christine."

"That might be all it was, Jimmy. You know people see shadows and think it's monsters."

Weber knew that was true, but he also knew that Donald MacGregor was a real life monster, not the shadowy stuff of nightmares.

"We don't have the manpower to keep someone here all the time, you know that. But I'll have Jordan stay here through the day, and the deputies will keep swinging by. In the meantime, keep the doors locked, just in case."

"I know the routine, Jimmy. This ain't my first rodeo. I've had other husbands show up here trying to cause problems before."

"I know, but MacGregor isn't just another husband trying to get his wife back. This guy takes crazy to an all new level."

"I know. And if he shows up here, he's gonna be a dead man. Don't you worry about that. You go home and start getting ready for your big day. I'll see you after a while at the courthouse."

Weber radioed the off-duty deputies to return home, thanking them for coming out when they were needed. Then he cautioned the rest of them to maintain their vigilance. Hanging up the microphone, he headed home to get dressed for his wedding.

Nick Russell

Chapter 37

"I want to see you as much as you want to see me, Jimmy" Robyn said. "But we both know it's supposed to be bad luck for the groom to see the bride before the wedding."

"Robyn, I've seen every part of you there is to see," Weber said.

"And you're going to see a lot more of it real soon, mister, I promise you that. I've got to get dressed, Jimmy. We need to be at the courthouse in less than an hour."

"Yeah, I know. I'll see you there."

"I can't believe we're finally going to do this!"

"Me, either. I've looked forward to it for a long time."

"I know you have. Thank you for all of your patience with me when I was going through my craziness," Robyn told him. "I love you, Jim Weber. I love you, and I promise that I'm going to be the best wife a man ever had."

"I love you, too, Robyn. With all my heart."

He could hear her mother calling her in the background and she said, "I've got to go. See you soon."

Weber ended the call as Parks came into his bedroom and said, "Don't we look like a couple of handsome dudes? I'm not sure we want to waste all this on just two women, Bubba. How about we forget this whole wedding thing and jump in my plane and fly to Vegas and see if we can get lucky?"

"First of all, we're not going to Vegas. Neither one of us can handle the women we've got here, Parks. And second of all, if we tried pulling a stunt like that, I think Robyn would walk out in her front yard and shoot us out of the sky. And I wouldn't blame her one bit."

"Okay then, you win. Here, let me fix that tie for you. Whoever taught you to tie a tie anyway? Hey did you hear that? Tie a tie. I'm a poet and I didn't know it. If you don't believe me, look at my feet, they show it. They're Longfellows."

"The way I hear it, that's about the only thing long on your body," Weber said, chuckling as Parks adjusted the knot on his tie.

"Yeah, yeah. You keep on believing that if it makes you feel better."

As they were pulling on their jackets, Weber said, "I guess I really don't need my pistol, do I?"

"I don't know, is her father going to have a shotgun?"

"Probably not," Weber said. He started to put the Kimber .45 Ultra Carry that he usually wore off duty back in his dresser drawer, then said, "Oh, what the hell? I'd feel naked without it."

"A man shouldn't be naked at his wedding," Parks said. "Especially a guy who falls into the short fellow category, if you get my drift."

"You're a funny man, Parks," Weber said, sticking the gun and its inside the pants holster behind his hip as they went out the door. "Tell your story walking."

~~***~~

They were two miles from the courthouse when they passed Marsha's red Chrysler Pacifica minivan waiting at a stop sign.

"Well, there's your bride and her parents," Parks said. "It's still not too late, Jimmy. This Mustang of Robyn's can outrun them."

Before Weber could reply, his cell phone rang. He picked it up off the console and glanced at the display. "Dispatch better have a damn good reason for calling me now," he said as he pushed the button to answer.

"Sheriff, I've got Christine on the other line. She said Donald MacGregor is behind her and trying to force her off the road! His wife is with her."

"Where are they?"

"They had just left SafeHaven and turned onto the main road when he came up behind them and hit the back of her car. She said she's driving fast and is just passing the Rawley place. Hang on. She just said he rammed her again. I've got deputies on the way but they are on the other side of town answering a call for a suspicious vehicle that resembled MacGregor's."

"Tell her to hang on and not stop," Weber said. "We're on the way."

He dropped the phone and floored the accelerator, the powerful 5.0-liter V8 engine of the Mustang pushing him and Parks back against their seats.

"What the hell is going on, Jimmy?"

"MacGregor's trying to run Hillbilly off the road. It sounds like he may have called in a false report to send the deputies to the other side of town. We're closer."

"Shit! Okay, let's take this son of a bitch down!"

His cell phone rang again but Weber had both hands in the steering wheel and couldn't answer. Parks picked it up and pushed the button. Weber could hear Robyn's voice but couldn't understand what she was saying.

"We've got an emergency," Parks told her. "MacGregor's trying to run Christine off the road. No, you guys go on to the courthouse. We'll see you there."

Weber made a hard left turn onto the road that went out to SafeHaven, the Mustang's tires screaming in protest. He glanced in the rearview mirror to see the minivan following them.

"Dammit, they're not going to the courthouse."

"Does that surprise you, Jimmy? There's no way something like this is going to go down and Robyn's not going to be a part of it."

"Do you have your weapon on you, Parks?"

"Yeah, Robyn made me promise to bring it in case you changed your mind at the last minute and tried to make a run for it. She told me not to kill you, but maybe to just wing you and slow you down a little bit."

"I swear to God, if MacGregor hurts Christine or his wife, he's never going to see the inside of a jail cell!"

"I heard that. But first we've got to catch him."

"That won't be hard," Weber said. "Here they come now."

As he spoke he saw Christine's old Isuzu Trooper lurch sideways from a hard hit from the big pickup truck following it. A lesser driver might have gone into a spin and rolled the high centered SUV, but Christine had grown up a tomboy, racing an old pickup on the winding mountain roads around Big Lake before she was even old enough to have a drivers license. She managed to get control of the vehicle and keep it pointed in the right direction.

"How are we going to handle this, Jimmy?"

They were approaching the oncoming vehicles at a rapid rate and Weber said, "I don't suppose I can lean back far enough that you can shoot past me and hit him, do you?"

"I'd be afraid to try it as much as we're bouncing around on this bumpy road."

"Okay then, I'll make it easy for you."

The Isuzu and the truck chasing it shot past them and Weber stomped on the brake pedal and cut the steering wheel hard to the left. There wasn't enough room to make a complete U-turn in the middle of the road and they took out a mailbox at the end of someone's driveway before he got straightened out and stomped on the accelerator again, closing rapidly on the pickup.

He tried pulling out and passing on the left to give Parks a chance to shoot, but MacGregor was too quick for him, moving toward the center of the road to block them. Weber knew the lighter Mustang sat too low to the ground to execute a PIT maneuver, and he also knew it wasn't safe for Parks to fire at the back of the truck, with Christine and her passenger in the vehicle in front of it.

"Son of a bitch," he shouted in frustration as he tried to pull up beside the truck again and was blocked. The right front of the Mustang impacted the truck bumper, jolting them violently.

"Robyn loves her car, she's not going to appreciate this, Jimmy."

"Christine will appreciate it a lot less if we let that asshole kill her and his wife. Hang on and be ready!"

He swung wide to the left, off the road and into someone's yard, pushing the accelerator as hard as he could. The Mustang lurched and bounced wildly, but he was able to gain on the truck. As he pulled up alongside of it, Parks stuck his .40 Glock out his side window and began firing at the truck. Bullets punched their way through the metal while the hot spent brass casings ejected from the pistol flew around the inside of the Mustang. One bounced off the top of Weber's forehead and another his cheek but he ignored them. His ears were ringing from the sound of the pistol in such a close space, but he had no time to wonder what kind of damage might be done to his hearing. Parks fired again and again, seeming to have no effect. The sheriff wondered for a wild moment if Donald MacGregor was some kind of subhuman or otherworldly creature that could not be killed by bullets. Then Parks' last shot seemed to do the trick.

The truck veered off the road to the right, then overcorrected, smashing into the Isuzu before shooting directly into their path. Weber stomped on the brake pedal but it was too late. The Mustang plowed into the pickup in a violent explosion of glass and smashed metal. Neither man in the car felt the airbags deploy and slam into their faces, and both sat stunned for half a minute after the impact. Then, realizing the danger still wasn't over, they piled out of the car as MacGregor stood up from the far side of the truck and laid his AK-47 across the bed and began shooting at them.

The high velocity 7.62x39 bullets shredded the inside of the Mustang. One came through the door Weber was crouched behind and he pulled his Kimber out and started to fire back when he realized that there were vehicles and cars in the background. There was too much danger of hitting an innocent bystander. Spotting a big ponderosa pine tree ten feet to his left, he made a mad dash for it, knowing the trunk would protect him from the bullets coming his direction. Meanwhile, Parks had moved to the back of the car, hoping the engine block would stop any rifle bullets headed his way.

"You okay, Parks?"

"Yeah. But I'm out of ammo."

They heard sirens screaming in the distance and Weber knew help was on the way. He just wasn't sure if it would get there in time. He realized the shooting had stopped and when he peered carefully around the tree he saw that MacGregor had run back into the road and was using the butt of his rifle to smash in the passenger side window of Christine's stalled Isuzu. The man reached inside and grabbed his screaming wife by the hair, pulling her out the window. They left their positions and ran toward them, but Weber was sure she would be dead before he or Parks could get to her side. MacGregor had dropped the rifle and was pistol whipping the helpless woman with his Ruger .357 magnum as he and Parks ran toward them. Weber cursed, knowing they would not make it in time to change what was about to happen.

Then, for a moment he thought he was hallucinating when he saw a woman in a white wedding dress come around the side of Marsha's minivan and launch herself forward, slamming into MacGregor and knocking him off his feet. In the next instant he realized that no matter what custom dictated, he was going to see his bride before the wedding after all.

He and Parks came around the back of the Ford pickup to see Robyn and the much bigger man rolling on the road, locked in combat. Robyn had him in a headlock and was trying to exert pressure on his neck, but MacGregor didn't seem to be bothered, shaking her loose and onto her back. He punched her in the face once and then again, and then Weber and Parks were on top of him.

The sheriff had been in some serious fights in his life, but he didn't know when he had ever taken on someone as strong and as deranged as Donald MacGregor was that day. He and Parks were punching the man and trying to subdue him, but not having much success at it. An elbow jammed into his mouth and Weber tasted blood. Then a fist caught him in the eye, knocking him backward against the side of the truck. MacGregor came at him, raining down vicious blows, and Parks attacked the man from behind, punching his fist into MacGregor's kidneys. Later, both lawmen would say that it was like something out of a horror movie. No matter what they did, nothing was slowing down the madman.

At some point Weber became aware that Robyn's father had joined in the battle, and seconds later two deputies were on the scene, and between all of them they finally took MacGregor to the ground. But the man wasn't done yet. He head-butted Weber in the face and the sheriff saw bright flashing lights inside of his head. He could hear yelling and cursing around him and wiped blood away from his eyes enough to see that MacGregor, bloody and battered, had somehow managed to get to his feet again. Blood dripped from the flesh wound Park's bullet had made on his left arm, but if he felt it at all he didn't show it. He took two steps toward his wife and suddenly Deputy Cooper was there blocking his path.

"Freeze or you're a dead man," Coop ordered, his finger on the trigger of his pistol.

For a moment Weber thought MacGregor might not give up. His rage was so overpowering that all conscious thought had left him. Maybe it was the look on Coop's face, or maybe he just ran out of steam, but for whatever reason he stopped and looked at the deputy. Slowly, he raised his hands, surrendering.

But Coop wasn't ready to let him off that easily. "You no good bastard. You like beating on women, don't you? I can tell you right now, you've hit your last woman. And you're not going to go to jail and sit on your ass the rest of your life either."

Weber saw his deputy's finger turn white as it started to take up the slack of his pistol's trigger."

"Don't do it, Coop!"

"Why not, Jimmy? You give me one good reason why I should let this maggot take one more breath."

"No, Coop. That's not the way we do things. You know it and I know it."

"Maybe it's time we did things differently, Jimmy. There was a time when people would take someone like this and string him up and be done with it."

"That was then and this is now," Weber said. "If you pull that trigger, you're no better than he is, Coop. I know you're pissed off, and I know how much you hate him. And believe me, I feel the same way you do. But you need to think about what happens after you pull that trigger."

"After I pull the trigger it's all over."

"No, Coop it's not all over. It may be all over for him, but your world's going to go on. Do you want to spend the rest of your life sitting in a prison cell, or do you want to spend it with Roberta? Because I'll tell you right now, if she was here she would tell you the same thing I'm telling you. He's not worth it."

Nobody standing there that morning knew what was going to happen in the next seconds. Weber hoped that Coop would come to his senses and not throw his life away to punish MacGregor. But at the same time, he knew that if it had been Robyn who had been brutalized the way Roberta was, he was not sure what he would do if he was standing in Coop's shoes.

"Go ahead, asshole," MacGregor sneered. "Shoot me, I don't care. It's better than life behind bars. You'd be doing me a favor. Shoot me if you've got the balls to do it."

A smile came across Coop's face and he said, "You're right, I would be doing you a favor. But I don't feel too damn favorable toward you right this minute. The people you hurt are all going to get better with enough time. Your wife's going to go on to find another man. A man who will treat her right. And she's going to have a good life. We're all going to have good lives, breathing free air. So instead of shooting you, I'll let you live. And every day for the rest of your life as you sit in your cell, I want you to remember that we're all out here enjoying every minute of every day. And when you go to sleep on that narrow hard bunk, I want you to know that we're sleeping in feather beds. I want you to know that someday that wife of yours is going to sleep in the arms of a real man. I want you to know that you don't mean anything to anybody. You're just a bad memory. Remember that everybody's going to forget all about you sooner or later. He lowered the barrel of the pistol and said, "Cuff him, Dan."

Nick Russell

Chapter 38

"I just talked to Judge Ryman," Dolan Reed said, as emergency room doctors and nurses tended to everybody's injuries. "He said he can reschedule the wedding for whenever you guys want. There's no rush."

"No way," Robyn said. "This wedding is happening today!"

"Are you sure, honey? After everything you've been through, maybe it would be best to postpone it."

"No, Daddy, we're not postponing anything. When I got up this morning I planned to be married to Jimmy when the sun goes down. And come hell or high water, that's what's going to happen!"

"But just look at you," her mother said. "Your dress is a mess, you've got a black eye, and him," she said, pointing at Weber, "he looks horrible."

"No, Mother," Robyn said, smiling at Weber sitting on an exam table next to the one she was on. "He doesn't look horrible at all. He's the most beautiful man I've ever seen."

"Robyn, I'm putting my foot down. I refuse to take part in a spectacle like this. You need to…"

Robyn got off the exam table that she was sitting on, pushing the nurse who was dabbing at her eye aside, and said, "Mother, go to hell. I've listened to your bullshit for as long as I'm going to. You don't want to take part in what you call a spectacle? Fine, I don't want you there. Now shut up and get the hell out of here!"

~~***~~

"Are you sure you want to do this? Weber asked. "Your mom ran the limo driver off and we don't even have a car to drive away from the courthouse in."

"Don't you worry about that," Chad said, pointing to his patrol car parked at the curb in front of the courthouse. Someone had written Just Married across the back window. "It's got a lot more miles on it in than your Mustang did, but that car is not going anywhere ever again."

Weber and Robyn laughed, and she said, "It's perfect, Chad. Thank you." Then she turned to Weber and said, "Get your butt up in front of the judge, Mister. It's time for you to make an honest woman out of me."

"No baby, it's long past time," he told her, kissing her before he turned to walk inside.

Robyn linked her arm through her father's and said, "Are you ready to walk me down the aisle, Daddy?"

"You bet I am," he said with a loving smile.

"Then let's do it," she said. And arm in arm together, they walked into the courthouse.

Here is a sneak peek at *Big Lake Ninja*, coming soon from Nick Russell

"Well, what do you think?"

"It's beautiful," Big Lake Sheriff's Department administrative assistant Mary Caitlin said as she admired the new Mustang. "It's the same color as your old one, isn't it?"

"Pretty close. They call it ingot silver. This one has the EcoBoost turbo four-cylinder instead of the V-8 my old one had. But it's pretty darn fast," Deputy Robyn Fuchette said.

"Yeah, fast enough that I thought we were going to get a ticket coming home from the Valley in it," her husband, Sheriff Jim Weber, said.

"Well, congratulations," Mary said. "A new husband and a new car. Life just doesn't get much better than that, does it?"

"I think that the car's got a lot less miles on it than the husband has," Weber said with a smile.

"That's okay, as long as she keeps both of you well lubed and exercises you on a regular basis, you'll be fine," FBI agent Larry Parks joked.

Their conversation was interrupted when a maroon F-150 pickup truck pulled into the parking lot of the Sheriff's Department and a man got out, approaching them.

"Hi, Sheriff. Nice looking car."

"It's Robyn's," Weber told him. "She needed a replacement, since I kind of killed hers on our wedding day."

"Pretty wife and a pretty car. You're a lucky man, Sheriff."

"Thanks. What I do for you, Doug?"

"Well, this is going to sound crazy, but I think a ninja tried to kill me."

Weber looked at him quizzically. "What do you mean, a ninja tried to kill you?"

"Just that. Like I said, I know it sounds crazy. It was pretty scary there for a while."

"What the hell happened, Doug?"

"I was headed out to the Neufield place to give them an estimate for replacing some fencing for them, and there was a big cardboard box sitting in the middle of the road. I didn't want to hit it, not knowing what was in it, so I got out to move it. I was just bending down when I heard a sound, and when I turned around there was this ninja with a sword. He had it in both hands and took a swing at me with it, like he was trying to cut my head off."

"What happened then?"

"I jumped backwards and tripped over the box and fell on my ass. I swear I could feel the wind as the blade went over my head. It was that close!"

"Then what happened?"

"He came at me again and tried to cut me in half with that damn sword."

"You're kidding me."

"I'm serious as a heart attack, Sheriff. I managed to get up on my feet and I ran away. When I turned around he wasn't there anymore."

"Did you see where he went?"

"No, sir. I got back in my truck and I hauled ass out of there and came here to tell you about it! I'll tell you what, Sheriff, I about crapped my pants when he came at me with that big old sword!"

"Where exactly did this happen, Doug?"

"On Providence Road. Just past where the Turner place used to be. I came around the curve, and like I said, there was this cardboard box sitting there in the middle of the road. It was like he set me up. Wanted me to get out of the truck so he could try to kill me."

"Let's take a ride out there," Weber said. "We'll follow you. I want to see exactly where this happened, Doug."

~~***~~

"See, there's the cardboard box," the man said when they

arrived at the scene of the attack, pointing at a box on the side of the road.

Weber walked over and picked up the box. It was about 36 inches' square and folded closed. It felt empty and when he opened it there was nothing inside.

"The box was just sitting in the road when you pulled up to it?"

"Yep. It was like someone put it there to stop me when I came along."

"And then the ninja came from out of the woods. What direction did he come from?"

"I really don't know," Doug said. "I was just bending down to the box and he came at me."

"Where were you standing exactly? Which direction did he come from?"

The man thought for a minute and then said, "Right here. I got out of my truck and walked up to the box. I was bending down, and all of a sudden I heard a noise. I looked up and this crazy person dressed all in black was running toward me with a sword."

"Then he approached you from your left side?"

"Yeah, I guess. Like I said, I think he was there to ambush me. I don't know."

"Then what happened?"

"I fell down and scooted to the side of the road. I guess I still had the box with me, I don't know. It all happened so fast."

"And that's when he tried to cut you again? There by the shoulder of the road?"

"Yeah, right there," the man said, pointing. "He raised the sword over his head and swung it down at me. I don't remember exactly what happened. Maybe I rolled to the side or something to get out of the way. Then I got up and ran like hell."

"Did he chase you at all?"

"If he did, I don't know. I wasn't looking backward. I ran all the way to the curve before I finally stopped. I swear to God, Sheriff, it was a craziest thing that ever happened to me."

"Doug, do you have any enemies that you know of? Anyone

who would want to harm you?"

"Gosh, no, Sheriff. I pretty much get along with everybody."

"And you have no idea why you were singled out like this?"

"No, sir, I don't. I keep asking myself why somebody would do something like this to me, and I keep drawing a blank."

"Can you give me any idea of what this person looked like?"

"He looked like a ninja. All dressed in black with a hood over his face with two eye holes in it."

"Was he tall or short? Any idea what he might have weighed?"

Doug thought for a minute, then said, "To be honest, I couldn't guess. It all happened so fast. I don't think he was very big."

"Did he say anything at all?"

"Nope, not a word."

Looking around again, Weber walked to the side of the road where Doug said the attacker must have come from. There were no footprints or anything to indicate who had been there or when. Thick Ponderosa pines grew almost to the edge of the road. It would have been easy for someone to hide behind one of them, waiting to attack. If that's what happened. Weber had no reason to doubt the man. Doug Mullins was a good citizen, a respected businessman, and not one prone to making things up or exaggeration.

Weber looked at Parks and said, "This has gone way beyond kid stuff, hasn't it?"

"I guess it could be a prank," Parks said. "But if it is, it's the kind of prank that can get somebody hurt. Or killed."

"He keeps saying someone was trying to kill him," Robyn said. "Do you think he was singled out, or was he just the person who happened to come along?"

"That's a good question. Whether he was the person this ninja was trying to get to, or just a random target of opportunity, I imagine it seems pretty personal either way when someone's trying to chop you up with a sword."

They walked back out onto the road and Weber said, "Why don't you go ahead and take off, Doug? We're going to poke around here for a little bit longer. If you think of anything else, give me a call."

The man walked to the door of his truck and opened it then turned around and asked, "Why me, Sheriff? I don't bother anybody. I just do my job and go home at the end of the day. Why would somebody want to kill me?"

"If it's any comfort to you, I don't think that you were the intended target," Weber said. "We've had several reports of somebody dress up like a ninja running around causing mischief. I think whoever is doing it is some stupid kid who has escalated things way too far."

"I don't know if it was a kid or a grown-up," Doug said. "But whoever it is, I think I'm going to be seeing him over and over again in my dreams for a while."

He nodded at the sheriff, got in his truck and started it, then drove away. Watching the pickup disappear back around the curve, Weber hoped that whoever was pulling these dumb stunts wouldn't make the mistake of doing it again. Doug was a pretty mellow guy, but there were plenty of people around Big Lake who carried guns on their person or in their vehicles, and the next time something like this happened, it could turn out tragically for everybody involved.

At the time, the sheriff had no idea of the tragedy to come, and he would wonder afterward if there had been a way to prevent it.

Made in the USA
Las Vegas, NV
17 October 2023